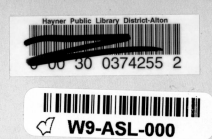

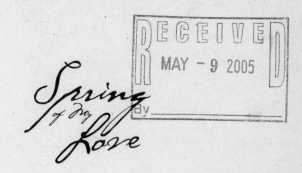

RECEIVED
MAY - 9 2005
BY_____

Spring of My Love

Spring of My Love

Ginny Aiken

Revell
Grand Rapids, Michigan

© 2005 by Ginny Aiken

Published by Fleming H. Revell
a division of Baker Publishing Group
P.O. Box 6287, Grand Rapids, MI 49516-6287

Printed in the United States of America

Library of Congress Cataloging-in-Publication Data
Aiken, Ginny.
    Spring of my love / Ginny Aiken.
        p.   cm. — (Silver Hills trilogy ; bk. 3)
    ISBN 0-8007-5876-5 (pbk.)
        1. Women landowners—Fiction. 2. Fathers—Death—Fiction. 3. Land tenure—Fiction. 4. Colorado—Fiction. I. Title.
    PS3551.I339S68 2005
    813'.54—dc22   2004020025

Scripture is taken from the King James Version of the Bible.

The LORD shall guide thee continually, and satisfy thy soul in drought, and make fat thy bones: and thou shalt be like a watered garden, and like a spring of water, whose waters fail not.

Isaiah 58:11

1

The mountains' silence overwhelmed her. Its endless echo rang grim and hollow; it drove in the certainty of her situation. She was now beyond any doubt alone.

Papa's sudden death, as far as Angel Rogers could tell, had occurred plain and simple because his heart gave out. It seemed Papa had indeed lived too hard before he met Mama and settled to a "proper" life, as he'd often said.

Knowing what led to his passing did nothing to ease Angel's grief.

She leaned on the handle of the heavy shovel and surveyed Papa's final resting place. He would have wanted it right by Mama's grave, so Angel had fought the hard, cold earth until her hands bled. In the end, the two people she'd loved most lay side by side.

She'd never known loneliness before. It was all she knew now.

How could silence be so loud?

Nothing stirred. The squirrels had packed away their stores

for the winter, and the birds had flown south. The bears had gone to ground, and every green thing, aside from the scrub pine, had died.

Dead.

Mama and Papa were dead.

Only Angel remained in this corner of their small valley, the only home she knew.

She wanted no one to suspect her predicament. Eighteen was no great age, but it was enough for her to recognize that dangers might await a woman alone. Papa had often spoken of his wealth, not in currency or coin, but rather in something perhaps of more value than silver or gold, even here in Colorado. The spring on their ranch ran clean, clear, and abundant. In this land so prone to drought, what little silver the nearby Heart of Silver Mine still yielded couldn't buy what the earth didn't give: water to satisfy parched land, cattle, horses, men.

She would have to protect herself.

Herself and her land.

Papa had fought the elements too long and too hard for her to let their patch of land slip out of Rogers hands. One way or another, Angel would do it. By dint of Rogers determination, and by the grace of Almighty God, she would.

Even though she didn't know quite how just yet.

At her side, Sunny moaned, or so the big, shaggy dog's mournful sound struck Angel. She bent to one knee and scratched the animal between her ears.

"Yes, girl. You're still here. I can't go forgetting that, now, can I?" Sunny's sad brown eyes met hers.

"You miss Papa, too, don't you?" Angel swallowed a sob. "Well, don't go fretting. You and I have too much to do to wallow in mourning and grieving and tearing up like this. He's with Mama and Jesus now, and there's no better place to be. Not even here."

She reached out a leather-gloved hand and patted the slight

mound of her father's grave. "Don't you worry either, Papa. I'll be fine. Remember how you and Mama always told me that Jesus's hand was big enough to hold me and whatever troubles I might find? I reckon it's big enough to hold this ranch and these mountains, too."

She stood and shivered in the frigid wind that had kicked up. With a final glance at the earth she'd just packed down over her father's spent body, she hugged the lapels of Papa's wool coat close over her chest, clasped the shovel handle and set off toward the house. Sunny, scenting home, ran ahead, her yellow tail waving its long, full fringe in the chill.

The sight of the cabin affected Angel as it never had before. It had always represented love and welcome, but now it spoke of her plight. Mama, who'd died four years earlier of the influenza, wouldn't be at the woodstove, her watchful eye on the savory supper she'd brought to a simmer. Despite the passage of time, the memory still came to Angel more often than she cared to admit. Now Papa wouldn't tromp in either, his heavy stomps dislodging snow, ice, and earth from his boots.

She had enough supplies to see her through to spring, for which she thanked Papa's wisdom and the Lord's bountiful provision. Plus, she had Sunny to keep her from going mad. After that? Well, she had to leave that in the heavenly Father's capable hands.

He'd have to be her protector in every way.

She'd never learned to use Papa's shotgun, not because he hadn't tried to teach her, but because she hated its sound, its power, the destruction it caused. Now, however, she wondered if she hadn't been mistaken in her refusal.

There were many, Papa had said, who would do anything to get what they wanted. They always wanted more land—especially if that land brought a good water source, as Rogers land did. Angel didn't know the first thing about protecting what was hers.

A cold whisper on her cheek told her the snow she'd smelled in the air since early that morning had arrived. From the thick, fluffy texture of the flake and the leaden shade of the sky overhead, she knew a heavy blanket would cover the ground before it was all over. She'd be snowed in.

Good.

Some satisfaction broke through the misery she'd felt since she found her father slumped over his Bible two mornings ago. Horror had filled her—what would she do with his solid body? How would she give him a decent burial?

But God had seen her through. It seemed He was still doing so, if this storm was any indication of His benevolence. The isolation of winter, which had always seemed harsh and endless, now stretched out as a welcome reprieve.

She had the winter, only that one season, to prepare for what might be an onslaught of greedy seekers. *In your hands, Lord Jesus. Sunny, the ranch, and I are all in your hands.*

🙢

One glance at the skimpy growth of grass on his land told Jeremy Johnstone that this year would be worse than the last. When he'd bought his spread two years earlier, he'd known his future depended on one thing: water.

The lazy little river that wandered around the southern border of his property swelled with snowmelt each spring. This past winter, as well as the one before, had brought little snowfall—a couple of big storms had covered everything, and the icy temperatures had kept the snow on the ground. But it hadn't added up to much in the way of water. Spring's rains had been more absent than not. Now, in late June, the banks of the river looked like dirty old china, cracked and crumbly.

Jeremy tugged off his hat and used his red handkerchief to sop up the sweat from the persistent morning sun. Not quite ten o'clock yet, and the temperature was high enough to roast a steer on the run. Where was God when a man stood to lose his very last dime on account of a dry sky?

He craned his neck to glare at the blank blue bowl overhead. Not a cloud to be seen anywhere. A frustrated sigh ripped from his chest, and he slapped his hat against his thigh. Small puffs of dust spread upward and outward from the denim and straw, making his tough situation more real.

A ways behind him, his herd made woeful sounds. They still hunted fresh pasture with little success. He'd already spent what to him was a fortune to buy feed, and he couldn't afford to hire enough men to drive the herd up north to richer pastureland. Not if he also wanted to get his ranch through another winter. If only he had a more ample water source nearby.

Well, the underground source was ample. But by the time the water reached his little river, large amounts had been redirected to other branches. Branches like Rogers Creek.

He'd heard Old Man Rogers was tough as rawhide. Wouldn't surprise him if it was true. The crusty codger would have to be to live through all Jeremy had heard tell he had.

Oliver Rogers, if folks were right, was a real western original. Jeremy hadn't met the man, but he'd been told the fellow had come out west as a baby-cheeked boy. They also said he'd done as much as Kit Carson and had become a real mountain man, was maybe even the last one left in Colorado.

Jeremy had also heard tell the old man had died.

Rumor had it he'd passed on in the early winter—he hadn't been seen in town since late fall. If rumor was anything to go by, then by all means, rumors in Hartville carried extra weight. He'd never known another place so given to gossip, even though Pastor Stone spent much of his pulpit time preaching against the sinful habit.

Jeremy suspected that rumor sprang from a root of truth.

If that was so, then who was manning the ranch? Old Man Rogers's wife had died a while back, and they'd had only a freckle-faced, carrot-topped girl. Had the daughter left the ranch? Did she now live in Hartville? He sure hoped she wasn't stupid enough to try to run the spread on her own. If nothing else, livestock needed more than the soft hand of a big-eyed miss.

Then again, Old Man Rogers had never gone in for cattle.

Jeremy spat in disgust.

Sheep.

Who in his right mind would fill the notch in the Colorado mountains with an army of the pasture-shearing beasts? Maybe all that rough living had addled the man's mind. Otherwise, why would he have brought those woolly pests out here?

To think that Rogers wasted that clear, fresh water on nothing more than curly, fatty fur. Cattle. Now they were more worthy creatures—not to mention horses. Especially Jeremy's cattle and horses.

He'd wager the daughter was ready to sell by now, if she hadn't already done so. He hadn't heard anything about a sale. He'd only heard rumors of the father's death. Surely word of Rogers Creek changing hands would have reached his ears by now. If it had happened at all.

Had Oliver Rogers really died?

Pastor Stone said he hadn't done a funeral, and folks said the Rogerses were devout and faithful Christians despite the old man's wild youth. Repentance and reform must have been Mrs. Rogers's starting points.

Jeremy squinted toward the green crotch between the two peaks—Rogers land. It lay just beyond his and touched on the foothills to his north. And, more importantly, Rogers Creek, that stronger branch of his water source, blessed the soil in that valley. His livestock needed the pasture those baaing beasts were surely destroying. He needed to fatten up his animals. He had to sell well this coming fall.

His future depended on it.

If he didn't realize a decent return on his two-year investment, he'd be sunk.

Broke.

Finished.

He had to make Old Man Rogers's daughter see reason. His money would bring him a better return if he used it to buy another source of water. She had to sell. A girl couldn't run a ranch, and certainly not if she'd moved into town. The only reasonable solution to her predicament was the same as his. She simply had to sell.

To him.

And in time to do his cattle some good.

Jeremy had to move fast.

❦

The Sunday following his decision, Jeremy rode out to Rogers Ranch after church. He hadn't seen that distinctive shade of Rogers red among the bowed heads of the faithful at Silver Creek Church. Sure, Hartville counted more than just one redheaded resident, the hardest to miss being the wife of the town's lawyer. Mrs. Miranda Carlson was tall, green eyed, and, some said, a real firebrand. Her hair, though, reminded Jeremy more of old, fancy wooden furniture.

Rogers red was more the color of a ready-to-eat carrot—orange, if a man was honest, and Jeremy fancied himself a stand-up sort.

Because of that honesty, he allowed himself a moment to take into account the likelihood of disaster. The worst that could happen was that Old Man Rogers would greet him at his place, none too happy with whatever excuse Jeremy cobbled up for the visit. He couldn't very well try to buy out the man who'd cleared that land and worked it for years. There'd just be no reason.

Not that he wished anyone dead, of course. He just had a real, distinct need. And Angela Rogers—Angel, as the old man's girl was called—might be able to help him. If Oliver Rogers had indeed died.

Jeremy sent up a prayer as he approached Rogers Ranch. Details of his surroundings began to register. The place was tidy, with its solid log cabin and the barn back a ways off to his left. A horse stood at the rail of a modest corral, and a couple of fat chickens pecked the ground just on the other side of the circle. As he approached, the old steed shook its head and snorted. The chickens scattered with much feather fluttering and loud clucking.

To the left of the cabin, a sizeable garden, lush with young vegetable plants, gave promise of future bounty. Behind the garden, up the broad, green slope of the foothill, he spotted the much-despised white blobs—Rogers's sheep. To him, they looked more like a plague of lice than livestock.

To his dismay, they also looked healthy and well cared for, as did the horse, the chickens, the bovine who'd just stuck its head out the barn door . . . and the skinny, denim-trousered, buffalo-plaid-shirted, double-braided, pitchfork-bearing redhead at its side.

"What do you want, mister?" she asked.

Jeremy blinked at her contrary tone of voice. "I'm here for a neighborly visit with your pa. Is he around?"

The tautness at the corners of her mouth hinted at her unease . . . or could it be grief?

She jabbed the blunt handle of a pitchfork toward the back of the property. "He's out thataway right about now."

"Then I'd best head on over so's he and I can have us a nice talk."

Angel's hazel eyes darted in the direction she'd pointed, and she stepped closer, the tines of the fork pointed at his knee. "I don't think so, mister. It'd be a sin to disturb him. So you just state your business, and I'll be sure to tell him all about it later on."

Before Jeremy could object, a sheep appeared at her side and butted its furry head against her thigh. Without a look at the animal, she patted its cream-colored topknot. "Back up, Snowball. I'm busy."

Snowball wasn't about to be put off. The sheep lowered its head and laid into the girl's leg again, this time with more serious effort. Angel's knee buckled and she stumbled. As she tried to get back her balance, the pitchfork waved in the air above her head, and Jeremy feared for her safety. If she dropped the nasty thing and tripped on the handle, there was no telling what kind of harm she might do.

He dismounted and hurried to her side, but he reached her as she righted herself, her grip on the implement as sure as before.

"Maybe you ought to put that thing down before you do yourself some damage—"

"You stay right there, mister, and no one will have any damage done."

Although Jeremy didn't know if she'd actually go through with her threat, the jab she gave the fork seemed plenty serious to him. He backed up a step.

Snowball, who didn't seem patient at all, shoved Angel again, and this time she couldn't stay on her feet. The pitchfork flailed again, and Jeremy knew an opportunity when he saw it.

"For crying out loud, girl," he muttered and closed his hand on the fork's wooden handle. "I'm not here to hurt you. You're only in danger from yourself and this crazy thing."

Her big hazel eyes widened, and her nostrils flared. "You'd best be gone, mister. My father won't be taking too lightly your bothering me. It'd be a sin if you didn't heed."

Again Angel's odd way of saying things caught Jeremy's attention. This was the second time she'd brought up sin. Then again, seeing as how she'd grown up out here alone with her ma and pa—most recently with only the old man—maybe she'd picked up their way of talking. Especially since Old Man Rogers was said to have done more than his fair share of sinning in his wild youth.

The girl put Jeremy in mind of a high-spirited, unbroken filly. He took care to use his best horse-breaking voice. "Easy there, girl. I'm not here to hurt you or sin against you or your pa. I'm your neighbor from down south of you, and I figured it was right about time I stopped by and say how-do."

"Well, then, mister, now you've done just that. You can be on your way, and I'll be sure to tell my father about you. Thank you much for your . . . neighborliness."

The soft quiver he spied when she raised her chin told him there was more here than what she said or he could hear.

"I just—"

"Baa!"

Before he knew what had happened, he'd landed on his behind. His legs waved in the air, and the sheep stuck its nose right in his face.

"What kind of folk are you, anyway?" he asked when he'd raised up onto his elbows. "I've heard tell of those who keep guard dogs, but you're the first I've known with a guard sheep."

To his amazement, a giggle escaped Angel's mouth.

At the same time, her eyes sparkled and a peach tint spread under her cinnamon freckles. Jeremy could hardly believe what he saw before him. Despite the manly clothes, plain, copper-penny braids to her waist, and boyish bravado, Angel was a very pretty girl.

She came to his side, took her pitchfork from where it had landed when he fell, and hugged the cantankerous Snowball. "The Lord works in mysterious ways, I always say."

Jeremy shook his head and picked up his hat. "I'm as Christian as the next fellow, but I've never thought sheep instruments of His grace. They're more like curses upon His creation."

Angel's good humor disappeared. She tipped up her chin. "I'll have you know, sheep are indeed part of God's creation, just as much as you and I are. He loves them, and you'd do well to pay them the respect they deserve, if for no other reason than that He made them and put them on this earth."

The flashes of green in her changeable eyes told Jeremy he'd have to at least pretend to stomach her flock if he was ever to have a chance to talk with her father.

If the man was still alive.

He stood and crammed his hat back on to shield his eyes from the glare of the sun. "Hey, you can't blame a fellow if he isn't particularly disposed toward a critter that just butted him onto his . . . er . . . well, you know."

A twinkle replaced the sharp shards of color in her eyes. "Couldn't miss how you landed, mister. And it may just be a good idea if you take it as a fair warning. We do well for ourselves here, and we don't cotton to strangers wandering about our property. None of us do—not even the animals."

Hands raised in surrender, Jeremy took a step back. "I didn't come to wander. I just came to be neigh—"

"I'm not deaf, mister. I heard you the first time. You came to be neighborly, and like I told you up front, you've been neighborly enough already. I'm sure my father will see your gesture as he should. So you can just turn yourself right around and head back home. We're much obliged for your effort and all."

She was a wispy thing, all flowing lines and slender frame. But Jeremy now knew the delicate package packed a will of iron . . . and carried a wicked weapon in that pitchfork of hers. He'd never been sent packing quite so thoroughly in his twenty-six years, not since his aunt Gertie—Lord rest her orderly soul—had last scolded him for one of his youthful pranks.

There wasn't much a man could do in this situation. "Since you've made your wishes plain, ma'am, then I guess I've no choice but to be saying my farewell. Please give your pa my regards."

"I'll do that—"

"Baa!"

The wail carried a world of pain. Angel cast Jeremy a glare, then spun and ran to the barn. She never eased her grip on the pitchfork.

He considered this sudden twist. Should he leave and avoid further riling the girl? Or should he see it as God's helping hand in his time of trouble? Maybe he could help Angel with whatever was wrong with that hurt animal and at least show her he wasn't her worst enemy.

Even if her pa might see him as just that.

Jeremy called on the Lord for . . . well, he didn't quite know what for, but he did know that without heavenly help he was unlikely to succeed in anything he undertook. His adolescence and Aunt Gertie had taught him that much.

In the doorway of the barn, he blinked at the change in light. He took the time to really listen. From somewhere in the far right-hand corner of the dark building, he heard Angel's voice. Sweet, gentle murmurs gave it a softer quality than he'd heard up until then.

"Easy, Maggie. Easy, now."

Another pain-filled wail tore the air.

Even though he had no patience for sheep, Jeremy didn't have it in him to ignore an animal's misery either, and that was just what this creature's call told. Once his eyes adjusted to the shadows, he approached.

"What's wrong with her?"

Angel shot him another scowl. "I told you to go, mister. We don't need you here."

He ignored her words and knelt at her side. "My name's Jeremy Johnstone, not mister. I'd be right honored if you'd call me Jeremy. If you don't feel easy doing that, then Mr. Johnstone's fine with me."

She turned back to the sheep.

Jeremy peered at the animal. Despite his inexperience with sheep, he'd spent years around livestock at Aunt Gertie and Uncle

Frank's farm, and his last two years had exposed him to any and all circumstances of a creature's life. This ewe was having herself a time of birthing.

"Is the lamb backward?"

Angel nodded.

"Have you tried to turn it?"

Another nod.

Her silent answers were fast eating up his patience. "Well?"

She shrugged. "Well, nothing. I couldn't turn it. It's too big and she's too small."

The sob that hitched her voice told Jeremy more about Angel than anything he'd observed until then. The ewe's suffering was breaking her heart, and quite possibly, she dreaded its probable death if the birth didn't happen soon.

"Look, Miss Rogers, I might not know much about sheep, but I've helped many a cow, horse, and dog deliver their young ones. I'd like to help. It'd be a crime if I didn't even try."

Angel's big hazel eyes studied him over one shoulder while a graceful hand swept over the laboring ewe's swollen side. Jeremy held his breath. Where was the girl's father at this critical moment? Had Old Man Rogers gone off and left her by herself to handle what was plainly a rough time?

He didn't think so.

With an ever greater sense of certainty, Jeremy felt that Oliver Rogers had indeed passed not too long ago. Angel was alone on the ranch. As he watched the sheep convulse with another contraction and heard Angel's indrawn breath, Jeremy realized how defenseless she was.

And how brave.

She needed help, and somehow his need of water had brought him to her side at just the right moment. He knew what he had to do.

"Where's there water and good, strong soap?"

"There's a bucket near the door," she said, her voice soft,

husky, "and I've a cake of Fels-Naptha soap right by it. Towel's hanging off a nail above it all."

Jeremy folded his shirtsleeves out of the way, sudsed then rinsed his forearms, and dried off. Moments later he returned to Angel and her sheep. "What's her name?"

"It's Maggie."

He reached a hand toward the animal. "There, there, Maggie. Everything's all right. I'm just going to check to see if I can give the good Lord a hand today."

Angel gasped and turned, her eyes wide and warm with splashes of gold. Jeremy met her gaze. He prayed he could rise to the challenge, even though he wasn't certain what that challenge really was. What mattered most right then?

The life of a sheep?

Easy access to fresh water?

Or the trust of a lonely, vulnerable woman?

2

Jeremy offered up a brief prayer, then turned to the ewe. He'd helped birth his fair share of animals in the past, but something told him this time was different. Not because he'd never before dealt with sheep, but because of the young woman at his side. Her fear came at him in waves.

He spoke to Maggie, his words a crooning chant. "You're not alone, little mama. The almighty Father is here with us, and I'd wager His mercy will bring you through this just fine."

The ewe twitched her nose, then quaked again with another contraction. Jeremy took note with relief. She hadn't worn herself out beyond the point where she could help with the delivery, as too often happened in difficult birthings.

"Is she . . . ?" Angel's voice broke. "Will she . . . ?"

Although he knew what she wanted to ask, he didn't have an answer for her—at least not yet, not the one she wanted—so he didn't finish her question. The silence in the barn grew tense, long.

Angel's shuddery sigh made him turn. She said, "Here."

Jeremy nodded toward the tin she held out, his hands still on Maggie's tight belly.

She took off the lid. "It's clean rendered lanolin. You'll need it to lubricate your arm if you're going to try to move the lamb."

"You've done this before, I take it."

"Papa needed my help often enough."

Her words confirmed what he'd suspected. Oliver Rogers was indeed dead. But Jeremy knew when to keep his peace.

"Since she knows you better than she does me," he said, "why don't you hold her head? And please keep talking to her."

Angel moved deeper into the pen and did as he'd asked. Jeremy scooped out a generous amount of grease from the tin and applied a liberal coat on his arm. Then, after yet another prayer, he reached into the ewe's womb.

With gentle determination he searched for and found a pair of tiny legs. He patted farther up the unborn animal's body to confirm that they were indeed the rear ones.

"Is this Maggie's first lambing?"

"Yes. She's just a yearling."

"Well, she's either a real small sheep or we have us more trouble than just a hind-ways-out birth."

A frown brought Angel's dark red brows together. "More trouble?"

He tried to feel past the lamb's spine but found the space too tight to learn much. "She might be having twins."

In the flicker of lamplight, Angel's hazel eyes widened, the gold more prominent than the green. "Two lambs would be wonderful, but will it . . . will Maggie . . . ?"

He gave her the only answer he had. "Pray."

Jeremy blocked out his awareness of Angel to focus on the animals before him. He took hold of the lamb's hind legs, then waited for Maggie's next contraction. As her muscles clamped down on his forearm, he began to pull the lamb. He kept up a steady, gentle pressure and shifted the infant from side to side; a turned-around delivery could turn tragic if the baby's midsection got caught partway out of the birth canal.

He sure hoped he wouldn't have to cope with a second lamb.

"It's coming," he murmured as the pasterns slipped out from

the ewe's birth canal. "Help me a little longer here, Maggie. We're almost done, sweetheart."

The side-to-side motion, combined with his constant pull, brought the lamb out just about to the halfway point, as he'd expected. If sheep were like cattle, then they now faced the most dangerous moment—birthing the ribs, slender bones that could catch and refuse to come out. If that happened, then the little one's life, as well as Maggie's, was in real danger.

Even though only a few seconds had gone by since the start of this contraction, to Jeremy it felt more like hours. "Hang in there with me, girl," he urged the ewe. "We just have a little while longer to work."

The pressure of the womb's muscles was still strong, so Jeremy pulled a bit harder and continued to work the little body out. He eased the delicate ribs one by one from Maggie's body and kept a lookout for the all-important cord. It could become pinched now that the birth was almost over, and once that happened, the lamb would draw its first breath. He had to make sure it didn't do so inside the mother's body.

Speed and sure hands were critical, so Jeremy took the lamb's hindquarters in both hands and drew harder yet. The little one slid out all at once, and he hurried to wipe off its nose to make sure it would breathe without trouble.

The bellows-like puff of the newborn's sides told him he'd succeeded . . . at least so far.

"Let me care for the cord," Angel said.

She soaked a length of cotton string in what smelled like pure alcohol, then squeezed out the excess fluid. With sure motions she wrapped the string around the cord two or three times before she knotted it. With the black-handled scissors she took from the pocket of her trousers, she snipped the cord, then dropped the scissors and pulled a small glass jar from her bottomless pocket.

A dark liquid sloshed inside the jar. When Angel opened it

Jeremy caught the unique tang of iodine. She did indeed know what she was about. When Angel maneuvered the lamb's navel into the jar to soak the stump in the medication, Jeremy smiled. There'd be no infection for her newborn lamb.

She then laid the lamb at Maggie's head. The ewe made a soft sound and went to work drying off the little one's coat.

"Well," he said, "we'll see right soon if she's about to have another one after all."

"In either case, I need to fetch molasses water for Maggie."

"Good. She'll need it to make enough milk, especially if she has to feed two."

Angel stepped away; Jeremy was impressed—impressed and surprised. Her efficient skill impressed him, while her decision to leave the barn right then came as a surprise. Either she'd decided to trust him or her concern for her animals was greater than her fear.

He didn't get the opportunity to mull it over to any great length, since Maggie's breathing changed again. Before the contraction built to its crest, he slipped his hand inside the ewe to feel for what he suspected was on its way out.

He found the small legs, back ones again.

"All right, little mama," he murmured. "Looks to this cowboy like you're going to work just a mite longer today."

Because the first birth had left space in Maggie's body, Jeremy turned this lamb on its side, and the ewe's second delivery proved easier than the first. By the time Angel returned, he'd cleared the second lamb's nose, tied her cord and doused it in iodine, and set her at her brother's side. Maggie busied herself drying her babies.

"Aren't they sweet?" Angel asked.

"They're tiny miracles."

When he realized what he'd said, Jeremy was sure he'd lost his wits. Sheep . . . miracles? Grass-shearing, water-guzzling blight was more like it. But in the face of Angel's enchantment with the critters, he knew he'd be wise to not rile her again.

Better to keep silent.

Angel moved the newborns to Maggie's udder, and Jeremy heard her catch her breath as she waited to see if they would nurse of their own will. When both little ones latched on, she sagged onto the bedding at their side.

"Thank you, Father," she murmured, her eyes closed.

"Amen."

When she didn't comment on his response, Jeremy gathered the wet bedding material. Any dampness in the pen could lead to pneumonia in a newborn, and although sheep were the bane of his existence, he was too much a rancher to let even these critters run that risk.

A while later, Maggie and her offspring now content in their clean pen, Jeremy and Angel left the barn. The sun still hung high in the sky, and he paused to consider how much time he'd spent at the Rogers spread already.

"Please, mister," Angel said. "I don't have anything fancy, but you've been a blessing to me, and the least I can do is feed you a meal."

His innards rumbled in response to her words, loudly enough to bring a smile to her lips.

"Looks like I can't turn your offer down in any kind of polite way," he said with a wry grin. "But I hate to put you out. You've been busy in the barn, and you don't have to go to the trouble of filling up my complaining belly."

"I've a chicken stewing in the kettle, and biscuits won't take but minutes to make. Won't be any trouble to make enough for you."

He jumped at the chance to see the inside of the tidy cabin a short span away. "I've a powerful fondness for a good biscuit, and goodness knows I'm a poor hand at cooking."

Angel chuckled and led the way to the pump in the yard behind the cabin. Another bar of the robust Fels-Naptha soap sat in a bowl, and a blue-and-white-striped length of toweling hung from a nail by the back door to the house.

After they'd both made good with the cleaning supplies, Angel led the way inside. While she went to the large woodstove at their right, Jeremy studied his surroundings from the doorway.

She kept the cabin as tidy as she did the garden and outbuildings. A plain wooden cupboard stood near the stove, and from it Angel withdrew a large, tight-lidded tin. A plain plank shelf over the cupboard held an array of crockery. She chose a large yellow-ware bowl and dumped in a measure of flour from the metal container.

On his approach to the hefty table in the middle of the kitchen, Jeremy matched his steps to the rhythm of her spoon against the sides of the bowl. He doffed his hat and sat on one of the solid ladder-back chairs. She worked with efficiency and grace, and before long she returned to the stove, a metal sheet dotted with blobs of dough in hand.

Jeremy's curiosity again took the upper hand, and he went on with his inspection of Angel's home. On the left side of the room, next to the fireplace, an upholstered chair and the table and lantern beside it told him where Angel spent her evenings. Jeremy suspected the woven basket at the foot of the table held needlework of some kind.

On a nearby wall, a wealth of well-worn books filled a set of shelves. Folks said Mrs. Rogers was a schoolmarm before she wed old Oliver, and the small library suggested an educated owner. She'd more than likely used her training to teach her daughter.

Farther down the opposite wall, a door closed off what Jeremy figured was a bedroom, while overhead, a banister and rails of peeled branch fenced in a loft. A many-colored quilt lay over the banister, its complicated piecing and stitching proof of someone's great care. He wondered if the late Mrs. Rogers had made it or if Angel was a woman of many talents.

A bowl of stew appeared on the table before him, thick with vegetables and pieces of chicken, and fragrant with savory seasoning. When he noticed Angel's pointed look, his ears heated.

His nosiness allowed no excuse. "Nice place."

"Thank you. Papa worked hard to build the house for Mama right after they married, and she took pride in keeping a comfortable home." She put a plate of biscuits in the middle of the table, a steaming pot of coffee next to it, and sat across from him. "It couldn't have been easy, not back then. It isn't easy now, and I know they worked mighty hard to make things good for me."

The question burned in Jeremy's throat, but he knew better than to ask it right then. He feared talk of her father's death would send her after her pitchfork—or, worse yet, a shotgun. He didn't cotton to meeting old Oliver Rogers on the other side of life just yet.

"You've done well, I'd say."

She gave a mild shrug. "If you don't mind, mister, would you ask the blessing?"

He arched a brow, but she refused to meet his gaze. Instead, she stared at her bowl of food, her hands somewhere below the edge of the table.

"I don't mind," he said when the silence grew long. "Father God, I thank you for all you give us each day. You put food on our plates, give us cover from the weather, and even watch over our stock. Bless this meal, the hands that made it, and us who'll need it to keep us working as we try to follow you. Amen."

He nearly missed her soft amen on account of the throaty yowl at his side.

"Sunny!" Angel cried. "Settle down. Right now."

The big yellow dog gave no sign of heeding her mistress's command. The yowls grew louder.

Jeremy had a way with animals, but he didn't know just how to get around the mouthful of bared canine teeth. He sat still, since he reckoned it a safer choice than reaching out to try to make friends with the shaggy critter.

Angel went to her dog. "You stop it right now, you hear? You don't fool me."

"I reckon she's not used to strangers," Jeremy said. "She's only fixing to protect what's hers."

"Not hardly." Angel gave him a sheepish smile. "She's the world's biggest beggar. What she wants is the food on your plate. Sunny hasn't met a stranger, much less an enemy, to this day."

Jeremy studied the animal's deep brown eyes. "Let's see if a biscuit will do the job."

"Oh, please, no. Once you give in to her, you'll have not even a moment's peace to eat. I've worked awful hard to break her begging habits."

"Couldn't you let the discipline go a bit today? I can stand a little wheedling here and there. Besides, we've the lambs' birthing to celebrate. Sunny can join us if I give her a biscuit treat. And I might just make myself a new friend. A man can never have too many of those."

She rolled her eyes in obvious disgust, then shrugged.

He held the bread out to the dog, and the snap of the strong jaws almost cost him his fingers. One gulp and the biscuit disappeared down the dog's gullet. Then her big pink tongue swiped nonexistent crumbs from her lips.

Jeremy chuckled. "I think Sunny and I will get on right fine. We're both partial to good biscuits."

Back at her chair, Angel shook her head. "Don't say I didn't warn you when she coaxes every last morsel from you. And don't complain about an empty belly after supping at my table. I put plenty before you, just not enough for that great big beggar of mine, too. I've a bucket of scraps tucked away for her."

"I'll take my chances."

Once Jeremy took a bite of his biscuit, he felt a great deal of sympathy for the dog. Flaky and tender, the biscuit melted right on past his throat.

"No wonder Sunny's a beggar. You make mighty fine biscuits, Angel Rogers."

"Thank you," she murmured, her attention on her plate.

From there, the meal took place in silence, and Jeremy savored the best food he'd had in days. Well, the best since Rosario Fuentes, his foreman's wife, had left to deliver the couple's first child and then recover from the birth. After Maggie had safely birthed her lambs, Jeremy and Angel had shared the success, and even when they'd entered the cabin, he'd felt, if not welcome, then at least at ease. But now a strange tension stretched between them. Angel refused to meet his gaze, and Jeremy wondered if she had her pitchfork on her mind.

He'd been patient long enough.

"Just when did your pa die?"

Angel's cheeks paled and her eyes opened wide. She opened her mouth, but no sound came out. Instead, she struggled to catch her breath, and her fingers shook enough for him to notice.

He watched her fight for calm, but her high, thin-sounding voice gave her away. "I told you before. He's out back—"

"Please don't do that. You're plainly a Christian, and I can tell you're trying not to fib, but the tale you're weaving comes awful close to a lie."

The knuckles of her clasped hands whitened as she tightened her grip. She stared down at them as if she'd never seen them before. She drew a deep breath, then squared her shoulders and brought her head back up. When her gaze met his, he again saw green fire in her hazel eyes.

"Fine, mister—"

"Jeremy or Mr. Johnstone will do—if you please."

Her head bobbed once. "Mr. Johnstone. You're right. Papa died at the start of winter, but I don't see how that has anything to do with you."

"Seems to me it has everything to do with me. Or with my ranch."

Her nostrils flared and she narrowed her eyes. "Then you'll oblige me and leave now."

"Not until I've had my say." She went to speak, but Jeremy held up a hand. "Hear me out. I mean you no harm."

He gave her the time to decide what to do. As the seconds ticked by, Sunny rose from where she'd lain by the fireplace and crossed to Angel's side, her dark eyes fixed on him. Jeremy didn't doubt that if for any reason the shaggy golden creature decided he'd become a threat to her mistress, she'd attack with those powerful jaws and big teeth—no matter what Angel said about the animal having yet to meet a stranger or foe.

Angel gave another sharp nod but said nothing. She stared at him, defiance in her eyes.

"Do you have any kin?"

Her startled expression told him she hadn't expected the question. "No . . . That is, none anywhere near. Papa had no one left, but I suppose Mama's cousins still live somewhere in Georgia. Why do you care?"

"Because you need them, and they need to do right by you."

"They don't know me, and I've never even learned their names, so I can't see why we're discussing them." She stood. "I told you to leave, and I meant it."

Jeremy stayed put. "Seeing as you're all alone out here—"

"I'm not alone. I've my sheep, my horse, my chickens, Sunny, and my Lord, thank you very much."

The snooty tilt of her chin began to irritate Jeremy. This wasn't going at all as he'd imagined it would.

"The animals can't protect you against . . . well, against anything that might come at you."

"At least you didn't say the Lord couldn't do as much. I trust Him."

"So do I, but you can't trust men, and everyone around these parts knows all about your land. It's a good ranch, and you're just a girl all alone. You can't handle it on your own."

"I don't handle it on my own. The Lord is watching out for this land, for me, and for my animals. Even you told Him that before we ate. Did you mean what you said to God, or were you just talking pretty?"

He surged to his feet. "Why, of course I meant it. That is, I was telling Him how much I appreciate what He gives, but that doesn't mean I think you're not risking too much out here now that your pa isn't here to watch out for you. If you make foolish choices . . . well, foolishness has nothing to do with what God can or can't do."

"I'm no fool. I watch out for myself, and as I already told you, I leave the rest to Him." She crossed to the door. "Now, as I also told you, I'd be much obliged if you'd get yourself off my land."

"Not before I tell you what I can offer."

"I don't want it."

He raised his arms in exasperation. "You don't even know what I can pay."

"Rogers Ranch isn't for sale."

"Everything's for sale sooner or later and for the right fair price."

She frowned. "Not a very honorable way to look at life."

"An honest one." He crammed his hat on his head. "Look. I saved up a good pile of money all those years I dug silver out of that mountain up over there. I spent a big chunk of it two years ago when I bought my spread—"

"When the Carlisles packed it up and went back east."

"That's right. And I've done a right good job of running that ranch. All I need is steady access to water. And that's where you come in."

"Not me. God."

He blinked hard and tried to make sense of what she'd said. "What do you mean?"

"Well, God set my creek here and not over there to the south." She smiled. "It's His earth, and everything is according to His pleasure."

Jeremy couldn't argue that. "It still doesn't stop me from making you a sound, fair offer for your land."

"It also doesn't stop me from turning you down. My land's not for sale, Mr. Johnstone. Now leave. Please."

She was stubborn. He'd give her that. "Fine. I'll head on out now, but you can count on me coming back. I don't give up easy."

"Mama always said I was more determined than Papa's old mule, Horace."

What was a man to say when a woman said something like that?

"You be careful, now," he said. "Not everyone who'll come out here for your land—or, to talk plain, your water—is going to care what the Lord thinks of him. There's plenty who'd do anything to get their greedy hands on what they want."

He paused. It was obvious she already knew there were those who'd lie and cheat. He wondered, however, how innocent she truly was.

"And your property isn't all they'll want." Her eyes widened again. This time he'd wager he saw fear in the dark gold depths. "You're a pretty little thing, Miss Rogers. Among us men, there are many who aren't principled when it comes to women. Who knows how far they'll go to get their hands on everything you have—on the ranch and on your self."

3

"Pretty little thing!" Angel said in a fair imitation of Jeremy's arrogant tone. "Did you hear him, Sunny? Me! Little."

The dog responded in well-modulated and multipitched yowls, her loving gaze on her mistress.

Angel picked up and waved Jeremy's used tin plate. "Why, I'm as tall as Papa was, and he wasn't the shortest of men. Besides, that Johnstone fellow mentioned fools. I'd say he's the one to best wear that title, don't you think?"

Sunny woofed a succinct response.

"I knew you'd agree with me."

Angel appreciated a dog who had yet to realize she was a dog. The two of them often carried on spirited conversations, and Sunny had never yet left her side—except when she kept her buddy Maggie company. Constant and loyal, the animal brought joy into Angel's workaday existence.

She dropped Jeremy's plate into the dishpan. Drops sprayed her checked shirt, and the moisture felt good in the too early, too high summer heat.

"He's the fool if he thinks I'm going to sell him Papa's ranch. Besides, I'm not lonely. Not one bit."

She'd discovered in the months since she found Papa slumped in his big chair by the fireplace that she enjoyed the easy pace she'd set up for herself and her stock. Not that she didn't miss her father, and she'd never stop wishing Mama was still with her, but Angel now knew she didn't need the constant company of others.

She spent her days working—hard. The ranch took a toll on a body, if you ran it right. But that was fine with her. She liked the satisfaction of doing a good job. And she hadn't had the chance to feel alone since those first few weeks after she buried Papa.

She'd felt the Lord at her side every minute of every one of those days, weeks, months. He'd made His presence known to her in a number of ways, the peace with which He'd blessed her the most obvious of all. That peace never lessened—well, it hadn't until Jeremy rode up to her house earlier that day.

Angel drew a shaky breath. "Oh, fine. I'll admit it, Lord. That cowboy did rattle me. But that's no reason for me to just up and take whatever he wants to give me and then prance off Papa's ranch. I've nowhere else to go, and I plain don't want to. Not until you tell me it's time for me to leave."

She dried the few utensils she'd used to prepare the meal she'd shared with the rancher, put them away, then headed back outside. From the angle of the sun in the western sky, she reckoned it was about seven o'clock. She had time to finish the last chores of the day.

At the barn, she filled a bucket with dried corn. Back out by the corral, she called to the chickens. "Here, ladies." The handful of grain she cast drew an immediate response. "Oh, and you, too, Rufus," she told the rooster. "Can't forget you. I'd have no flock without you."

In wide, sweeping waves she scattered the corn over the yard. The fowl skittered around her, their beaks busy with the food. She welcomed the ruffle of feathers, the clucked calls, even the cock's crow; they played a song to her rancher's ears.

She smiled up to heaven. "Thank you, Father."

As she turned back to the barn, she glanced toward Jeremy's ranch. She froze.

Atop a huge russet horse, Jeremy stared at her, his face shielded by the shadow the wide brim of his hat cast down. The square set of his shoulders, the proud tilt of his head, and the determination she'd read in his gaze as he'd made his offer left her no doubt that he'd meant every word he'd uttered.

He'd been there while she'd cleaned up inside. He'd never left.

From what he'd said, she knew Jeremy Johnstone was a self-made man. He'd worked hard and had used his money well. Now he saw only one obstacle in the way of his continued success—her.

He would be back. He wouldn't let his dogged resolve fade. He meant to have her land—her water.

Angel turned her back to the man etched against the purpling sky. One step after another, she made her feet draw a straight line to the barn. He could stay and watch her as long as he wanted—it was none of her business how he wasted his time. But she prayed she'd made clear her position. She wasn't about to hand him what belonged to her. No matter how much he wanted it.

A cold shiver ran up her spine as she entered the barn, and not because of the slightly cooler temperature inside. She wondered what her father would have thought of the cowboy and his determination.

Was Jeremy the kind of man Papa had in mind when he'd voiced his many warnings? What kind of scruples did Jeremy have? He'd been quick to speak of the lack of scruples in those he believed would follow him.

How would he negotiate? Those negotiations wouldn't bring him satisfaction. Even though Angel knew she wouldn't sell, she also knew the cowboy didn't believe he wouldn't sway her.

To what lengths would he go to reach his goal?

The next morning Angel went about her work determined to forget Jeremy's invasion of her small, peaceful world. But try as she might, his words remained seared in her memory.

As was his steely blue stare. He struck Angel as a man who never gave up and always got his way.

Well, she didn't give up either. She always succeeded.

Except when she tried to forget their discussion the day before.

"Oh, Sunny girl," she muttered. "Here I promise myself I won't waste another thought on that fellow, and I'm back at it just minutes later. What am I going to do?"

Sunny sneezed and shook her head. She had nothing to say.

"Angel Rogers! Where are you?"

Thank you, Father, for the distraction.

"Wynema Howard!" she called, "What are you doing out here again so soon? Are there no more folks in need of a photograph or two?" She didn't wait for an answer. "Oh, who cares? It's good to have you here. I'm in the barn. Maggie birthed twins yesterday. Come and see them."

A clatter broke out near the barn door. Mutters followed.

Angel stifled a giggle. "One of these days," she said on her way to help her friend, "you're going to realize that you need to either affix all these contraptions to your body or hire help to take them with you."

The young photographer from Hartville was a caution. Always somewhat disheveled, she wasted no time or effort on fluffs or furbelows—something the two women had in common. Where they differed was in their approach to folks in general. Angel preferred to avoid them altogether and chose to surround herself with her animals. Wynema liked nothing more than to spend hours taking the likeness of even the most disagreeable curmudgeon, whom she'd likely describe as an interesting subject.

Wynema shot Angel a glare from where she'd bent over to retrieve the tripod she'd dropped. "You think I should hire a silly miss who'll have nothing more on her mind than what she'll look like in her next picture? Hah!"

Angel giggled again, unable to squelch the mischief that from time to time took over. "You could always hire a man."

The lady photographer snorted. "What good would one of those do me? He'd be forever telling me how to do what I have to do and know how to do better than he'd ever know. I have yet to meet the man who isn't more of a fool than . . . than . . . well, than the next man."

A fool . . . a man . . .

"Wynema?"

Angel's visitor dragged the tripod toward the birthing pen. "Yes?"

"Do you know a man by the name of Johnstone? Jeremy Johnstone?"

"Johnstone? The rancher?"

"That very one."

"Can't say that I know him, but I've seen him around Hartville. Less often since he quit working at the Heart of Silver Mine and bought himself that ranch a couple of years ago." She set up the tripod just beyond the gate to the birthing pen, then turned to stare at Angel. "His spread's somewhere out around here." She narrowed her eyes. "Is he giving you trouble?"

Angel bit her lower lip. "Maybe."

Wynema smacked her fists on her hips, and her hat tumbled off her head. It dislodged a hank of plain brown hair on its descent. She blew at the mass from the corner of her mouth but achieved nothing. "Now what kind of fool answer is that?"

"The only one I have right now."

Wynema tapped her toe against the dirt floor of the barn. "Well? Do I need to call a dentist to pull the words out of your mouth? Explain yourself!"

"He was here yesterday." Wynema's concern turned to a mutinous glare. Angel placed a hand on her friend's shoulder. "Wait. Don't get angry—not yet. He only came to offer to buy my land."

"Only? He only offered to buy your land? That strikes me as awfully high and mighty of him. And him looking just like an innocent choirboy, with all that yellow hair and blue eyes . . . Turns out he's quite full of himself, isn't he?"

Angel thought back on the events of the day before. "No . . . I can't say he was anything like that. He did help when Maggie had trouble with the birthing. He came right into the pen and brought those babies out of her when I couldn't even budge them. All three could have died had he not helped."

"Hmm . . ."

"No, really. He wasn't nasty or anything, just . . . determined."

Wynema laughed. "Well, then I'd say he's met his match, don't you think?"

Angel shrugged.

"I say he did." The photographer fiddled with the tools of her trade and, in moments, set a dark and serious-looking camera, black shroud and all, atop the tripod. "If I couldn't talk you into selling and moving into town with me, then I know a pretty-faced cow wrangler with a pocketful of dollars isn't about to do it either."

"That's true."

The photographer's gaze turned speculative, and Angel felt, as she often did in her friend's presence, that she might be the subject of Wynema's next photographic essay. She didn't cotton to that one bit. Wynema saw more than Angel wanted her to see far too often.

It was time to change the topic. "Well," she said, "since you're here and with your contraptions—"

"Stop right there, missy!"

Uh-oh. She hadn't been fast enough to escape Wynema's quick

wit. "I'm not going anywhere other than to introduce you to Maggie's babies—"

"Seems to me you're in a sudden hurry to drop the matter of Mr. Johnstone. I wonder why. Is it because he irked you with his offer? Or is it because I reminded you the Lord blessed him with a pretty face?"

Angel's cheeks warmed, and she turned toward the sheep. "Neither," she said in a voice as firm as she could muster. "I just don't reckon it'll do us any good to keep talking about something that's of no great importance. I'm not going to sell Rogers Ranch, and Mr. Johnstone's not going to buy it."

"Hmm . . ."

Maggie chose that moment to give out a welcoming baa.

Angel seized the opportunity. "Come look at the lambs. You haven't seen a sweeter pair."

Wynema hesitated a moment or two, just long enough for Angel to offer a prayer for relief from her friend's curiosity and perception. She thanked the Lord for His response when Wynema knelt at her side.

The two women spent a pleasant morning with the lambs and shared laughs as Wynema plied her trade, this time for no other reason than her passion for photography. She took endless likenesses of the newborns and their dam, all the while she chatted up a storm.

Angel let her ramble, glad to have something else in mind besides yesterday's visitor, his irritating offer, and his frightening warning. It wasn't until after they'd eaten their noontime meal that Wynema returned to the earlier, uncomfortable subject.

As she clattered into her latest purchase, a shiny buggy, Wynema wagged a long, slender finger at Angel. "Now, you listen and listen good. You know as well as I do that we've had quite a drought around these parts—never mind last winter's one horrid storm. It was hardly enough to make mud when it melted."

"I know that better than you do."

"But what you don't know is the talk around town."

"Oh?"

"Oh yes. There's any number of landowners around here who're just this far away from going belly up."

Angel took note of the lack of space between Wynema's thumb and index finger. She grimaced.

"Well," the photographer continued, "I can also tell you there's just that many of them who're willing to about kill to get their hands on what you have. That creek of yours is worth more than all the land in Colorado right about now. Land is nothing more than dirt unless it grows grass for cattle and horses to eat. If nothing grows, stock can't eat, and if they don't eat, they won't get fat enough to bring a rancher anything to put in the bank when he sells."

Angel didn't respond.

"Haven't you heard a word I said? There's been more than a few killings around these parts for as little as a horse found on someone else's land. When I said these men are willing to kill, I'm afraid I spoke God's truth—He's witnessed sinning as you can't imagine when it comes to greed."

"Papa said as much."

"And he would know." Wynema took up the reins. "He saw more of the West and our fair Colorado than just about anyone else ever has and maybe ever will. You watch yourself all alone out here—"

"Now you sound like Mr. Johnstone. Whose side are you on?"

"Yours, silly goose. If nothing else, I'm determined like you. I have to be—I work a man's trade in a man's world, and I've had to fight for everything I have. But no one's livelihood has ever been threatened by my camera or chemicals or papers. Your water and your sheep may look like both the enemy and salvation to any number of greedy men."

Angel sighed. "I've read my Scripture as well as any other woman has. I know it's a fallen world. But I'll get nothing done if I fret and fuss and worry about which brute will come out here to make me the next clumsy offer. I'm sure that's not why the Lord put me on His earth. All I can do is work as I always have and trust Him to watch over me."

Wynema looked as though she wanted to say more, but then she sagged. A moment later she straightened again. "I'm sorry. You're right. There's little you can do. Besides, I guess there's no earthly good in scaring you, is there?"

"No. And tell me this: if you were me, would you leave?"

The photographer sputtered like a boiled-dry teakettle, then said, "No."

"See?"

"Now *you* tell *me*: do you have a shotgun?"

"Sure. Papa's old one."

"But can you use it?"

"Ah . . . er . . . well . . ."

"Just what I thought. Heaven help you, girl, because it looks like you won't do it yourself."

With that dire declaration, and with a shake of her head, the young photographer took off for Hartville, the small mining town where she lived and worked a ways up the mountain north of Rogers Ranch.

Angel watched her friend drive away, her gaze on the buggy until it disappeared in the shadows of the mountain's trees. As she often did, she recalled Psalm 121 from memory. "I will lift up mine eyes unto the hills, from whence cometh my help. My help cometh from the LORD, which made heaven and earth."

❦

A week after he helped deliver Angel's latest additions to her flock of pasture lice, Jeremy hadn't come up with a better argument against her hardheaded stance. He knew she shouldn't be out there by herself, but he didn't have the fancy words or the polished ways of an educated man to convince her of that.

And it still hadn't rained.

Everyone was testy, and a meeting had been called in Hartville to discuss matters. Of course, he'd go.

He tightened the cinch on his gelding's saddle, all the time aware of his foreman's gaze. "Don't know what good jawing's going to do, Esteban."

The man shrugged but didn't speak.

"Well, it sure won't make it rain, now, will it?"

"No, Mr. Johnstone, it won't. So why you going to—what you call it? Jawing?"

Jeremy rubbed his damp forehead on the sweat-drenched sleeve of his upper right arm. He'd changed out of the rank clothes he'd worked in all day only a quarter hour ago. "Blasted heat."

He glared at the dusty ground, kicked it with the toe of his boot. "Babbling," he muttered. "That's all's going to happen tonight. A lot of talking that won't bring us a single change in the weather."

"Then why you go?"

Why indeed?

"I guess a man's gotta find like-minded fools who're suffering as he is, at least every once in a while."

Esteban gave him a pitying look. "Sounds crazy to me."

"Maybe I have gone crazy."

The Double J Ranch foreman knew when to keep his peace.

It didn't help Jeremy's temper. He smacked his dusty hat against his thigh. "Why does she have to be such a stubborn mule?"

"You have no mule, Mr. Johnstone."

"You're right, Esteban, I have no mule. I just have to deal with a woman more wrongheaded than a mule and with more water than she and those sheep need."

"Ah . . ."

"What does that mean?"

Esteban shrugged.

"Oh no. You can't say that 'Ah' like that and not explain yourself."

"It's a woman. What more is to say?"

"Yes. A woman. A woman with a ranch and a creek and sheep."

"Ah . . ."

Tiring of the pointless conversation, Jeremy swung into the saddle. "I'm leaving. Two of your 'Ahs' is too many for me. Go home to Rosario. See if you can talk her into coming back to cook for me. I'm hungrier than a bear at the winter thaw."

"Rosario is woman, too, Mr. Johnstone. I no believe Rosario come cook for you again. She wants stay in the home with the little one and cook for me."

"Figures," Jeremy muttered, then took up the reins. "Go home and eat the feast she's likely made for you while I go make do with whatever's left at the Silver Belle."

"Apple pie good there."

"Not half as good as my mother's was."

Esteban smiled, then turned away, shaking his head. "*Buenas noches*, Mr. Johnstone. I see you in the morning."

"Hopefully, in the strongest, longest rain Colorado's ever seen."

When his foreman didn't answer, Jeremy took up the reins and headed to a middling meal at the town's most popular restaurant and the lousy meeting he suspected would ensure a bad case of dyspepsia once he managed to fall asleep.

❦

A miserable four hours later, Jeremy's hind end was sore from sitting. His middle housed a roaring fire from the food he'd wolfed down in order to make it to city hall in time for the meeting. The arguments had soured his supper, just as he'd expected. And as he'd also feared, nothing came from the hours of wrangling the matter.

Now he stood at the door to the large room and watched the still-lathered ranchers disagree with each other some more. He was waiting for Marcus Sutton, Hartville's banker, so as to discuss his options before he had to act with no toothsome choice before him.

The well-upholstered banker finally shook off those who'd claimed his attention and approached the door.

"Evening, sir," Jeremy said. "Could I trouble you for a short spell?"

Exhaustion drew lines from the corners of the man's eyes to the receding hairline at his temples. "I guess it is for the best if we discuss your situation now instead of later."

"That's how I see it."

Jeremy laid out his predicament, even though the banker had heard the same thing from just about every man who'd attended the meeting. Sutton showed great patience. When Jeremy came to the end, the older man sighed.

"I wish there was more I could do, son. Hate to see a fellow lose everything he's worked for, and especially because of something out of his control. But that's the way of the world, isn't it?"

Jeremy's anger simmered. A pounding took up just behind his eyes, the pressure right near unbearable. "I reckon so, but I figure you can see that with money I can feed my herd better. I can sell it for more if they're good and fat. That's how a rancher turns a profit. Once I do, I can pay back what I borrow, and I'll even bank some savings. In your bank."

"What if the rains continue to pass us by? How will you pay the loan?"

The banker's words clapped tension like a vise grip onto Jeremy's head.

"I can't be thinking on that possibility, sir. Sure you can understand that."

"Of course, son." Sutton laid a sympathetic arm on Jeremy's shoulders. "But I have to remind you of reality, now, don't I?

There's a chance this year will prove even dryer than the last two have been. I'd have to foreclose if you couldn't pay. Are you sure you want to risk that?"

Jeremy's stomach flipped. "I reckon that's the kind of chance I took when I left off working for someone else. I'll make good for myself, or I'll go under for myself. The mines will always be there, and I can always work them again if things don't pan out. But I have faith that they will. Besides, if I sell the herd and it's not fat enough to bring me a good return, I'm bound to lose the ranch for taxes anyway."

The banker didn't answer straightaway. His keen gaze scoured Jeremy's face.

"Did I say something wrong?" Jeremy asked.

"No, son, I can't say you did." Sutton rubbed behind his right ear with a thick finger. "But there is something else you can try. Something you haven't mentioned."

Hope caught fire in Jeremy's heart. "And that would be . . . ?"

"The Rogers girl."

"What about her?"

"Old Man Rogers is dead, isn't he?"

"She finally admitted it was so."

"Well, then there's the answer."

Although he'd never thought himself thickheaded, Jeremy felt that way right then. "Where, sir? She won't sell, so where's the answer?"

Speculation filled Sutton's gaze. He tapped Jeremy's shoulder with his beefy fist. "Just marry the girl. You'll get the ranch, a wife to keep house for you, and her water as well."

The earth dropped out from under Jeremy's feet. "You'd have me marry that stubborn, pitchfork-toting, sheep-loving, red-headed mountain madwoman?"

Sutton just smiled.

Jeremy shook his head. "I'd best go on home to bed. I need to get me some sleep. I'd swear I heard you say I should marry

Old Man Rogers's daughter. And I just plumb can't believe you meant it."

"I did—I do. The way I see it, whoever owns her land—and her water—will be the one who'll survive the drought."

"And lose his mind in the doing."

The banker laughed, shook his head, then turned to leave. "Never did ask me how to keep your wits, now did you? You just wanted to know what to do to keep your spread. Looks like there's only one thing to do if she won't sell. Go home and sleep on it. You might find the medicine for what ails you a mite better tasting in the light of day."

As Jeremy rode home, he doubted he'd notice any light around him, even if the sun blazed as brassy and hot as it had for days . . . weeks.

Marry Angel?

Nothing could be farther from his plans.

Lord? Are you out there somewhere tonight? Are you even listening to me? What am I going to do?

The silence of the mountains pursued him all the way home. Its endless echo rang grim and hollow; it drove in the reality of his situation.

At the ranch, he stabled his horse and sat on the porch steps. Hours crept by. He tried to keep his mind blank, wishing his lids would grow even a bit heavy. When the relentless yellow sun burned away the pale tint of dawn on the eastern horizon, Jeremy had no answer to his predicament. He was truly alone—God had forsaken him.

There was no rain in his immediate future. Not a cloud marred the relentless blue of the Colorado sky.

4

"There you are," Phoebe Gable said as she paid Angel for her weekly delivery of eggs and early vegetables.

Once spring arrived, Angel had resumed regular trips into Hartville to sell her surplus to the mining company's general store. That wouldn't give away her secret—no one would suspect Papa's death, since she'd begun to bring the goods to town after Mama died.

Phoebe, the new mine owner's recent bride, had become one of the few people Angel didn't regard with suspicion, just like Wynema, who stood by a rack full of tinned foods, and Letty Wagner, the town's doctor, who carried an armful of bandages and wore concern on her face.

"Thank you," Angel said. "And how are you faring, now I hear the mine's not producing as it used to?"

A faint line appeared between Phoebe's fair brows. "I won't deny that we've given the matter much thought, but Adrian has decided to run it as long as the vein produces enough ore to make weekly payrolls. Too many families depend on the men's wages, you know."

Wynema marched over from the rack of tins. "That's why I'll never let myself depend on a man," she said. "I'll always work my hardest and trust the Lord to bless my efforts."

"Goodness, Wynema," Phoebe said. "I hope you don't discount the possibility of wedding, at least some day."

"Well, I don't intend to hitch myself to some sad sort who'll want to run my life and my business and keep me fat with his babies."

Wynema's words surprised Angel. "What's wrong with you?" she asked. "I've never heard you so sour on marriage before."

"I'm no more or less sour on marriage. It's men that give me dyspepsia. I haven't met a one yet who doesn't have a plan to benefit himself. Not even your Adrian, Phoebe. Remember what brought him to town, if you will. And all the trouble his plot brought with him."

Angel had heard something about the mine's new owner last fall when she'd come to the store, and even at church on a Sunday, but she hadn't paid it much attention. It must not have been too awful. Phoebe had married him.

"Now, Wynema," Letty said, "you know full well that Adrian had few choices. He did the best he could, and he righted those wrongs as soon as he could."

Phoebe tipped up her chin. "My dear husband's actions were heroic—even if he didn't always think through their possible consequences. Besides, that's all in the past. I'll have you know we're a blissfully happy family."

The four women glanced toward the simple oak crib behind the store's counter.

Wynema smiled. "I'll grant you, Lee is sweet."

Phoebe glowed. "My son's a treasure, and my husband and I are blessed to have him, him and the new one to come."

"There's a lot to be said for ready-made families," Letty added. She and her husband had adopted a brood of their own, just as Phoebe and Adrian had adopted Lee. "And we hope to add to ours just like you and Adrian will soon do. A family is a gift and a joy, Wynema."

"Oh, fine," Wynema conceded. "There must be some benefit

to wedding a man—but you must agree that most are louts, rude and demanding and greedy to the end."

At the mention of greed, Jeremy's piercing blue eyes and tousled blond hair sprang into Angel's thoughts. "Perhaps it depends on the specific man."

Phoebe and Letty smiled.

"That's a most mature and wise way to look at the matter," Phoebe said. "I'll grant you, there are all sorts on earth, and we're all sinners, no more and no less. But some men are worth every minute of trouble they might pose."

"Aha!" Wynema crowed. "You see? Even you admit they're little more than troublemakers."

Again Angel couldn't fight off the image in her mind. "So how does a woman deal with a troublemaker?"

Three pairs of eyes locked in on her. The diminutive but spirited doctor reached out and took Angel's hand. "Who's making trouble for you, dear?"

Angel bit her lower lip. Although it went against the grain, something told her she should share what she knew, what had happened. These women could be trusted.

Before she could utter a word, however, Wynema snorted. "It's that Johnstone cowboy, isn't it? Has he gone to the ranch again?"

"Johnstone?" Phoebe asked. "Is that the young man who'd taken his earnings from the mine and bought himself a great ranch near the foot of the mountain well before Adrian came to town?"

Angel nodded.

Letty glanced at Phoebe, who looked just as puzzled as she did, then turned to peer at Wynema. "I can't say I know Mr. Johnstone very well, but he sent for me when his housekeeper, his foreman's wife, went into labor two, maybe three, weeks ago. I found him polite, generous—he paid my fee—a man of prayer even."

"As did I," Angel said, "but—"

"It's the greedy part he's learned much too well," Wynema put in. "He wants Rogers Ranch."

The other women gasped.

"What do you mean?" Phoebe asked.

It was time to tell her tale. Angel left out not one single detail, not Jeremy's compassion for Maggie, not his decision to share his meal with Sunny, and certainly not his determination to buy Rogers Ranch. She didn't, however, mention Papa's passing.

"Well!" Letty smoothed a bouncy brown curl from her forehead. "I see what incensed Wynema. I, too, am a woman doing what many consider a man's work. There've been more than a few who've made their opinion clear."

"You're young, Angel," Phoebe added. "Many would think it wrong for a girl to ranch."

Angel stood tall. "I shared the load with Papa ever since Mama died, and since he passed away—"

"What?" Letty looked horrified. "Your father's dead and you didn't send for me?"

Angel's shrug seemed insufficient, but she had nothing more to say.

Phoebe's gaze grew sad. "You never said a word."

Wynema laid an arm on Angel's shoulders. "She didn't want folks telling her what to do. And on that account, I agree with her."

"Fair enough," Letty said. "But perhaps I could have helped him. When did he fall ill? How long did his illness last? Why didn't you send for me?"

"I'm sorry, Doc, but there was nothing anyone, not even you, could have done. I woke up one morning early in the winter and found him in his chair by the fireplace. At first I just thought he'd fallen asleep there, but then when I touched him, I knew."

Compassion warmed the doctor's silver gaze. "Dear girl. I truly am sorry. It must have been difficult for you."

"Forgive me for even bringing it up," Phoebe said, "but . . . well, did you . . . what I mean to say is—"

"I understand," Angel said to ease her friend's discomfort. "I dug his grave and buried him right next to Mama. It's what he would have wanted. And I did read his favorite Scriptures—hers, too. I reckon the Lord counted it a decent Christian burial, don't you?"

"You see?" Wynema said. "She can't just up and sell her land to that Jeremy Johnstone fellow. Her folks are there. That's her land. If she can bury her pa and run the place, why, there's no reason for her to even entertain the notion."

Angel didn't speak.

Phoebe, also silent, kept her gaze on Angel. She then turned toward the store's wide front window, stared outside, and finally turned to Angel again. "It's all about your creek, isn't it?"

"It would seem so."

"Ah . . . ," Letty said. "My Eric came home from that meeting last night in a state. He's troubled. He worries about those who depend on the weather. Cattle don't fare well in drought, and many families stand to lose everything."

"I reckon that's the way of it," Angel said.

Whimpers came from the crib, and Phoebe fetched her fretting son. "I suspect this boy needs a clean diaper and a full tummy."

The expression on Phoebe's face left no doubt as to her feelings for the baby. Angel smiled.

Phoebe covered the small head with a gentle hand and closed her eyes, clearly savoring the moment. Then she glanced down at her child. "I can't say I blame a man for trying to provide for his family," she said. "Does Mr. Johnstone have children?"

Letty drew her brows together. "I didn't see any when I went for Rosario Fuentes's birthing. I don't think he'd have a housekeeper if he was married."

"Still," Phoebe said on her way to the store's backroom. The former owner had let her turn the space into a cozy apartment, which she now used to care for Lee during store hours. "Just as you want to protect what's yours, surely you don't blame Mr. Johnstone for wanting the same."

Angel picked up her hat and stepped toward the front door. "I don't blame him. I just don't mean to sell Papa's ranch—my ranch."

Letty joined Angel at the front of the store. "I'm not especially worried about Mr. Johnstone. He seems a decent sort. He'll likely pester you from now until forever with repeated offers, but I doubt he'll do any worse. It's the others, those who have yet to learn that you're out there on your own, who worry me."

Angel winced.

The doctor patted Angel's arm. "I suggest you prepare yourself. I don't know how long it'll be before everyone for miles and miles knows of your father's passing, but I suspect ranchers will make a beeline to your door as soon as word gets out."

"I'm afraid you're right," Angel said, dread hard in her middle. "And there's not much I can do to keep them from coming. All I can do is pray the Lord will help me send them on their way."

"I'd keep that big yellow dog of yours a hair on the hungry side," Letty added. "A hearty growl or two could go a long way to keep you safe."

Wynema dragged her tripod and joined Angel and Letty. "I just hope a firm no and a growl are all it takes to send your rejected buyers packing. Because from what I've seen, there's no telling what a determined man will do when an obstacle doesn't yield."

Her father's warnings rang in Angel's memory. Her stomach lurched. "I pray I don't have to find out."

☙

On Main Street, Angel bid Letty farewell. The morning's conversation followed her all the way to the livery. As she approached the open Dutch doors to Amos Jimson's establishment, she noticed a cluster of men gathered outside Seth Narramore's Silver Belle restaurant. They all had their eyes fixed on her.

One of them, a tall, heavyset man dressed in a fancy suit, caught her eye. He wore no particular expression on his face. The others, dressed in the denim and boots of working ranchers, wore anger and bitterness on their faces and had challenge in their stance.

Angel shivered and picked up her pace. Inside the livery, she drew a deep breath. The musk of animal mixed with hay and leather, familiar and comforting, soothed her rattled nerves. She glanced around the tack-covered walls and found Nelly, her mare, in the stall to her right.

"Afternoon, Miss Rogers," said David, Amos's young stable hand. "You ready to head on home?"

The image of her cabin, snug and secure, came to life in her head. She nodded to the boy and moved toward her horse. "It's where Nelly and I belong."

David scattered a forkful of straw in the stall next to Nelly's, then propped the implement on the wall and came to Angel's side.

"She's a right fine horse," he said.

"Papa took good care of her, of all our stock. He said a sound animal would pay back the time and food you spent on it with many more years of service than if you misered around with it."

"And right that is," Amos said, his voice booming from the other side of the stall. "How's the ranch treating you, Miss Angel?"

"The work never ends, but I don't mind. It's home, and I love it there."

Amos didn't speak right away, and Angel glanced at him. His brown eyes remained on her, an odd expression on his broad, black face. She liked the man, always had, and she remembered the times Papa had said Amos was as good as God made men.

His scrutiny gave her pause. "Is there something you want to tell me?"

"Well, there, Miss Angel, there's plenty I want to say, but I'm trying to figure what the good Lord wants me to tell you."

"I'll listen to anything you say."

Amos chuckled. "There ain't many as would be willing to confess that, girl. They'd be afeared of getting stuck here in the muck and madness of the livery for a right long lifetime."

"Papa did say you liked to share your wisdom."

Amos laughed. "Reckon that's Oliver's way of saying I hadn't yet learnt to hold my tongue. How's he doing? Haven't seen him in a right long time."

For a moment Angel wondered if she should continue her pretense, but Amos's decency invited trust and honesty. "Papa died this past December. I miss him something fierce."

"So sorry, Miss Rogers," David said, then slipped away.

Amos took a moment to absorb the news. As Angel watched, telltale dampness filled his eyes. His mellow bass voice came out rough. "Gonna miss that old coot. Reckon not near as much as you will though."

The knot in Angel's throat tightened. She nodded, then turned to Nelly to keep from bursting into tears. She hadn't cried for a couple of months now, and she didn't intend to do so again any time soon.

A comforting weight draped her shoulders. "Now, you listen to me good, girl," Amos said. "Anything you need, you just come call on Amos. My Sadie'll likely skin me, but I ain't gonna try and talk you outta staying at that ranch. I remember your pa telling me, all proud and all, you know, that you were as stubborn as the old mule he had all those years he went prospecting."

A laugh hitched out past the knot of sadness and grief. "Thank you, Mr. Jimson. I reckon you're the only one who won't."

"That many of them trying to get you to go?"

"Not many, but Wynema and Doc Letty warned me against staying."

"They got some smarts to them, those two women do. But I can't blame you for wanting to keep all you've ever known, now, can I?"

Angel shrugged.

The sound of horses awaiting their owners nudged her toward her interrupted task. She saddled Nelly, the motions automatic and satisfying.

"Morning, David."

Angel cringed at the familiar voice. The last thing she wanted was another encounter with Jeremy. Maybe she could wait in the stall until he left. Surely a cowboy with a large herd couldn't afford to linger in Hartville this time of day. Her flock needed less constant attention than his cattle likely did, and she'd overstayed already.

Male voices, one young and one mature, approached. It would seem Jeremy's gelding occupied the stall on Nelly's other side. There'd be no avoiding the man.

She tipped up her chin. "Good afternoon, Mr. Johnstone. Fancy finding a diligent rancher like you away from your spread."

Jeremy's blue eyes widened. "Can't say I expected to meet you in town, myself, Miss Rogers. How're Maggie and her newborns?"

"Maggie's a wonderful mother. The little ones are growing."

"Good," he said, but with a wince.

"Do you feel unwell?"

"As well as you might expect, considering the state of affairs."

"You'd be talking about the weather, then."

"Among other things on this rancher's mind."

"Water. And how to chase me and my sheep off my land to get it."

Jeremy started. "You don't mince words, Miss Rogers. I can't say as I haven't thought about Rogers Creek more than once a day."

Angel tightened her grip on Nelly's bridle. "My answer's still the same, in case you were wondering."

His humorless chuckle grated on her nerves. "Can't blame a fellow for trying. Or hoping."

"Seems foolish to waste your time. You know my answer."

"Sometimes hope's all a man's got to keep him going."

"Ahem!"

Both faced Amos.

"Seems to me the neighborly thing would be to share our Father's riches," Amos said.

"What?" Angel cried.

For a moment, a light sparked in the cowboy's eyes. But then he scoffed. "Water's good," he said, "but after her woolly monsters are done with her pastureland, there isn't a blade of grass for a cow to lick. Those critters of hers are a curse on the land, Amos."

Angel glared. "If you gentlemen will excuse me? Those accursed critters need me at Rogers Ranch. I'll take my leave of you now."

Instead of moving out of the way, Amos blocked Nelly's path. "Don't go leaving with your feathers all ruffled, now, Miss Angel. I'd wager Jeremy here ain't the only one who'd give a gizzard to get his hands on your creek. And them as would are unlike Jeremy, who's come to you? Am I right?"

She nodded.

"Well, there you have it, girl. He came to you, and I'd wager— if I was a betting man, which I surely ain't—that he made you a decent offer."

She raised a shoulder.

"I can't say that'll likely be so with the others what are sure to come. And you all alone out there and all . . ." Amos's face took on a worried look. "Can't say I'm all settled about it, girl. There's a right big load of bad in many a man. Maybe . . ."

As Amos's words trailed off, Angel's stomach lurched. She

remembered the men outside the Silver Belle. There had been anger in their faces and who knew what kind of malice in their hearts. Papa—and Jeremy, to her regret—had been right about one thing. There was danger in her future.

"I'll trust in the Lord," she said, clinging to her one truth. "And keep to myself. As for sharing Papa's land . . . Can't say as how I can see my way clear. I have to keep Rogers land in Rogers hands, Amos." She tugged on Nelly's reins and gave the men a pointed stare. "I'll head back now, if you don't mind."

Amos looked as though he wanted to argue on, but then he shook his head. "The Lord Almighty pour His blessings on you, girl. I'm afeared you're going to need every last one of them. And right soon, there."

"I'll take whatever the Father gives me and thank Him for it."

Jeremy stepped aside. "I can't say I'll be giving up hope anytime soon, Miss Rogers. Take care on your way back, now."

She acknowledged the polite tip of his Stetson with a nod, then led Nelly into the stable's open center. She swung her leg up over the horse and sat astride her saddle. Anyone who saw her like this had to know she was more than a silly girl with gossip and knitting on her mind.

"I'll take care of my ranch." She urged Nelly through the doorway. "I suggest, Mr. Johnstone, that you do the same with yours."

Angel rode down Main Street and felt myriad stares upon her. She usually drew attention, since she'd rather walk all the miles from the ranch to Hartville than ride sidesaddle or even burden herself with petticoats and a gown. But today's looks felt different, hotter. The ruinous heat of the summer day didn't make the difference.

She had what the men outside the Silver Belle wanted—needed.

And, she supposed, they also knew she wouldn't give it up.

After he put the ranch to sleep that night, Jeremy went in the house. A groan escaped his lips. He didn't have the energy, much less the wish, to cook himself a meal, never mind clean up after.

"Great timing, Rosario," he mumbled at the kitchen doorway. The icebox had milk and cream from his cow and eggs from the chickens he kept. But his stove wasn't lit; it hadn't been for days now.

He sighed. He'd have to open another can of beans and eat them plain. And cold.

A scan of his pantry shelves confirmed the limits of his choices. He had beans, a few tins of vegetables, a can of brown bread, and a can of pickled tongue. None of it appealed to him.

Even a skillet of eggs and bacon would be better than this. But one look at the iron stove was all it took. He didn't have it in him to go back out, chop wood, stoke the stove, wait for it to heat, and only then cook food.

What he really wanted was to go to bed. Even though it was still light outside, he felt as though it could have been the middle of the night. He sighed. Maybe eating was overrated.

Then his stomach growled, and the hunger pangs told him fasting wasn't an option.

"Mrreow!"

Mouser, the cat Rosario had said she needed to keep rodents away, rubbed his head against Jeremy's shin. "Hello there, fella. What've you been doing?"

The carcass a couple of feet away showed him Mouser's deeds.

"I'm glad you're earning your keep," Jeremy said, "but I wish you wouldn't drag these things into the house."

He wrapped his hand in a sheet of newsprint and picked up the corpse. He chuckled on the way to the back door. "Wonder what Eric Wagner would think if I told him how I use his paper at times."

The tomcat yowled when Jeremy threw his prize into the embers where Esteban had burned a pile of rubbish. Then, tail at an indignant height, he stalked off, no doubt in search of a new trophy.

Jeremy smiled, but when his stomach sent up another hunger pang, he gave in. "Oh, fine. I can see I'll have to head on over to Hartville again. Seth Narramore's shoe-leather steaks are better than this twisting in my gut all night long."

An hour later he rode into town. Amos called out a warm greeting. "How'd ranching treat you today, Mr. Johnstone, sir?"

Jeremy grimaced. "Ranching's fine, Amos. It's the weather that's about killed me."

"Sure can understand. It's been dry as dirt here in town, too. All's a body can do is pray himself up a storm."

"Wish I could do just that. I've been praying for more than a year now, and this blasted drought's still with us. Reckon the Lord's turned a deaf ear on me these days."

Amos frowned. "Watch your mouth, there. The Father's always a-listening. We just gotta know what we're really wanting, and if it might could be out of His plan."

"I'm supposed to sit back and lose all I've worked for on account of my ranch not being part of God's plan? Then why was it His plan for me to buy it in the first place?"

"Ain't my place to question the Almighty, Mr. Johnstone, sir. I just listen and obey. That's all's a body can do."

On his way to the massive doors to the street, Jeremy asked, "Would you be so easy with waiting if you stood to lose this place?"

"Jeremy Johnstone," Amos called. "Now you listen to me and listen good, son. I lost me everything back in that there War Between the States. But as God Almighty in heaven is my witness, I'd lose it all again if it meant staying in His blessed will. All's I have here—" A powerful arm gestured around the stable, toward the house next door, his fine horses. "Ain't one bit of it mine. I

59

won't ever forget that. I done learnt over all these long years that trouble comes a-calling on the man who does."

Jeremy grimaced. "You're right, Amos. I reckon I forget that while I work all day and see the cattle not hardly gaining any. I'd do well to remember it's best to trust in Him and obey."

"Have yourself some faith, there. Our God reigns, and He'll keep on reigning if it pours and even if that there sky never does send us another drop again."

The conversation offered Jeremy a measure of comfort on his way to the Silver Belle. Partway there, he stepped aside to let a herd of young ladies pass by on the boardwalk.

The fractious redhead didn't number among them. Dahlia Sutton, the banker's daughter, however, did. Jeremy doffed his hat and nodded. "Evening, Miss Sutton."

"Good evening, Mr. Johnstone," the fine-looking brunette said in her thick, rich southern voice.

One of her companions leaned close, whispered in her ear, and then giggled. Dahlia tipped her head sideways and studied Jeremy. So did all the others.

Without another word for him, but in whispered consultation with the gaggle around her, Dahlia proceeded down the boardwalk in the opposite direction. That measuring look she'd given him triggered off a crazy idea.

The Suttons were the wealthiest residents of Hartville, aside from Adrian Gable, the mine owner. And Dahlia sure was a sight for sore male eyes.

Hmm . . .

The scent of cooked meat mixed in with the perfume of apple pie derailed his train of thought. But only until he finished his supper.

As the owner of the largest ranch in the area—if he could feed and sell his herd—he was quite respectable. He didn't drink, didn't cuss, didn't visit the places on East Crawford Street, not for the women and not for the card tables either.

Dahlia's saucy smile danced in his head.

Maybe marriage wasn't such a bad notion after all. Just not to that redheaded mountain woman with the flock of pasture-killing sheep. Surely Sutton would want his daughter well settled. Surely the man wouldn't let her husband's ranch go belly up. Not when he had the money to prevent it.

5

She was no longer alone.

Angel took her time to stand. Moments earlier Sunny had darted from her side to splash through the shallows at the edge of the creek and clot the gold fur on her legs with mud.

The silence of the mountains, once just daunting, now grew ominous. Angel had grown accustomed to being the only person around, so she trusted her instincts.

She sensed another's presence but saw nothing . . . no one.

Where was Sunny?

Peace had a velvet touch. But right then she felt as though she'd rubbed down with a burlap sack. This taut silence could only mean one thing: trouble. It evidently had a life of its own; it breathed down her neck.

She'd done nothing to court it. She'd come out to the creek after slogging through all those chores on the hottest day so far this year. The cool water had drawn her, and she'd crouched to drink. Its sweetness had refreshed her, and just as she'd contemplated a quarter hour's rest in the shade of the two willows this side of the bank, the peculiar awareness, that sudden certainty, had struck.

Someone was watching her.

Fear threatened, but she fought it. Indignation set in. Why

should trouble come find her? She belonged here. Whoever hid among the pines scattered among the birch and aspen had no business on her land.

She prayed for strength, for courage.

"Sunny!" she called, determined to again face an unwanted visitor with the air of a landowner. "Where did you go?"

A cheerful woof rang out in the direction opposite from where she'd sensed the presence.

"Come on, girl. Let's get on home."

On her way back to the cabin, Angel scanned the trees and the undergrowth for the intruder. At first, all she saw were stray scraps of Sunny's fur, as the dog was still shedding healthy amounts of her cottony undercoat. But as she reached the outside edge of the stand of trees, a speck of blue, a foreign color among the branches, caught her attention.

And then it was gone. She pretended nothing was amiss, hard though it was. Even more difficult was to take smooth, unhurried steps when all she wanted to do was run and lock herself inside the cabin, to block the door with Mama's tall oak chest of drawers.

Wind rustled in the grasses to her left, and Sunny's ecstatic barks made her sigh in relief. She wasn't sure the dog would offer any kind of help should the situation turn dire, but she felt better knowing she wouldn't face danger alone.

The Lord was with her, true. Surely He'd keep her safe.

"Look at you," she said when Sunny jumped and put her front paws on Angel's shoulders. "You're nothing but a great mud ball. I don't know if there's enough water and soap in this state to clean you off." Angel took advantage of the opportunity to break into a trot. "Come on, you dirty girl! We can't let that dry on you. Let's race. Can you beat me home?"

They reached the yard, and although Angel didn't want to spend another second outside, she also didn't want to deal with the mess Sunny's muddy frolic would make inside the house.

She pumped a bucketful of clean water, scraped off as much muck as she could with her hands, then crouched to lather up the golden fur.

"Howdy, ma'am."

Angel's breath caught in her throat. Trouble had just caught up with her.

She stood, squared her shoulders, and met the stranger's gaze full on. "Who are you, and what do you want at Rogers Ranch?"

Her direct question appeared to surprise him. He took off his brown Stetson and revealed thinning brown hair. He spun the brim with rough-looking, stained fingers and darted looks in every direction but hers.

"Ah . . . well, I just thought maybe you'd be wanting some help, what with all the chores a body has to do on a ranch like this."

Angel crossed her arms. "What would you know about my chores?"

The washed-out blue of his eyes didn't hint at anything close to honesty. Shifty was the best way to describe this invader.

"Er . . . well, you see." He swallowed hard, and his Adam's apple jerked in his thin neck. "It's like this, miss. I've lived near all my days on farms or ranches, and I do fancy myself a fair hand with all it takes to run them. I'm sure a little slip of a thing like you'd welcome a strong man to lean on."

The absurdity of the man's words almost made Angel laugh.

She made the most of her height and stood tall, her shoulders back, her fists on her hips. "I don't know where or why you got the notion I'd welcome anyone to my place, but seeing as I'm taller than you and know my way around here in the dark, I'd say you're barking up the wrong tree."

He narrowed his eyes. "The only one barking around here is that blasted cur of yours. I'll tell you this, girlie. You're no match for the land. When it burns you up from too much work and too little smarts, why, then Albert Pringle will be looking for you to

64

come begging for help. I'll be either in Hartville or Rockton—I'm sure you'll find me when you need me."

"I don't beg, mister." Angel kept her voice steady, her resolve strong. "I pray."

Pringle turned and started down the path toward Rockton. "Bah!" he said over his shoulder and glared. "Pretty words won't be getting you out of trouble, girlie. Mark my words. You'll be coming after help afore too long."

As she headed for the cabin, Angel turned her gaze toward the mountains, a certain psalm ringing in her heart.

❦

"It's a pure crying shame," Daisy Butler, budding reporter at Eric Wagner's newspaper, the *Hartville Day*, said to Wynema. "Not a one of these ranchers can be faulted for his handling of his business, and still they're all on the knife's edge of failure."

Wynema shoved a swath of straight brown hair off her brow. "I knew it was bad, but I had no idea how bad until I went to the Rumple place to take photographs for your story."

"The poor Rumples. And those poor, poor animals, too."

"It about breaks your heart to see the calves all so bony."

The two women fell silent for a moment. Then Daisy began to pace the manse's parlor. Pastor Stone and his wife had taken her in at a time of great need.

"I'm glad your friend Angel has that creek of hers," Daisy said. "She's not likely to lose any of her flock."

"She says sheep weather drought better than cattle do."

"Maybe it's because they eat every last scrap of green they find." Daisy stuck her pencil into the blond knot atop her head. "That's the reason the cattlemen hate them so. They say sheep ruin pasture because they crop the grass so close to the ground."

She crossed the room again and darted a worried look at Wynema. "That's something to consider, at least on your friend's part."

65

"I told her and told her and told her they'd resent her until I couldn't spit out one single word more," Wynema said, her voice taut. "Angel Rogers is the stubbornest woman I know."

Daisy laughed. "Who best to know one than another? You're hardly the wishy-washy sort."

Wynema shot a lofty look Daisy's way. "A woman has to know where she stands, I'll have you know. Elsewise, men will tromp all over her and hers."

The young reporter's humor faded. "I've heard all sorts of dreadful complaints about Angel and her sheep. The ranchers have been to meet with Mr. Sutton, Pastor Stone, Sheriff Herman—even Amos and Mr. Wagner have gone along to hear them out."

"Have any of them threatened Angel?"

"Not that I know of, but how many are angry enough to do her harm?"

"Do you think they'd go that far?"

"This is Colorado, you know. They've lynched women here."

Wynema clapped her hat on her messy topknot and crossed to the door. "There's so much rottenness in men's hearts. I warned her, but she doesn't want to listen. And she doesn't know what to do with her pa's shotgun—won't even try to learn. She's out there with only that sweet, silly, loving Sunny for protection. Sunny's a great friend, but she's everyone's friend."

A frown drew parallel lines between Daisy's fair brows. "Does she know how much danger she could really face?"

"I told you, Daisy. I warned her, and it seems her pa did, too. She won't listen—not to him or to me. Even Doc Letty and Phoebe brought up the matter a few days ago."

"Well, then," Daisy said by the hall tree near the door, "it's probably time to bring someone else along. Would she listen to Mr. Wagner? Maybe Pastor Stone. Or do you think we should speak to the sheriff, too?"

Wynema opened the door. "Seems to me, she's stubborn enough that we might have to enlist them all to talk with her."

"I'd like to know this Angel Rogers." Daisy descended the steps to the manse's front walk. "Even though I think she's making a foolish decision, not taking care to protect herself, she sounds like a woman to reckon with."

On her way down the steps, Wynema's camera bobbed against her middle. "That she is. And I hope we can do something so she can be her hardheaded self for a long, healthy time out on that ranch she loves so much."

"As do I."

The women walked for a brief, silent time. Then Daisy said, "You know what?"

"What?"

"There's one thing we haven't done. At least, not yet."

"What's that?"

"Pray."

Wynema stopped. "No better time than now."

She held out her hand. They lowered their heads and in reverent tones took the matter to their Maker.

❦

After church on Sunday, Jeremy checked his reflection in the window of the Heart of Silver Mining Company's general store. After careful study, he straightened the knot of his tie just a hair. He'd bathed early, dressed in his finest suit, and taken pains to plan out his day.

He was going courting this afternoon.

But it was early yet to carry out his plan, and he was hungry, so he walked to the Silver Belle. He chose his meal with more attention to his clothes than to his taste in food. He didn't want any gravy drips on his Sunday best.

It amazed him how long he got away with nursing his cup of coffee; Seth just filled it up time and again. Then, too, Seth didn't ever chase anyone away, no matter how crowded the place got. He just lumped strangers together at whatever chair he found empty. Sunday noons never got quite as crowded as other days of the week. Many of the Silver Belle's regular patrons wrangled invitations to chicken dinners or roast beef suppers from folks who took pity on them.

Jeremy had turned down Letty's offer earlier that day. Not because her food wasn't tasty—her cooking was right good, some of the best he'd ever had—but because meals at the Wagner ranch were wild adventures that often wore a man down. Their five rapscallions, while well mannered enough, had the spirited get-up-and-go of a wild pony who didn't cotton to the notion of a saddle. They also knew Jeremy was a sucker for little wheedlers who wanted a grown-up to play with.

He dared not attempt his afternoon visit distracted, not to mention scruffed up, in any way.

At 2:00 on the nose, he stood, paid Seth for the dry steak, plain boiled potatoes, mushy, overcooked carrots, and endless river of coffee.

He strolled down Main Street toward the eastern part of town, where the wealthier folks lived. One could hardly miss the change, what with the large, fancy houses that lined the side streets the farther east he went. He turned onto Aspen Way and took in the grandness of the mansion at the end of the circle up ahead.

Marcus Sutton hadn't spared a cent when he'd had the place put up. Peaks on the roof and fancy cut-wood trims and windows and shingles and dressed-up chairs scattered all over the porch. He'd even had a cupola built on the roof and two turrets at the front corners of the house, for goodness' sake. Jeremy had heard tell the inside showed even more of the man's taste for pricey things.

Jeremy reckoned just a few of the gewgaws on the outside of the Sutton place would buy enough feed to carry his cattle quite well past this season's drought.

Once on the veranda, he took the polished silver knocker and rapped it twice against the silver plate on the huge, dark wooden door.

The door didn't make a sound when it swung in a moment later. Bess O'Hanrahan, her gray hair slicked into a knot at the back of her head, her white apron starchy-crisp enough to break if he brushed against it, looked him up and down.

She smiled. "You're a sight for sore eyes, you are, boy-o. And how've you been faring, now you're a rancher?"

When Jeremy first arrived in Hartville, he'd been lucky enough to rent one of the rooms the cheery Irishwoman had let out in her home. But after her husband died in a mine accident, those reasonable rates no longer covered the note on the house. Sutton's bank foreclosed on the property, while Mrs. Sutton took pity on the widow and benefited from Bess's skills.

"If it weren't for the weather, then I'd have not a single complaint."

Bess clucked. "Can't be counting on what's beyond you, lad. The Lord in heaven's the only one who calls the rain His own."

"Afraid you're right, Mrs. O." Jeremy swallowed hard and called up every ounce of brass in him. "Is Mr. Sutton home?"

"Indeedy so. And in a fine mood, he is, I'll have you know. Would you like to come inside a spell while I tell him you've come?"

"That would be fine."

Inside the grand entry, Jeremy noticed how just about everything his eyes could see had a gleam to it. The wood floors shone. The marble top on the dainty little table against the wall glowed. The dangly pieces in the many-armed light fixture overhead sparkled. Even the wide colored-glass window high on the wall over the stairs twinkled as it let in streaks of red-, blue-, green-, and gold-tinted sunshine.

Fancy. Just like the banker's brightest gem: Dahlia Sutton.

"Jeremy," Sutton said. "I didn't expect you. What can I do for you?"

Jeremy wondered how much he could really believe that offer. "I've a question for you, and it's of a more . . ."

Blast it! Now that he was here, he didn't have a spit and polished speech to fall back on. Well, he was decent, honest, and hardworking, and he came with only honorable intentions. That would have to do.

"It's a personal matter, sir," he said. "Is there somewhere we could talk—private-like?"

Sutton's eyebrows drew close. "Private, eh?"

He nodded.

"Well, son, we can talk in my study." The banker turned, and Jeremy followed him down the hall to their left. "We can even share a smoke."

"A chance to talk is all I need. I don't fancy tobacco."

"A brandy, then."

"Don't fancy spirits either."

Hartville's richest man gave Jeremy another puzzled look but said nothing as he opened the door into a somewhat darker room. Where the entry had been washed in light and color, Sutton's study wore quieter trappings. Shelves full of books went from the floor to the ceiling on all the walls, and the windows, two long ones behind the huge desk, had heavy red drapes closed over them.

"Have a seat." Sutton indicated the winged armchair across the desk. He took the leather chair on the other side. "What brings you here today?"

Jeremy sat and found that the collar of his shirt had just grown too tight. He ran a finger around the inside and regretted his lack of refinement. He prayed for God's help to reach his goal.

"Well, sir," he said, "I did some thinking after we talked the other night, and it strikes me that you did have a good idea or two."

Marcus smiled, and reached for the tobacco box on the desk. "Do you mind if I do?"

"It's your home, sir. I'd never dare tell you what you can and can't do here."

The fat cigar took longer to prepare than Jeremy would have thought possible. It seemed the smoker had to snip off a bit at one end, tamp down the other, sniff the whole thing, close his eyes and smile, and only then strike a match and light up.

"Well?" Sutton asked as a foul cloud gathered over his head. "What did you want?"

"I want—that is, I'd like . . ." He was botching the whole blasted thing!

With the banker's keen gaze on him, Jeremy stood, took a deep breath, and just let it all out. "I want your permission to court your daughter, sir."

Sutton gaped and dropped his stogie. He disappeared behind the desk, scrabbled around for the burning item, rapped something against wood, and muttered a curse. He then grunted and wheezed, cursed some more, and finally peered over the edge of the desk.

"Excuse me, Mr. Johnstone. I must be having trouble with my hearing. Did I hear you say you wanted to court Dahlia? *My* Dahlia?"

Jeremy squared his jaw. "That's what I said."

Sutton scratched the pink spot at the crown of his head where gray hair seemed to have surrendered long ago. "Son, it strikes me as though you misheard everything I said to you the other night. I recollect telling you to marry Old Man Rogers's girl. She's the one with the creek."

"She may be the one with the creek, sir, but she sure as shooting isn't the one with the marrying traits. Why, she's nothing but a wild mountain man in the skin of a girl. She even dresses the part."

The banker held his cigar just inches from his lips. "Let me say it again, Jeremy Johnstone. And this time, listen to what I say. Angel Rogers has the water to grow the pasture you want. Marry her."

"And, if you'll pardon me, Mr. Sutton, I'll repeat what I said, too. She's not hardly the kind a man needs for a wife. She may have water and pasture, but I can feed my cattle if I can pay for the feed."

"Oh! So now you tell me you want my daughter to get your hands on my green."

Jeremy refused to be cowed. "I'd like to court your daughter, seeing as she's a right lovely woman. And I doubt you'd let her spouse go under, since she'd have a rough going if he did."

Sutton's laugh held no humor. "You're a brassy one, I'll grant you. What makes you think I'd let my daughter marry you?"

Jeremy shrugged. "I've heard talk that you wouldn't let any man marry her, on account of her fine taste in good things and you wanting to make sure she keeps on having them. I may not have the cash just now, but I own the largest ranch and the biggest herd for miles around. If I succeed, I'd make sure every last one of Miss Dahlia's wishes came true."

The banker rounded the corner of the desk. "But that's the question, isn't it? *If.* There's no telling if you can make it through the summer, never mind beyond that. I'm not about to let my daughter move into a shack and live the life of a miner's wife. Especially not in a Colorado winter."

"Nothing wrong with hard work, sir." Jeremy held himself tall. "At least you'd know I'd never hit her, I wouldn't go catting in the brothels, and I wouldn't waste my pay on drink or cards. That's more than many can say."

"Bah!" Sutton's wave sent a chunk of ash onto the thick black, cream, and blue rug underfoot. "You're a decent enough sort, Johnstone, but not the kind to make my girl happy. Do as I said. Go marry the Rogers chit. She'll give you what you want."

Humiliation seared a path to Jeremy's heart, then settled in his gut. He understood too well what Sutton had tried to nicen up. The banker didn't consider Jeremy good enough to wed his daughter.

"Well, then I regret taking up your Sunday afternoon." He turned and crossed to the door.

"No bother at all." The banker's voice turned expansive. "Just remember what I said. My Dahlia's too delicate a rose to cast out into the harsh life of the usual Colorado wife. You need a tough little thorn like Angel Rogers. She and her creek should serve you well."

Jeremy shot him a look over his shoulder. "You rest assured I'll remember everything you said. Everything."

He would, too. He might not be a fancy swell with a family's money and clean-hands kind of work, but he wasn't stupid. That's why he wasn't about to go after Angel any time soon. He didn't want to imagine what a man might suffer hitched up to a pigheaded cuss like her.

That pitchfork didn't bode well for the fella.

He also remembered the look Dahlia had given him. He hadn't seen distaste in her snapping eyes the other day. Surely, she'd have a say in her choice of husband.

Jeremy meant to put himself square in the running.

6

After Jeremy put away the plate on which he ate that night's beans, bacon, and biscuits, a knock came at the door. He didn't expect anyone. Esteban had gone home like he always did once he'd finished his day's work, and Rosario hadn't set foot in the ranch house since the day her water broke.

Unease followed Jeremy to the door.

"May we come in, please?" Eric Wagner, the tall owner of the *Hartville Day*, stood on the front porch, his brown hat in his hands. To Eric's right side, Jeremy saw Pastor Stone. To the left, Amos and Sheriff Herman waited in silence.

Worry stampeded the unease to a pulp.

He stepped back and let the men in. "Have a seat."

He waited at his favorite hide-covered chair by the fireplace as the others chose their spots. Once everyone sat, an uncomfortable silence filled the room.

"Well," he said when he realized his guests felt as ill at ease as he did, "I reckon you have more to keep you at home than here, so I have to wonder what kind of trouble I've got myself into."

Eric stood. "You're in no trouble, and we hope to keep any from breaking out."

"I'm afraid this cowboy hasn't followed where you've led."

Someone else rapped on his door. "If you'll excuse me."

Eric nodded. "It's likely Adrian Gable and a couple of others."

Jeremy did find the mine owner on his front porch, and with him were Douglas Carlson—Hartville's lawyer—and Roger Andrews, the Pinkerton agent who'd helped Adrian out of a sticky mess some months earlier.

Eric stayed on his feet, so Jeremy chose to do the same and pointed the new arrivals toward the remaining empty seats.

"Now, please," he said, "have mercy on me. I don't reckon I've ever seen the bunch of you gathered in one place—besides church or town hall. What kind of trouble am I in?"

"None, as I already said." Eric seemed the leader of the group. "But we do have a worrisome situation to discuss with you."

Jeremy scratched the hair at the base of his skull, more than a little befuddled. "Get on with it, then. If you please."

Eric glanced at the others. They nodded. He turned back. "It's about the weather—"

"There's not a blamed thing I can do about it, Mr. Wagner."

"Please call me Eric, and I know your position only too well. It's because the drought's hit you hard that we're here."

"How so?"

"You need pasture for your cattle, unless you can move them north for the summer to Montana or some far-off place that has more grass for them, right?"

Jeremy nodded.

"That's a costly proposition, I'd imagine."

"Very. It'd wipe me out."

"Well, there seems to be a decent supply of grass not too far from your property, up by Rogers Creek."

Jeremy let out a tired sigh. "I already made Old Man Rogers's daughter an offer for the place, and she near ran me through with the biggest, meanest pitchfork I ever did lay eyes on. Besides, there's not enough left on the ground after her fat wool balls are done with it to feed one scrawny cow, much less help my herd. It's not just her water that matters."

75

"More than likely," Eric said, "you approached her head-on. By offering to buy her land, you alarmed her, and she reacted in the opposite way you'd hoped, so—"

"I think it's best if I take it from here." The pastor struggled to his feet. "Ah! These old bones creak more each day." He shook his head and then faced Jeremy. "There's more than one way to solve your problem, and from my point of view, the most compassionate way is to prevent the worst we fear could arise."

Jeremy hooked his thumbs on his belt loops and braced himself. He didn't like the look in the reverend's eyes.

"You see, son," the gray-haired gent said, his brow marked with deep lines, "that little girl's all alone out on that ranch. Oliver spent years keeping himself and his family apart from the regular comings and goings of the town. From what he told me, I assume it was natural for someone who saw as much as he did those years he spent taming the frontier, but it sure didn't help prepare his daughter for the day he passed on."

Although the men studied Jeremy with expectation, he had nothing to say. He couldn't see how this had anything to do with him.

The pastor sighed. "A friend of Angel's brought to our attention that she doesn't even know how to use her shotgun—doesn't want to learn either. Not that I support reckless shooting, you understand, but reasonable protection is always prudent."

"Still don't see where I can be of help," Jeremy said. "I told her to look up her mother's kin back east, but she bristled like some riled up polecat and sprayed me with scorn."

Pastor Stone came over and laid an arm over Jeremy's shoulders. "Son, that's just what we came to discuss. How you ought to deal with Angel Rogers. She needs a man, and you need her land."

Jeremy reared up. "There's nothing that'll make me offer marriage to that wild mountain woman, and I told Marcus Sutton that more'n once already. So if that's what you're all thinking you can talk me into, I suggest you head on home straightaway."

Jeremy's guests exchanged nervous glances, then sat back to await the pastor's next words.

"How well do you know Angel?" the reverend asked.

"Well enough that I don't want to know her any better."

"She's an accomplished young woman, very intelligent, well taught—her mama was a schoolmarm before she married Oliver, did you know?"

Jeremy nodded.

Pastor Stone went on. "From experience, I know she's a splendid cook, keeps a neat and comfortable home, is a fair hand with animals, and is as decent, honest, and straightforward a woman as the Lord ever made."

"She's also wild, disagreeable, bad tempered, contrary, surly, and rude. Not the sort I'd ever hitch myself to for the rest of my born days."

"Do you have any other solution to our two problems?"

"I have only one problem—saving my herd in this lousy drought."

Pastor Stone shook his head. "The Lord calls us all to love our neighbors as ourselves. Would you really turn your back on a woman alone?"

Discomfort made Jeremy's conscience itch. Angel's predicament had returned to his mind more than once since he helped her deliver Maggie's twin lambs. But she'd made her position only too clear. "She has no intention of giving up her land."

"She wouldn't have to," the man of God countered, "if you two wed."

"But I don't want her for a wife!"

"Ahem!" Amos shifted his great bulk on the settee, which let off a creak. That got everyone's attention. "Do you have yourself a better choice in mind, then, son?"

"I do, and it's none of anyone's business who she is."

"Can she help you with the ranch?"

"She has means." Sutton's words came back at him and put

the same foul taste in his mouth as they had the other day. He was good enough for any woman, no matter what Sutton said. Jeremy would make sure Dahlia knew that before long, too.

Sheriff Herman took advantage of the lull in the conversation. "Look here, Johnstone." He rocked back and forth on his boot heels. "This here's a good place to live. Sure, we have us our share of bad sorts to take in hand, but I aim to keep them in check."

"I've no complaint with how you keep the peace."

"Well, now. Every man has to lend me a hand in keeping the law. And that's where you come in. I been hearing some nasty stuff's been said about that Rogers girl, what with the land as dry as kindling and the forest not much better. There's those who are pert near desperate."

"They're not my business."

The lawman's rough-cut features took on a mulish cast. "Beg to differ—begging your pardon, you understand. Law and order's everyone's business, and if some crazy fool goes and hurts that little girl, why, you'll be looking pretty bad in everyone's eyes. Especially since you coulda done something to prevent it."

Jeremy glared at the posse in his parlor. "Since when does a man have to court a woman to keep the law in a town? And why one who needs his arm twisted into courting her? A woman he doesn't even like. How'd you all want to be told who you should and shouldn't take for a wife?"

Adrian gave him a pointed look. "Since your objections strike me as too strong, I have to wonder if you're perhaps fighting your wounded pride as much as you're fighting us. Did Miss Rogers's rejection of your offer sting you in more ways than just your concern for your ranch? Seems to me she's awfully pretty. A man might take her lack of interest in his proposition in a personal way."

"Not true." Jeremy ignored the warmth in his cheeks. "I told you, I'm already courting a young lady, one who'll help me even more than that redheaded mountain woman ever could."

Douglas peered at Jeremy through his spectacles. "And what's wrong with red hair? I can vouch for the excellence of at least one red-haired wife."

Jeremy raised his arms in surrender. "Fine. If only to send you home as soon as possible. I'll try talking to Miss Rogers one more time. But I'm not agreeing to marry the girl. No sir. I'm not at all interested in that sheep-loving madwoman one bit."

He led the party to the front door and steered them all out. As they went down the porch steps, he could have sworn he heard Adrian murmur, "With that much fire in his refusal, we'll just have to wait and see what cooks up between those two."

Jeremy shuddered and closed the door on the very notion of him and Angel hog-tied for life.

ॐ

Angel had just covered the kettle of soup when she heard a clatter on her porch. She smiled and opened the door for Wynema.

"I didn't expect a visit." She took the tripod from the photographer and leaned it on the wall by the door.

Wynema marched straight past the sitting room and into the kitchen, where she divested herself of her camera, the pouch where she carried the paraphernalia essential to her trade, and her plain black derby.

"I went to Thomas Woodruff's spread today—he wanted a family portrait by the oak mantle he brought in from back east. So I thought I'd see how you were on my way back to Hartville."

"As always, I'm fine. And how about yourself?"

Wynema gave Angel one of those disturbing, all too perceptive looks. "I'm concerned about you. The rumbles in town grow louder each day. There's many a man getting desperate, and who aims to keep himself from failure. Has anyone besides Johnstone come to bother you?"

Since Wynema wouldn't quit her badgering until she got what she wanted, Angel told her about Pringle's visit. As expected, the photographer responded with another plea for Angel to come to her senses.

"For goodness' sake, woman, you have the shotgun. Don't just let it sit idle and gather rust while these louts come after you."

Angel nibbled on her bottom lip. "You know, I never thought I'd give it a thought, but I must confess I've considered taking it out to practice."

"Phew!" Wynema collapsed onto the sturdy oak kitchen chair. "Now you make some sense. But tell me. Do you even know how to load the thing? So as not to kill yourself in the process, I mean."

"I saw Papa do it at least a million times. I'm sure I'll figure it out." Angel went to the cupboard next to the stove. "I reckon you haven't done a thing to feed yourself this evening, have you?"

"You know as well as anyone that I've not been blessed with, as Phoebe would say, cooking gifts. I make do fine though."

Angel laughed. "Yes, through the mercy of kind friends who take pity on you. Why don't you wash up while I serve us a meal."

"I suspected you'd do as much." Wynema gave her a mischievous wink. "I can't ever turn down your cooking, just as anyone who turns down Phoebe's Shaker-style food has surely gone stark, raving stupid."

The women prayed, then settled in to an enjoyable supper. They discussed their work, the goings-on in town, and, inevitably, the endless drought. Which brought the conversation right back to the most uncomfortable topic of all—for Angel, at least. Wynema had no trouble discussing whatever she pleased.

"So," the photographer said after they'd savored the last of Angel's wild berry preserves on feather-light biscuits. "Have you given any more thought to Jeremy Johnstone's offer?"

Angel hesitated; she refused to lie. "Not a serious one."

"Well, then have you given any thought to the man's looks?"

"Wynema!" Angel's cheeks warmed. Her recollection of the man was crystal clear. "What would make you ask such a thing?"

"Most women I know seem stuck on landing themselves a good catch. He strikes me as more decent than most—excepting his greedy side, of course. You could do much worse than him, I reckon, and you might do well with his protection at your side."

"I don't need a man to protect my ranch. I trust in the Lord, and in Him alone. He provided this place for Papa, and now He's entrusted it to me. I can't let Him down and be a poor steward of all He's given me."

"No, but think of how much greater a blessing you would have if you and Mr. Johnstone joined the two spreads."

"What's Mr. Johnstone's is his, and what's mine is mine. I'm not after more, Wynema. I just want to honor Papa's hard work."

"Don't you think your father would have jumped at the chance to enlarge his property?"

"He turned down the Carlisles when they came and offered the ranch to him first. I recollect his words: 'I have what the good Lord's given me, and that's enough for me. More would be like a glutton after more food.'"

For a long moment, Wynema stayed quiet as different expressions rioted on her face. Finally, she took a deep breath. "Have you ever . . . I mean, do you wonder—"

She came to a stop. Angel gave her friend the chance to collect her thoughts. They must be thorny ones, indeed, seeing as how the always talkative woman had such trouble with them.

The dishes they'd used needed a wash, so Angel carried them to the counter where she'd earlier set her dishpan. She poured hot water from the teakettle she kept at a simmer on the stove, then lathered up a cloth and set to her task. Behind her, Wynema groaned a couple of times, stood, paced, and sat again. She finally let out a belly-deep sigh.

"Do you ever wonder what it'd be like to be some man's wife?" she blurted out in a mad rush of words.

Angel dropped the graniteware plate in her hand. Its clatter against the floor drowned out her surprised "What?"

Wynema's throat, her cheeks, and even the tip of her uptilted nose turned the color of raspberry preserves. "I mean, Mrs. Stone and Doc Letty and Phoebe all have nothing but praises for the wedded state. I don't see a reason to tie the knot with a man who'll demand things and give orders and that kind of thing, but the three of them can't be wrong, can they? And since everyone marries, they can't be the only ones who think it dandy to live with a male. Don't you think?"

She left Angel speechless.

"Or," Wynema went on, "do you reckon their favorable opinion of marriage is on account of the men they married? Is that the key? Does it take finding a real good one among the bad ones to make it all worthwhile?"

"I—I'm sure I wouldn't know. I've only met a few men, and aside from Papa and perhaps Pastor Stone, maybe Amos Jimson at the livery, none of them strikes me as a particularly good proposition."

"Well, I don't have much bad to say against Eric Wagner, and I suppose Adrian Gable did have his reasons for his muddleheaded actions in the past . . . but are they the only exceptions to the general rule?"

When Angel again had no answer, Wynema shrugged. "Can't say I've much knowledge on the subject either." She looped the strap of her hefty black camera over one shoulder, then plopped her hat on the lopsided bun on her crown. "Guess there's no point in wondering, is there?"

"I prefer to keep my attention on my business and leave the rest in divine hands."

"Well, you see, I've a bit of trouble with that leaving the rest part," Wynema said in a sheepish voice. "I always have this urge to just do something about things. Can't seem to let them alone sometimes."

"Ask the Lord for more faith in His perfect provision. You'll see. He won't ever let you down."

Wynema strode through the sitting room, gathered the tripod from where Angel had propped it by the door, and then turned back to her friend. "I'll do that—if you promise to learn to use that gun. You do, don't you? Promise, I mean."

Angel moved her head in a vague way.

Wynema would not be thwarted. "That's not any answer, Angel Rogers. Now, do you promise to do something smart for yourself, or will you keep on being foolish?"

Faced with her friend's considerable determination, Angel caved in. "Very well. I promise to do something with Papa's shotgun. Now go. You don't want to ride home in the dark."

"It's summer, and there's hours to go before dark, silly. You just want to get rid of me because I made you uncomfortable."

At Angel's shrug, Wynema added, "But it's all to the good if you do the right thing."

Angel opened her mouth, but Wynema stopped her. "I'm going, and I pray you'll take the better part of the evening to think through all I told you. A woman can't afford to let others—men—take advantage of her."

Then, with a proud tilt of her chin, she sailed out and clambered into her buggy. As she rode away, she called back, "Don't let that rust grow one bit thicker, now!"

Angel gave a wry chuckle. It was unlikely she'd be able to ignore Wynema's warnings. In truth, she'd thought much about her predicament. Why would everyone think that just because she wasn't a man she couldn't run her ranch? She'd grown up at Papa's side; she'd watched and learned and then did everything with him.

About an hour after Wynema's departure, a knock at the door startled Angel from the quilt piece she'd begun to embroider. She set the linen aside and headed for the door.

"Evening, ma'am," the dust-covered man in denims and a plaid shirt said. "It's a right fine one, and I'd be honored if'n you'd grant me the privilege of escorting you for a walk."

Stunned silent at first, Angel looked at the man's well-worn boots, the spurs on them, the lean horse he'd tied to the hitching rail near the barn. She narrowed her eyes.

"I don't reckon it'd be wise to go with strange men, not even on my ranch. State your business or get off my land."

He blinked. "Now, now. No need to bristle up, there. I ain't especially strange, not once you get to know me. And that's just what I aim to do—get us acquainted, you see."

"To what end?"

"Why, to the same end all men want when they see a fine woman like yourself. I said I come with honorable intentions."

Angel crossed her arms and all the while wished for the pitchfork she'd used to keep Jeremy at bay. "Since I've never seen you before now, and am not dim-witted, I'd say you'd be wise to turn around and find yourself a fine woman elsewhere. I'm not for sale, nor am I in the market for a man. They seem to come with too high a price for me to consider them any kind of bargain."

The man struggled with his expression, but Angel caught the spark of anger in his eyes. "That's a right fine way to respond to a man you ain't been introduced to, Miss Rogers. I'll take my leave now, but I'll be seeing you again. And I'll make sure that next time we're introduced proper-like. Evening, ma'am."

As he left the porch, Angel said, "Don't bother yourself. It won't make a difference. None at all."

She caught the brunt of his rage in the glare he shot her way. His horse got the rest of it when he mounted and dug his spurs into the animal's sides.

Angel shuddered. The woman who married that man could expect only the same treatment.

❦

The day after the unwelcome meeting at his home, Jeremy washed up after supper, changed into a clean shirt and denim trousers, wiped down and polished his boots—even though he knew they'd be dusty by the time he arrived—and headed for Rogers Ranch.

He'd promised to approach the mountain woman again, and he was a man of his word. He was also a man who knew his mind. Nothing would change it when it came to the matter of a wife.

In his heart of hearts he knew he could win Dahlia's affections, and that was what he meant to do. Daddy or no daddy.

As he turned onto the road that led to Angel's spread, a rider on a roan tore past him as though Satan himself had nipped at the horse's tail. Jeremy shook his head. He hoped the fool had plenty of water for his mount wherever he was headed. Poor beast would need plenty to drink, and a good wipe down would be in order.

A short while later, Jeremy dismounted at the rail near Angel's barn. The silence surprised him. Had she heeded his warnings and left the place after all?

"Miss Rogers!"

Sunny's yowl came from the barn, but the large yellow animal didn't come to meet him, and she didn't sound quite right. Whether in friendship or not, he'd yet to meet the dog who didn't charge at a visitor's arrival.

The silence was too great.

He called out for Angel a second time.

Again his answer came from Sunny, this time wilder, higher pitched than before.

With a sense of dread, he hurried to the barn. Back by the lambing pen, a lantern hung from a nail on the wall. The gate to the pen was open, and as he approached, Sunny barked.

She kept it up until he reached the gate, and when he did, he wished he hadn't. The sight before him was too gruesome to bear.

Maggie, the recently delivered ewe, lay on the hay that covered the floor, her cream-colored coat red with blood from the gash in her neck. At her side, one of the lambs had its neck bent at a wicked angle, and blood covered it, too.

In the far corner of the enclosure, Angel cowered, the other lamb in her arms. Horror blazed from her eyes. Her shudders came hard, one after the other. He smelled her fear from where he stood. At Angel's side, Sunny struggled to rise, but it appeared that at least one of her legs was broken.

"Dear God . . ."

Without needing to be told, Jeremy knew what had happened. The men who had come to him to plead on Angel's behalf had been right.

He'd been wrong.

Now two good animals were dead, and an innocent woman had been terrorized. All because she owned the land where Rogers Creek flowed, where God had placed it.

And because he'd failed to act when he should have.

He was responsible for Angel's plight.

7

"Forgive me, Father," Jeremy prayed, "and help her forgive me, too."

He let Sunny sniff his hand. "It's me, girl. Remember the biscuit?"

She tried to wag her tail and paid for it with a cry.

Jeremy came closer, his gaze on Angel. Her eyes stared straight ahead, but they seemed to see nothing, not even him. She didn't react to his presence, his voice, his approach.

He continued to talk to the dog, his voice calm and sure, soft in the unnatural silence of the barn. For a moment he wasn't sure whether he should help the dog or remove Maggie's body from the pen. But Maggie was beyond help, and Sunny and Angel needed him.

He didn't fit well into the space, but he didn't care. He'd knock down the walls before he'd quit what he had to do.

"Let's see now, Sunny. What'd they do to you, girl?"

With a gentle touch he patted all four legs, and found that two were broken. Either someone's out-and-out wickedness had caused the injuries, or the dog had come by them while protecting her mistress and her home.

From the corner of his eye, he saw that even though Angel still stared ahead in that strange, blind fashion, the hard trembling he'd noticed when he first came upon them had stopped. Perhaps she would settle down more easily if he looked after Sunny first and then tried to help her. He suspected she needed time to realize she wasn't about to be hurt yet again.

He didn't even know if she'd been hurt—physically, at any rate. He didn't doubt that Angel's injuries went soul deep and might never heal.

"Dear God, have mercy on her."

He stood slowly and backed away from the victims. Sunny's legs needed splints, and he'd have to leave the pen to find some. At the gate to the pen, he again looked to see if Angel had noticed his movements, but aside from the fresh strong tremor that wracked her from head to toe, she seemed frozen, lost in the horror carved in her mind.

He hurried to the woodpile near the cabin's kitchen door and soon found a pair of scraps that would do the trick. He loped back, and although it felt as though his errand took hours, in truth only a few minutes passed. At the pen, Angel and Sunny remained as they'd been.

The dog thumped her tail when she saw him, then moaned.

"I'm glad to see you, too," he said. "But don't move. You don't have to. It'll only hurt you more."

Another quick check told him that aside from a handful of minor cuts, more than likely from her efforts to fight off the attacker, she'd escaped the knife that had sliced Maggie's throat. Sunny nudged his hand with her wet nose, then licked him.

"Don't thank me yet," he muttered. "I'm going to hurt you even more than you already are before we finish here."

Moments later her whimpers proved his prediction true, but he had to go on. Soon he'd bound both legs to the thin boards with strips torn from his shirt. Even though the dog had clearly suffered from his crude doctoring, she'd never once tried to fight him or even bared her teeth.

"You're a sweetheart," he said when he'd tied the last knot. "No wonder Angel keeps you by her side."

At the mention of her mistress's name, Sunny glanced at the woman close by, then whimpered again. She looked at Jeremy, turned once more to Angel, and cried yet another time.

"You want me to help her, too, don't you? But first I have to move you out so I can have me some space to move around."

Jeremy gathered the dog in his arms as gently as he could. At first Sunny resisted, her mournful brown eyes fixed on Angel, but then, likely worn out by pain, she quieted, and he brought her up close to his chest.

"I'm taking you inside now," he murmured. "Then I'll go back for Angel. Both you girls will be much better off inside the cabin."

He kept up the conversation as he crossed the yard. He hoped his words would soothe Sunny. He'd always had a way with animals, especially unbroken colts and fillies, and he prayed that talent didn't leave him now.

Something must have worked, because by the time he reached the kitchen door, Sunny had laid her head on his chest and her eyelids drooped low. Good. The poor animal needed sleep more than anything else.

Jeremy placed the dog on the braided rug by the hearth. She opened her eyes, thumped her tail, and whimpered, then let exhaustion claim her. She looked asleep by the time he gave her a final glance from the doorway.

He ran to the barn. Angel hadn't moved, but the lamb in her arms let out a weak baa when he entered the pen.

"Thank you, Father. At least one of Maggie's babies is still alive."

He knelt next to Angel and her sheep, unsure what to do next. In a whisper, he offered up another prayer, this one for guidance and wisdom.

"Well, ladies," he said, noting that the lamb she held was the female he'd delivered not so long ago, "if my talking helps horses and a dog, then I reckon it sure can't hurt either one of you. Let's see what we have here."

It took some doing to ease Angel's grip on the little critter, but Jeremy kept at it and soon had the baby in his hold. To his relief, she'd been spared the butchering done to her mother and brother. A knot on her curl-topped head, though, told him she hadn't escaped unhurt.

Then he faced a new predicament. Each time he tried to set the lamb aside, she wailed her objection.

"Hey, there," he crooned. "I need to look after Angel now. You'll be fine. I promise I'll take care of you as soon as I know how bad she's hurt."

Then he realized what caused the young animal's distress. She obviously smelled her mother's presence, and with a baby's innocence, she nudged the ewe's lifeless body. Maggie's failure to respond vexed her.

"I see I'll have to deal with your mama before I can do anything more."

A glimpse at Angel triggered within him the desperation he'd felt when he first found the slaughter in the pen. He had to get to Angel; she needed help more than the lamb, even more than poor Sunny had. She was clearly in shock and needed medical attention. But all she had was him.

He took hold of the dead ewe and dragged her into the nearest stall. He'd deal with her later.

Back in the pen, he sat at Angel's side, and the lamb trotted over to them. She plopped down and looked up at him with eyes full of trust. He prayed he wouldn't betray her again.

"Angel."

She didn't respond, didn't move, didn't blink.

He repeated her name in a soft voice over and over again. Then he placed a hand on her forearm. She spun toward him, fire in her gaze, and shrieked. "No!"

Before he could react, she dove at him, screamed, scrabbled, reached for his eyes. He twisted to one side, rolled on the ground, and came up to grab her. "Angel!"

She followed him, swung her fists at his head, and screamed, rage and horror in her voice.

"Angel," he yelled again, and this time he caught hold of her arms. "It's me, Jeremy. Jeremy Johnstone."

She fought him with a strength he struggled to match. He tried to wrap his arms around her, but she threw herself backward and flailed at him with her legs. Her fists never let up their assault on his face, head, shoulders, chest. The light in her eyes burned wild, and her pupils looked tiny, like black dots.

"Angel!" he roared yet another time. He tried to hold her still, nothing more. "You're hurt. I don't want to hurt you any more than you already are."

She lunged at his face, her short nails poised to rake his skin, but he was ready for her this time. He threw his arms around her, pinned her hands between their bodies, and toppled them both onto the straw-covered floor. He held her down with his greater weight, and all the time he repeated her name in his horse-taming voice.

"It's all right now, Angel. I'm here, and I won't let anyone hurt you anymore. Don't fight me, Angel. I'll take care of you. Just look at me. Look here, Angel."

The mad shrieks wavered and slowly lost their intensity. Little by little they turned to sobs. At about the same time, her fighting stopped. Jeremy suspected she'd tired herself out, not just from attacking him but from the nightmare she'd gone through before he'd arrived. He doubted she'd taken in a word he'd said.

Her eyes locked on his face, but he didn't think she saw him. The look in the hazel depths was still crazed, but he also thought he could see the start of bewilderment, as though Angel tried to understand, to recognize him, to make sense out of what had happened.

He talked on, and he knew that if ever there was any worth to that soothing tone he'd learned to use years ago, it was here and now. Finally Angel blinked. Recognition dawned.

"J—Jeremy . . . Johnstone," she murmured. Her sigh brushed his cheek before her head lolled sideways on the floor. Her body went limp beneath him.

Jeremy held his breath for a moment. He could hardly move in the close quarters of the pen, but he knew it wouldn't help her if his solid weight stayed on her a moment longer.

He took as much care as possible and eased off to one side. He lay there, aware of Angel's shallow breaths. She'd fainted. Perhaps it was for the best. He needed to get her to the cabin, and he didn't know what kind of fight she'd put up again—if she had any strength left in her.

He got to his feet and studied her condition. Her clothes were soaked through with perspiration, and splotches of blood had spattered all over her. One of her red braids had come undone, the wealth of hair strangely bright at such a grim time. She had no injuries, at least none he could see, so he crouched, slipped his arms under her slender frame, and picked her up.

Only when he held her against his chest did he feel the sticky wetness at the back of her left shoulder. His stomach churned. Rage set up a roar in his head. How could someone do this to a defenseless woman? How could they kill two sheep? Maim a dog? Why?

He bit off the curse that rose to his lips.

He needed water right away to cleanse the wound on Angel's back. As carefully as he could, he hurried back to the cabin, mindful of the little lamb at his heel. Sunny's woof greeted them, and he crossed the room to what he assumed was Angel's bedroom door. He kicked it open and placed her on the clean sheets spread on the neat bed. He then propped her onto her side so he could better judge the extent of her injury.

She moaned.

He felt sick.

Blood oozed in a steady flow from the gash just above her shoulder blade. Since he needed water and towels and bandages, he eased Angel's body over onto her stomach. He flinched at the pain-filled sound she made.

They needed Letty, but unless she suddenly showed up or someone came to visit and could fetch her, they only had him and his limited skill. He'd sewn together his share of raw wounds, but somehow this was different.

This was Angel.

In the kitchen, a kettle simmered at the back of the iron stove. He also saw a pitcher filled with cooler water, and he poured a blend of both into a deep basin he found under the cupboard by the stove. He gathered the pile of towels from next to the enamel bowl, then took everything into Angel's room.

At her side once again, he hesitated. He didn't know this woman; she hardly knew him. How could he touch her? And how would he look at that gash without taking off her clothes?

While he dithered, more blood seeped from the wound. "Blast your proper manners and all that other nonsense, Aunt Gertie!"

He couldn't do it. He wouldn't. And, indeed, he shouldn't even try to cope with this injury. Surely, Rogers Ranch had a buggy or a wagon somewhere.

But he didn't have the time to search. He'd have to carry Angel into town on his horse and pray that they got there before she bled too much more. It was bad enough that she'd been hurt because of him.

He couldn't live with the knowledge that she'd died on account of him.

❦

The rocking motion disoriented Angel. She opened her eyes. The sight that met them stunned her. She was in Jeremy's arms. And if her wits weren't any more addled than she feared, they were both astride a horse.

But perhaps it was some odd kind of dream. She felt light-headed, a bit dizzy, thirsty, and queasy all at once.

"Mr. . . ." Her mouth seemed full of lamb's wool; she couldn't get the simple word out. She closed her eyes, and darkness overtook her again.

A nattering caught her attention what seemed a lifetime later. Strangers spoke, and to her surprise, despite the swoony sensation in her head, she understood their words.

"Would you lookit that, Marthy?" a man said.

"Simply scandalous!" Marthy replied.

Angel opened her eyes and tried to see the scandal, but all she saw was Jeremy's grim expression a short distance away. The rocking hadn't let up. Neither had the sick sensation in her stomach or the muzziness in her head.

"Wha . . . ?" she got out.

The cowboy looked down. "Hush. You're hurt, and I've brought you to Hartville. We're on our way to Doc Letty's clinic."

Everything rushed back at her, heartache so strong that it overtook her fear. Her eyes burned from the feverish tears that filled them, and she doubted she could draw breath, her chest felt so tight.

"Maggie," she moaned.

Jeremy's clear blue eyes turned to her, sadness in their depths. "Yes, she's gone."

The knot in her throat and the queasiness in her middle worsened. A dry heave convulsed her. The sadness was too much to bear. It made her physically ill, yet the merciful blackness she'd known just moments earlier refused to return.

Grief overcame her and she surrendered. She wept, silently but with a pain so deep it seemed to spring right from the center of her heart. How had things gone so wrong? What had she done to bring on such horror?

Images rushed at her from behind closed eyes: A face shrouded in a red handkerchief loomed over her. Dark eyes blazed with an anger that hurt almost as much as the knife stabs she'd received in her back.

She'd fought him, but her hands had posed no match to his greater strength nor to the sharp blade he'd wielded with chilly and sure aim.

Papa had been right.

As had Wynema.

And Letty.

Phoebe.

She'd been wrong. And she had indeed been naïve. She'd trusted God with a child's ease, one she now questioned. What was the truth of trust?

But she really couldn't concentrate enough to think through such deep and difficult matters. There would be time enough for that once she went back to the ranch, Bible in hand. She belonged there, not in the cowboy's arms.

Not where he could make use of her weakness to take over her land.

"I . . . want . . . to . . . go . . . home."

"I'll take you back as soon as Doc Letty says you can go."

"No. Now."

Jeremy's square jaw tightened, and Angel saw a muscle work under his tanned skin.

"If I don't get you to the doctor right soon," he said, "you won't last long enough to spend another day on that ranch."

Angel shook her head. "Oh . . ."

The pain.

The dizziness.

The bile in her throat.

The frightening sensation that she was falling through air, through time . . .

☙

"Put her down on the examination table," Letty said. "I'll just be a moment. I must wash my hands before I touch her."

Good to her word, she was back at Jeremy's side only seconds

95

later. He'd already settled Angel on the platform covered with a snowy sheet. She'd made that odd moan again, that raw sound of heart-deep pain, and it tore something inside him.

Letty put a hand to Angel's pale forehead. "What happened?"

Jeremy took off his hat. "I'm not sure, ma'am. All's I know is that I went to Rogers Ranch to talk again with Miss Rogers here, and I found her in a lambing pen with a pair of dead sheep at her side. Her dog Sunny had two of her legs broken."

The doctor's silver eyes flashed. "Who did it?"

Equal fury flared in his heart. "I don't know, but when I do . . . why, ma'am, all's I can say is that they'll be sorry they ever laid a hand on this poor girl."

Intelligence shone in the angry gray eyes that raked him over. Jeremy felt the inspection clear down to his toes. Then, without another word, the doctor nodded and turned back to her patient.

Jeremy winced when she lifted Angel's torn shirt away from the deep wound. Letty gasped.

"Fetch Phoebe Gable, if you please, Mr. Johnstone. I'll need her nursing experience."

"Can't you just . . . A couple of stitches should close the cut right up, no?"

"There's a piece of blade still in her," the doctor said. "I suspect it's embedded in the bone. I'll have to do surgery on her shoulder, so please don't waste a minute more. Bring Mrs. Gable here."

The leaden weight of guilt sank straight to his gut. A knot tied his throat, and he couldn't say a word, so he nodded, clapped his hat back on, and went to find Phoebe.

No sooner did he tell the lovely blonde that the doctor needed her, than they were back on Main Street headed straight for Willow Lane. They ran up the front steps to the clinic and went straight to the examination room.

Jeremy moved back and watched the women work. Their grim

faces told him more than he wanted to know, but just what he suspected. Angel's life hung in the balance.

He prayed.

A while later he heard metal strike metal.

"There," Letty said, satisfaction in her voice. "At least that's out now."

"Would you like me to suture her?" Phoebe asked.

"Please. I'll see to that broken leg."

Jeremy groaned. His untrained once-over hadn't found the break. What was to become of Angel? Surely the stubborn woman wouldn't insist she could run her ranch on her own now. Not with her in this condition.

He took a seat in the waiting area by the front door. He clasped his hands between his knees, lowered his head, and again sought the Lord.

"Mr. Johnstone," Phoebe said moments later.

Her words jolted him from his rambling prayer. "Yes?"

"Tell me, if you would, please. I'm not a man or a rancher either, but is a parcel of land or a stream of running water worth a woman's life?"

He looked up into eyes as blue as his own. The air of peace he'd noticed around the mine owner's wife was still there. But today he also saw distaste, dismay, disillusion.

"Couldn't tell you what others think, ma'am. Her land and creek are worth fistfuls of dollars to many—even me. But her life?"

He looked past Phoebe to the still body on the table, covered with a pure white sheet. He thought of the years he'd dug ore from stingy mountains. He remembered the pride he'd felt when he put his money down for the deed to the ranch. He thought of his herd, good animals who now suffered from lack of water and grass.

He thought of Maggie, her lamb, Sunny.

Angel.

Was that water-rich ranch of hers worth her life?

She'd nearly died on his account. He owed her. And even though it could, and probably would, cost him his spread, Jeremy had to help her protect what was hers.

He'd give up his dream to atone for his sin.

"No, ma'am. Her land's not worth her life to me."

8

Jeremy left Letty's clinic, Phoebe's question still ringing in his head. He knew that no ranch was worth a person's life. But when he found Angel and the dead sheep, he'd learned that not everyone felt as he did. Whoever had attacked her hadn't meant to just hurt her. That knife in her back had been intended to kill.

Even though he wasn't sure what he should do next about his herd, he knew what he had to do right then. He headed for Sheriff Herman's office.

By the time he entered the building, his anger had reached a boil. No one should suffer what Angel just had.

"Well, howdy there, Mr. Johnstone," the lawman drawled.

The sheriff's lighthearted greeting hit Jeremy square in his gut. "I don't reckon you'd be so cheery if you'd seen what I just saw."

Herman's mud-brown eyes narrowed, and his smile vanished. "If I ain't seen it, then how can I be otherwise?" He stood behind his desk. "Tell me what you're so all-fired worked up about, and let me see how I feel."

"Angel Rogers was attacked earlier today."

"What do you mean, attacked?"

Jeremy dragged off his hat, dropped it in a worn chair nearby, and then planted his palms on the desktop. "In my book, attacked means only one thing. Someone went after her, and he meant to carve her up. He used a knife."

Jeremy's anger seemed to shock the sheriff. "You telling me that redhead girl's been hurt? With a knife?"

His stare would have to do as a response. Jeremy couldn't trust himself to say another word. He did muster a nod.

"Who did it?" Herman asked.

"Seems to me, Sheriff, that's your job—to find out who did it. I did my part. I found Miss Rogers, her dead sheep, and her hurt dog. I took care of the dog, and I'm on my way to see to the sheep. I brought Miss Rogers to Doc Letty. Now I figure it's up to you to do the rest."

The barrel-chested sheriff shook his head, and Jeremy hoped it wasn't in disbelief. He didn't know how he'd respond if the man doubted his word.

When the sheriff's dull eyes met his, Jeremy drew a sharp breath.

"What were you up to out to Rogers Ranch? How am I supposed to know you're not the one what hurt that girl? You ain't made no great secret you're after her water."

"Don't question my honor," Jeremy said, his words sharp and curt, his eyes on the sheriff's. "I went to her and offered to buy her out fair and square. I'd be right stupid to go and hurt her now, don't you reckon? I haven't done a thing to her, and here you think I went and did this . . . this disgusting thing."

For a moment the lawman just stared back. Then he ran a hand over his brow. "You got a point there, son. So if you didn't do it, then do you have any notion who might've?"

"I'd say it was the fool who rode his horse down the road past Angel's place like the devil himself was on his heels. Didn't get a good enough look at him, otherwise I'd have brought him to you—hog-tied, at that."

The sheriff sighed. "Strikes me, that's just what you would've done. Then tell me. Did you see anything at the ranch? Did he leave anything behind?"

The clink of metal on metal at the clinic echoed through

Jeremy's mind. "Sure did. He left the blade of his knife. After he cut the throat of one of Miss Rogers's ewes and wrung the neck of a newborn lamb, he went for Miss Rogers's heart—from the back, the filthy coward."

Sheriff Herman blanched, and Jeremy fought the same nausea he'd felt when he first discovered the extent of Angel's injury. He turned from the lawman to hide how hard the events of the day had struck him.

He swallowed a couple of times, walked to the window, stared at the mountain where for years he'd dug ore to save to someday buy his dream. A dream he saw fade with every minute that went by.

He looked over his shoulder at the sheriff. The man hadn't taken his gaze from Jeremy and appeared confounded. By what? Jeremy didn't know.

He made his point again. "He left the knife blade in Angel's back."

His words hit the sheriff with the strength of a fist. Herman took a pair of steps backward. He opened his mouth to speak, but no words came out. Finally he muttered an oath in a raw, low voice.

"Who'd do a thing like that? Especially to a woman—a girl?" he asked, his words rich with disgust. Jeremy's opinion of the man regained some of the luster it had lost when Herman questioned his honor.

"Someone desperate," Jeremy said. "Someone who's watched his life's work die before his eyes and knows he can't stop it. Someone who cares more about money than he does honor, decency, or the people who have what he wants. Someone who doesn't care about the day he'll face God and have to account for what all he's done."

"Well, son, way I see it, these someones you talk about ain't thinking much beyond keeping the next cow alive."

"That's what I said, but does that make them any less guilty before the Almighty's throne?"

"I must echo Jeremy's sentiment," Pastor Stone said as he entered the room. "You'll have to excuse my interruption, Sheriff Herman, but the moment I heard about this . . . this sick offense against an innocent woman, I had to come."

The lawman offered a wry smile. "I see you ain't come alone."

Eric Wagner and Douglas Carlson crowded in behind the pastor. "Did you expect us to ignore it?" Eric asked. "We've a killer on the loose—"

"She hasn't . . . ?" Jeremy asked, too horrified to put his fear into words.

Eric faced him. "I'm sorry. I didn't mean to worry you. But surely you agree that whoever stabbed Angel meant to kill her?"

Again the metallic clink rang through Jeremy. "I've no doubt."

Douglas stepped forward. "As the Rogerses' attorney, I'll tell you the ranch is hers. Her father wrote a simple and clear will."

"That might be the worst thing for her. The land and the creek are truly hers."

Eric frowned. "Let's not waste time on this. What do you intend to do, Sheriff?"

"Why . . . I . . ." The sheriff stopped, blustered a bit, then squared his shoulders. "I'll have you know I keep the peace in these parts pretty well, Eric Wagner. And I mean to keep on doing so. I don't need you to tell me how or when to do my job."

"Now, Max," the pastor said. "This isn't the time for false pride. A woman was hurt. That's what matters most."

Jeremy nodded, then hooked his thumbs into his belt loops. "So why are you here still jawing with us instead of on your way to Rogers Ranch?"

"Ah . . . er . . . because I reckon I'd best talk to the girl first."

"I don't think it'd be a wise thing to disturb the patient," Eric said. "Not when she's in as serious a condition as I understand Miss Rogers is. You wouldn't want to cross my wife."

Jeremy smiled at Herman's alarm. Angel's predicament was

anything but humorous, but to see the cocky sheriff taken down a peg? That the man dared not confront Hartville's small but spirited lady doctor offered much-needed relief. On a day like today, he'd take whatever helped him think of anything besides the butchery he'd seen.

Herman elbowed past the reverend in his hurry to reach the hall tree by the front door. He crammed a battered brown hat on his thinning hair, gave a quick swipe at the tin badge he wore on his shirt, and shot Eric a quick look.

"Give your lovely missus my best regards," he said as he stepped outside. "And you tell her I sure do hope Miss Rogers gets herself all the rest she needs. Yessir. Rest and sleep and peace is what that girl needs right now. I'll take care of the animal what did this to her."

Jeremy turned to the newspaperman, and they exchanged knowing looks. Douglas joined them in a hearty laugh.

"Thank you," Jeremy said.

The lawyer, the first to grow serious again, said, "For what?"

Jeremy shrugged. "I don't know . . . For not asking Herman to arrest me, for sending him to do his job instead of wasting time, for giving me a laugh on a day when sin and cruelty have come out on top."

"Don't forget, son," Pastor Stone said, "that the victory, the one that really counts, is already won. That victory belongs to the Lord."

The three younger men turned to the man of God, who didn't let any of them speak. "This is as good a time as any to call the Lord into our midst. Shall we pray?"

"I reckon God's the only one who can really right this fix," Jeremy said. "So I guess we'd do well to turn to Him. Lead us on, Reverend."

"Heavenly Father . . ."

❦

Her eyelids weighed too much. Angel couldn't think of a time when anything had taken as much effort as it took to lift them. But she'd never been a quitter, and she wasn't about to start now.

When she got her eyes to focus, her disorientation grew. Where was she? And why wasn't she home, at the ranch?

The golden glow of lamplight drew her gaze to her right side. "Mr. Johnstone?"

A sleepy "Huh?" came her way.

Nothing made sense, not this white room, not the vague woozy sensation in her head, certainly not Jeremy's choice of a spot to nap.

"Mr. Johnstone," she said, relieved to hear strength in her voice this time.

Jeremy's blue eyes popped open, and he jerked up from a slouch. "Angel! You're awake."

The familiar use of her name surprised her. They weren't so well acquainted, and what they knew of each other, they didn't especially like—at least, that was her recollection of their earlier encounter.

Another image flashed in her head. They'd had a much worse encounter. Fear, raw and imminent, caught her in its grip. She fought for breath but only gasped.

"Doc!" the cowboy yelled. "Doc Letty! She's awake, but something's awful wrong with her."

Blood . . .

Hurried footsteps approached, and a soft, cool hand covered her forehead. "Angel dear," Letty said. "Relax. You're safe."

Safe . . . but Maggie hadn't been.

Grief filled Angel, and tears flooded her eyes. "Where . . . ?"

"Don't try to talk now," the doctor said. "We're at my clinic, where Mr. Johnstone brought you. You're going to be fine."

Fine? How could she ever be fine after all that horror?

"Sunny . . . Maggie . . ." They hadn't been fine. And she'd never be the same again. ". . . want to go home."

"Of course you do." Letty's competent hands took Angel's pulse, then plied her chest with a rubber hose and metal bell contraption. "And you'll go back as soon as you're able to do so. I suspect it won't be much longer now either."

"My sheep . . . Sunny. They need me. My ranch."

"Pardon me, ma'am," Jeremy said. "Your critters are all doing fine. I made sure of it."

Of course he'd make sure the ranch ran well. "You've taken it." She struggled to sit, but when she raised her head, the world spun violently around her. "Oohh . . ." She fought the disorientation again. "You can't do that. I won't let you."

Bile rose in her throat. Her head throbbed. Pain pierced the wooziness, just enough to make her gasp at its intensity, but it did nothing to help her overcome the light-headed sensation. She moaned.

Letty's cool hands cupped Angel's cheeks and gave her something to focus on besides her misery.

"You were hurt," the physician said, "and you're still very weak. You lost a great deal of blood. But you will be fine—if you don't do anything foolish, like try to take on that great ranch of yours before you're ready."

As if the fact that she couldn't go back to the home she loved would help her recover. A sense of sorrow came over her, and Angel feared she'd failed her father—and so soon after his death.

"Miss Rogers," the cowboy said, "please don't fret. I only meant to ease your mind. I've been by your ranch two or three times each day—but only to make sure your animals don't need anything. And Sunny's doing right fine. Her legs are on the mend."

"I'll be back on my land soon." She fought the bitterness. "And you'd best be off it, mister. I won't sell, and I'll fight you for it. I won't let you kill me to get your hands on Papa's creek."

Her words hit their mark. Jeremy flinched, and his face paled under his tan.

Before he could recover, Letty made a dismayed sound. "You

have it all wrong, Angel dear. It's not like that. Jeremy's been here every night since he brought you in. He's watched over you like a mama bear does her cubs. And during the day he's had his foreman run his place so he can make sure no one tries to move in on yours."

Angel wanted to believe what the doctor said, but she couldn't forget the first time she'd seen Jeremy. "How do you know," she said, "that he's not the one who did this?"

That got a rise out of the cowboy. "*You* know I didn't do it. I came out and made you an honest offer. I'd never do anything like . . . like—"

"It wouldn't make any sense for him to work so hard to save your life and protect what's yours," Phoebe said from the doorway. "Not if he was the one who tried to kill you in the first place."

The mine owner's wife removed her hat and placed it on the chair Jeremy had vacated. "And I have it on good authority that he's done nothing but fret himself near dead over the care of your sheep. Especially since he took over without any idea what to do for them."

Another image flew through Angel's mind, and she remembered the hate-filled dark eyes of her attacker. She sighed. "It wasn't him . . ."

"I'd best be on my way now," Jeremy said, his words sharp and his tone curt. "I'd hate to see the doc's good work all spoilt because you won't listen to reason, Miss Rogers."

"It wasn't you . . ." She stopped, swallowed past the knot in her throat. "And it's Angel."

All three turned toward her.

"My name is Angel."

An odd expression bloomed on Jeremy's features, not one of pleasure, nor one of rage. Instead, distrust and bewilderment seemed to crash on his attractive face.

"Did you ask me to call you by your given name?" he said.

Angel went to nod, but the pain in her back stunned her. It took all her strength to whisper, "Yes."

A moment or two went by before he met her gaze. To her surprise, she saw pain, sadness, regret there. She also got the sense that he might be a decent man, one who had tried to do his best by her.

"I'm sorry," she added. Would she come to regret this gesture?

He pulled himself to his full height and shook his head. "No, Miss Rog—Angel. No need for you to be feeling that way. I'm the one who's sorry, and I'll always be."

He turned, smashed his hat on his unruly blond hair, and left the room. Moments later, in the sudden silence, Angel heard the door close.

"Well."

"My goodness!"

The two ministering angels chimed out their comments at the same time. Although she hadn't said a thing, Angel felt as stunned by Jeremy's words as Letty and Phoebe seemed to be.

If he hadn't been the one to hurt her, and if he really had no bad intentions when it came to her land, then what did Jeremy have to be sorry for?

On his way to Amos's livery, Jeremy spotted a group of young women on their way out of the Hartville Public Library. At the very center of their midst, Dahlia held court. The ladies seemed to chatter all at the same time, their words sprinkled with generous handfuls of giggles.

Their cheerful smiles came as a relief after all the time Jeremy had fretted and worried and worked for Angel's sake. Then she went and accused him of trying to kill her!

He was responsible for leaving her open to the attack, but he'd never injured another soul. And he didn't mean to start now. Not even when it came to a pigheaded mountain woman like Angel.

To think that some in town, the most unexpected being Pastor Stone, thought he should tie the knot with that contrary creature. After all that had happened—now more than ever—Jeremy knew no such thing could ever happen. Not only had he recognized that no land was worth the destruction he'd seen at Angel's ranch, but he'd also seen how unsuited they were.

As he'd always known.

"Good evening, there, Mr. Johnstone," Dahlia said, her thick-as-molasses southern accent a sweet balm to his wounded pride.

He dragged his hat off, gave her a courteous nod, and smiled. "It's a pure pleasure to see you, Miss Sutton. I trust you ladies have been having yourselves a right nice evening."

"Don't you know?" a mousy brown slip of a thing said. "Our dear Miss Dahlia's opened a most important academy for the women of Hartville. We're much obliged to her for all her efforts on our behalf."

Jeremy smiled and arched a brow. "Oh?"

Dahlia stepped forward, her movements feminine and smooth. "Indeedy so, Mr. Johnstone. I've decided my excellent education is too great a treasure to keep to my little old self. I've begun to share its wealth with the women of the town. I'm the directress of Miss Dahlia's School of Ladylike Arts and Deportment."

He blinked. Deportment? "I . . . see."

The beautiful brunette took hold of his arm. "Do honor me with your company a while, sugar, and I'll be tickled to tell you every last little teeny thing you want to know about it all."

Jeremy swallowed hard. "Of course. I'd be right pleased to escort you anywhere you wish to go."

Behind them, a young woman let out a breathy "Oohh."

He glanced over his shoulder and saw another fan her face with her gloved hand.

Dahlia addressed her admirers. "I'll see you all again tomorrow evening, you hear?" She then turned the full force of her charm on Jeremy. "I can trust you to see me home all safe and sound, now, right?"

If he hadn't been aware of the date, time, and place of their encounter, seeing and hearing all that left Dahlia's lips, Jeremy would have sworn he was right smack in the middle of a particularly awe-inspiring dream.

Perhaps his idea to court the banker's beautiful daughter was the smartest one he'd had yet.

"Miss Sutton, ma'am, you can count on me for anything at all."

A wide smile lit up her elegant features, and she clasped his arm all the tighter. "You're a fine, strong gentleman, Mr. Johnstone, one a lady can trust with confidence."

The momentary image of a cowering, bloodied Angel flashed in his head. Jeremy faltered, but he gritted his teeth and forced the memory from his mind.

"I sure do hope so, Miss Sutton. I surely do."

"Call me Dahlia, sugar."

That "sugar" business rubbed him the wrong way, but the invitation to a more personal acquaintance encouraged him. "And I'm Jeremy to my friends."

"Oohh!" Dahlia's coo came with a little wiggle right against his arm. Jeremy blushed and stepped an inch or two away—for propriety's sake, of course.

Dahlia didn't take offense but instead went on. "I do so hope we can become *dear* friends . . . Jeremy." She blinked fast and furiously. "Why, I've always said a lady can't have none too many of those. Wouldn't you agree?"

"I've said the same a time or two myself." He clapped his hat on his head, then covered her hand with his. "Now, Miss Dahlia, you were saying something about some academy or some such thing?"

"Oh, indeed, Jeremy, sugar. I've decided it's long past time for Hartville to get itself some of life's better refinements. My sweet mama made sure I did learn all the things that make a girl a lady. Why, it did strike me as plumb selfish of me to keep all that polish to myself. And I've never had a selfish bone to my body."

Jeremy's eyes followed the gloved hand that waved along the lines of Dahlia's fine, feminine figure. He gulped.

She went on. "I'm working real hard to teach the women in this little old town of ours how to hold their heads high among the rest of America's most gracious ladies."

Jeremy mustered a befuddled "I see."

They strolled on in the early twilight. Dahlia described in detail such things as table settings, flower arrangements, the proper treatment of servant staff, comportment—or was it *de*portment?—fashionable conversation, personal beautification, and a host of other things he'd never even heard of. Some had to do with foods for the elderly and the use of vinegar to clean nearly everything known to mankind.

To his relief, she didn't expect much from him. An occasional "Mm-hmm" kept her going. Even though he enjoyed her voice, lush with the sound of the South, her conversation seemed a bit on the far side of silly.

He reckoned it could be on account of all the time he'd coped with such weighty matters as thirsty, hungry cattle, an injured dog, and a ranch that belonged to a woman who'd been hurt just because she had what someone else wanted.

Serious matters, those.

". . . don't you think?"

Jeremy's cheeks warmed. "I . . . ah . . . agree."

"I do declare, Jeremy Johnstone, you're a most unusual man. You really do listen to a lady, and I'm tickled to see that you even understand."

Ouch! She'd complimented him, and he didn't deserve it, but Jeremy, even if he was as unrefined as Dahlia's papa thought, wasn't about to lose sight of his goals.

"Why, thank you, Miss Dahlia. I'm right pleased to listen to you—your lovely voice and your splendid plans. You've made my evening a pure delight."

How had he trumped up those flowery words? He'd never been one for fancy stuff, and here he'd earned flattery for a passel of grunts and nods.

"Oh dear," Dahlia said, her voice full of disappointment. "We're here already."

She faced him and laid a delicate hand on his chest. Her huge black eyes met his, and she smiled again, a more radiant smile than any that came before. "I do declare, Jeremy Johnstone. I can't ever remember a more pleasant walk on a summer evening."

"My pleasure, ma'am."

"We must do it again sometime."

"Any time, Miss Dahlia. I'm at your service. A man's right lucky when a lovely lady like yourself does him the honor to take his arm and welcome his company."

"Why, thank you, Jeremy, sugar. Now, don't go making yourself a stranger, you hear?"

"No, ma'am. I surely do hope to see you again right soon."

"As do I, sugar. As do I."

She danced up the front steps to her father's mansion—as Jeremy thought of the elaborate house. He watched until she slipped inside, savored the momentary satisfaction, then hurried to the livery.

Perhaps his fortunes had taken a turn for the better.

Perhaps wedding bells would soon be ringing . . . but for Dahlia and him. Not for the redheaded mountain woman who'd only brought a passel of headaches to his life.

"Mrs. Dahlia Johnstone," he murmured as he mounted his horse.

He had to admit, it did have a certain ring to it, the ring of a job well done, that certain ring of success.

His future success.

9

Angel's recovery proved to be a slow and difficult one that tried her patience. "I've a ranch to get back to," she argued when Letty refused—yet again—to let her go home.

"One that's doing fine, much better than most, even," the physician replied. "My dear Eric went out to see it for himself. He says Jeremy has done himself proud on your behalf. Everything is right as rain—that rain I wish would come before too much longer."

Angel sighed. She hated to feel helpless, and although she appreciated everything the Wagners, the Gables, the Stones, and even Wynema had done for her since that horrid day, she itched to return to all she held dear. The small bedroom in the eaves at the clinic was lovely, with its flowered wallpaper and rose-bedecked quilt, but it wasn't home.

And she missed Sunny.

"Very well," Angel said. She sounded childish, and she knew it, yet she couldn't help but think her recovery would be quicker if she were at home. There she wouldn't fret over what that cowboy was doing with her flock, her creek, her pasture, her home.

She sank back into the plump pillows on the bed, and the stab of pain in her shoulder told her in no uncertain terms that she couldn't yet handle much of anything on her own. Besides, a simple wriggle of her toes set off a blunt ache in her broken leg, and she still couldn't go more than a pair of hours without dozing off.

She wasn't ready to return. But she didn't have to like the current state of affairs.

"Doc Letty!"

The call for the doctor awoke Angel a few hours later. She heard the door downstairs open, the hushed conversation that followed, and then the hurried footsteps that rang out. Moments later the door opened and closed again, and an odd silence filled the small house.

"Lord God," Angel whispered. "It sounds as though someone somewhere is ill. Be with them. I've come to know how discomfiting it is to feel weak, unwell. Please help Doc Letty. And help me, too. Help me heal so I can go home again."

She lost track of time and even dozed a bit more . . . until a commotion downstairs startled her awake.

"Doc?" she called.

When she didn't get a response, she pushed herself up almost to a sitting position. After a deep breath, she called out again, this time in a louder voice. "Doc Letty? Phoebe? What's happened?"

"I'm coming," Phoebe said.

Something was very wrong. Her friend sounded troubled.

When Phoebe appeared in the doorway, the tears on her face made fear clutch at Angel's heart. She whispered, "Lord Jesus, help us."

Phoebe lowered her head. She nodded, then met Angel's gaze. "We will indeed need His help. It's Pastor Stone. He . . . he's dead."

"No!"

Angel fought the covers, dislodged them from her legs. She gritted her teeth, and with a great heave, swung even the splinted leg over the side. The exertion made her pant, but she nonetheless relished her minor accomplishment. She felt more like herself.

"How could that be?" she asked.

"It just is, Angel. Letty says he suffered from a heart condition. Mrs. Stone sent for her when he had what must have been some kind of seizure, but I suspect it was too late even then. Mrs. Stone never got a response, and by the time Letty arrived . . . well, he was likely at the foot of God's throne already."

Mama.

Then Papa.

Maggie, the lamb, the ranch. Now Pastor Stone.

Father God, am I to lose everything good?

She didn't know; all she knew was that she wouldn't stay in Letty's lovely little room one minute more. Not if she had to prop her leg on a cart and have a horse pull it for her.

"How is Mrs. Stone?" she asked while she worked to rise to her feet. She was a mite wobbly, light-headed even, but now that she'd put her mind to it, she could hold herself upright for the first time in days and days.

"Mrs. Stone is Mrs. Stone," Phoebe said. "She was weeping when I arrived, but before long she began to comfort everyone around her. She even fed us cookies and coffee after the undertaker did his job."

"I know how that is. I had to milk the cow right after I buried Papa." She prayed for strength and hobbled to the chest of drawers.

"What do you think you're doing?"

"I need my clothes, and please don't try to stop me. I must see Mrs. Stone—pay my respects. Her husband was one of God's own angels here on earth."

"I don't think it's wise for you to put weight on that leg quite yet, but I also doubt you'll listen to me."

"Aha! My trousers . . ."

Her elation vanished as she considered her situation. The

denim pants would never fit over the splint that held her healing leg in the proper position. "And I suppose my shirt's been burned or buried or something of the sort."

"Something of the sort."

Spirits deflated, Angel leaned on the oak chest and tried to come up with a solution, her determination intact.

"I suppose I wouldn't dislodge the splint if I wore . . ." She glared at Phoebe's simple navy skirt. "If I wore a dress."

Phoebe gave her a mischievous grin.

"It's hardly fair," Angel groused. "You're enjoying this, aren't you?"

"Oh yea!"

The peculiar Shaker response made Angel smile back in spite of her irritation. "I reckon a good number of the more proper ladies in town have had their pleasure gossiping about my clothes."

Phoebe nodded.

"If I recollect clearly, Mr. Johnstone—"

"He asked you to call him Jeremy. And, Angel, he's really not a bad sort."

Angel sighed. "Jeremy it is. Anyway, as I tried to say, Jeremy and I scandalized more than a few when he carried me into town on his horse."

Phoebe's eyes sparked, and her lips pursed with indignation. "There are more than a few here in town who are scandalized far too easily. I wouldn't give it a moment's thought."

Angel waved the comment aside. "I only meant that it won't be any less a matter of chitchat when they see me wear something—" She took a mental measure of her friend. "—of yours."

"Oohh! Do you really mean that?"

"Of course I mean it. How else can I get from here to the manse? I wouldn't care if folks saw me in this." She gestured at the pretty lace-trimmed cotton nightgown Phoebe had provided. "It covers all it needs to quite well, but I don't reckon it would reflect any too well on you, Letty, or Mrs. Stone."

"Don't give it a thought. We've weathered more than the sight of an injured woman on her way to pay her respects in something other than a proper, sedate suit." Phoebe's smile turned impish again. "But take a seat on the bed and wait for me. It'll take me but a moment to fetch something for you to wear."

An uneasy niggle bounced from corner to corner in Angel's mind, but she made herself ignore it and did as Phoebe asked.

True to her word, Phoebe was back a short time later, a brown-paper-wrapped parcel in her hand. Angel looked at it askance. "What did you bring?"

"You'll see."

Phoebe untied the cord she'd used on the package and removed the paper to reveal fabric—surely garments—in shades of deep red and cream.

Angel's little niggle grew.

"It's not some fussy, prissy thing, now, is it?" She studied the contents of Phoebe's parcel with a jaundiced eye. "You wouldn't bring lace and flowers and ribbons and bows just to try to make me stay in bed, now, would you?"

Phoebe chuckled. "Nay. It never occurred to me. I'm not that devious. Besides, you'd likely run out in the nightgown if I had done that. I brought you a blouse like mine, and a skirt very similar to this one I have on. I thought that with your bright hair and hazel eyes, the red would be much nicer than my blue."

Angel sniffed. "Pretty is as pretty does—Papa always said that. I can't say I care to fret over prettiness or any such foolishness. Sturdy clothes that let me work are all I need."

"I understand." Phoebe brought a soft-looking chemise and the blouse to Angel. "Just humor me a bit. Please?"

Angel sighed. "I'll try them on."

A handful of minutes later, she wore the unaccustomed garments, and although she'd expected to feel uncomfortable and restricted in them, she found that Phoebe had made wise choices on her behalf.

"Thank you," she said and slid her hand over a cream serge-covered hip. The other arm hurt too much from the struggle to first undress and then put on the dark red blouse. Even Phoebe's help hadn't kept the effort from making the pain worse.

For a moment Angel feared she'd swoon, it hurt so much. But she clamped down on her lip, closed her eyes tight, and fought the light-headedness. Her efforts paid off.

"I suppose I'm ready."

Phoebe stood just steps away, her eyes narrowed in careful scrutiny. She turned her head a tiny bit, closed one eye while she stared a while longer through the other one. In the end, she nodded and smiled.

"You look quite different, you know. I wonder if anyone will recognize you at first glance."

Angel patted her upswept hair with her good hand. "I don't know why you thought I needed to do this."

"I asked you to indulge me, didn't I? And you said you would —right?"

Angel nodded.

"Well, I'd like you to take a turn before the looking glass above the chest."

Angel held her breath and stepped closer to the shiny thing. She didn't know if she should worry, but she'd never been a coward, and she wasn't about to become one today.

With a prayer for strength, she lifted her gaze to the glass and gasped. "Mama . . ."

Tears filled her eyes. She'd never known how much she resembled her late mother, but the knot of red braid on the crown of her head revealed the high cheekbones and slender neck she remembered. Although the eyes that stared back were hazel rather than Mama's brilliant emerald, they had the same shape, as did the eyebrows above them and the straight nose between them. Even the light sprinkle of gold freckles on her skin reminded her of the woman she missed every single day of her life.

Tears fell—sad, yes, but also weighted with a certain pride. If she had to look like anyone, then she would much rather look like her mother than anyone else. And Mama had always taught her to hold her head high no matter what might come.

She sniffled and faced her friend. "I'm ready."

Phoebe gave her a radiant smile. "Yea, Angel, I'm sure you are. But I must wonder . . . Is Hartville ready for you?"

§

Angel stabbed the cane Phoebe had provided into the ground before her, then dragged her broken leg to meet the other. She repeated the awkward process over and over again. She refused to give in to the pain and exhaustion that threatened.

After she saw Mrs. Stone, she was going home.

The door to the manse stood open, propped ajar with a solid chunk of Colorado rock. Angel took a deep breath and tackled the challenge posed by the front steps. One by one she conquered them. Her breath burst out in labored gasps.

"There!" she cried at the summit. Then she registered the absolute silence inside the house.

A number of townsfolk had gathered inside. Not at all unusual if one considered the circumstances. The close scrutiny they all gave her, however, struck her as troublesome. It proved far more difficult to withstand than she'd imagined.

"Mrs. Stone?" she said.

The pastor's wife . . . Oh dear. It would be difficult to remember that the dear lady's state had now changed. Pastor Stone's widow came close, a puzzled look in her brown eyes.

"Who . . . ?" Her eyes widened and her mouth formed an *O.* "Is that really you, child?"

Angel felt as though the blush started down at her toes and stained every inch of her right up to the top of her head. "Yes, ma'am."

"Dear girl, you're the very image of your sainted mother!"

Tears threatened again, but Angel fought them. She nodded. "I'm as surprised as you."

Sibilant whispers spread across the room. Angel's mortification grew. "I came because . . . well, Phoebe told me about . . ."

She hated the clumsiness, so she shook her head to dispel it and then blurted out her condolences. "I'm so very sorry about Pastor Stone. I'll miss him a great deal, but I'm certain it won't be near as much as you will."

Mrs. Stone's sad little smile touched Angel's heart. "Indeed, my dear. I will miss that wonderful man. But we had many happy years together, and I trust the Lord has plenty for me to do before I go meet them both."

As she spoke, the older woman crossed the room, then faced Angel once again. "Why don't you come and sit on the settee? I'm sure standing there isn't doing that leg one bit of good."

"I'll say it's not." Letty's gray eyes flashed. "You've proven to be a most challenging patient, Angel Rogers. Why did you ever leave that bed?"

Angel squared her shoulders. "You didn't stay home to fold bandages or count remedies, now, did you? You're here for Mrs. Stone's benefit, and I could do no less. I loved the pastor as much as any of you did."

The gathered mourners halted their chatter and stared. Angel didn't care. She'd done the right thing, and she was about to do another one as well.

"I don't want you to think me ungrateful," she added. "But it's time for me to return home—"

"But you're hardly recovered yet—"

"I'm sure I will recover in due time, and I prefer to do it at my ranch. I've been away far too long. I do promise not to do anything that might undo your good doctoring."

The mutinous expressions that fought on Letty's face told Angel her friend and physician didn't like what she'd said. Not one bit of it pleased Letitia Morgan Wagner, M.D.

The spirited woman went to argue, but Angel didn't give her the chance. "Would you leave your clinic unattended—or attended by a stranger—any longer than necessary?"

She knew she'd won the battle when Letty's dismay replaced her disapproval.

"I surrender," the doctor said. "But I'll warn you, and with many witnesses present, as you can see. You must take great care—with that leg in particular. That is, if you don't want to end up with a significant limp for the rest of your life."

"I understand."

"And that wound on your shoulder has yet to heal. You'll need help with the dressings."

Angel frowned. She hadn't considered that particular challenge.

"I'll help her," Wynema offered as she entered the parlor from the kitchen in back. "It won't be a bother to stop by the ranch and see how she is. That way I'll rest easy that she's not up to some fool thing or other."

Angel didn't know whether to scold or thank her friend. In the end, she did neither. "I promise I'll take care. I want to get well and return to my regular life. I won't take silly chances."

Unused to a patient who argued, Letty finally surrendered. "I'll stop by every chance I get."

Phoebe stepped up. "I'm sure Lee will benefit from a ride out to Rogers Ranch a time or two. I can look after Angel's wounds when I go."

"I suspect," Mrs. Stone said, "it'll do me good to take time away from settling my husband's matters now and then. That promises to be a difficult chore, and a visit with Angel should give me a much needed distraction."

Angel frowned at her self-appointed overseers. "Ladies, I don't need you to fuss so much. I can take care of myself."

"Just like you took right good care of yourself that day a couple of weeks ago," Jeremy said from the doorway.

Everyone turned. Someone gasped.

Angel held her head high. "There's little a person can do against a madman with a knife and evil intent. That's not what we were discussing before you so rudely interrupted."

"And I reckon you think I rudely interrupted that day when I picked you up and brought you to the doc. Let's see . . . Ah, yes, Miss Rogers. Seems to this dumb cowboy, I interrupted your death."

More gasps accompanied horrified exclamations.

Angel couldn't speak. She'd never been confronted like this. And in front of all these people . . .

She tried to think, but her head filled with images of the struggle, of pain, of Maggie's blood, of Jeremy's gentle arms as he carried her into town.

She couldn't deny the man had saved her life.

But had he also taken her ranch?

She wouldn't know until she went back. And there were other things she wanted to know. "I've wondered why you did, Mr. Johnstone. Seems to me, you'd be closer to your goal if you'd just let me die."

Another rash of comments burst forth.

"You're a right stubborn . . . lady," he said. "And I'd say even some foolish, too. If you don't take care, you'll be adding to all these fine folks' grief before long. I doubt it'll do Mrs. Stone any good, so soon after the reverend's passing." He turned to the new widow. "My sympathies, ma'am."

Mrs. Stone murmured something Angel didn't hear and that had little effect on Jeremy. When he aimed his angry blue gaze back at Angel, she felt its power clear down in the deepest part of her heart.

"It'd be a pure shame," he went on, "if you put this good lady, and the rest of the town, too, through the trouble of having to bury you as well."

❦

"Angel?" Jeremy asked the Lord as he rode home a short time later. "Bah! That girl's no more an angel than . . . than . . . well, than any of her pasture-shearing sheep."

His outburst had no effect on the mountains' peace.

"I just plain don't understand her, Father. First she accuses me of trying to kill her. Then she argues with me on account of my saving her. What goes on inside that flaming-red head of hers?"

He took off his hat and swiped the sweat from his brow. "Here I've been busting a gut to work two ranches just to make sure nothing goes wrong with hers."

He heard the clop-clop of his gelding's hooves—nothing more.

"The least she could do is give me a polite 'Thank you kindly, Mr. Johnstone.' But no. She's the contrary sort, all right. And I'll never tie myself to her, not even for that right good land of hers. Never. You hear me, Lord? Never."

At the Double J Ranch, he settled his horse down for the night, then took off his dust-and-sweat-stained shirt on his way to the pump by the kitchen door. The cool water felt good on his hot skin, and he wished it would clear away his frustration with Old Man Rogers's daughter as easily as it did the grime.

Inside, he poured himself a glass of cold water from the pitcher he kept in the icebox—something he wouldn't be able to do much longer. The price of ice had risen beyond his means.

Thirst satisfied, he headed for his room. He undressed and got ready for bed and, before he climbed in, he took up his Bible. Maybe some verse somewhere would help him understand that mountain woman. He reckoned only God could know what was in a woman's head. After all, He'd made women.

Then again, not all women were like Angel. "Why couldn't she be a mite more appreciative, Lord? Like Dahlia Sutton. Now there's a fine figure of a woman. Respectful, charming, well prepared to make a man happy. And I aim to be that very man."

With that optimistic thought in mind, Jeremy dozed off.

Angel wept when Wynema drove right up to the barn. "I'm home . . ."

"But you'd best be careful here," the photographer said yet again. "Elsewise, I'll be back to pack you up for a return to town."

Angel reached out for her friend with a sniff and a blink. "Help me up, please."

On the ground—her land, the soil Papa had worked so hard— she turned to Wynema. "You won't be packing me up unless, as Mr. Johnstone so indelicately put it, it's to bury me. This is where I belong, and until the good Lord sees fit to move me, why, then this is where I'll stay."

"I've said it plenty often already, but I'm about to say it again. You're the stubbornest woman on earth."

Angel smiled, then used the cane to help her reach the door. At the door she paused to study the place. Oddly enough, it looked just as it had when she'd last seen it. There wasn't even a speck of dust on the furniture, something she and Mama had always battled and never felt they would ever conquer.

"It's so good to be home . . ." Then she realized what felt different, wrong. "Sunny! What did he do with her? Is that his plan? To rid himself of my one companion? Does he figure I'll leave if I get too lonesome?"

Wynema propelled Angel to the overstuffed armchair by the fireplace. "If I didn't know any better, I'd think your brain rather than your leg was broken. Of course he didn't 'rid himself' of Sunny. He told us he's kept her in the barn with the other animals, in a pen by herself so she won't hurt her legs any further."

Relief filled Angel. Then a sense of shame. Why was she so ready to believe the worst of Jeremy?

"You must understand," she told the photographer. "Mr. Johnstone wants my property—he made no secret of that. And I don't really know him all that well."

Wynema gave her one of those all too seeing looks. "I suspect you're about to come to know that man much better than you might imagine. He's taken the care of your property to heart. All he ever talked about while you were unconscious was how he had to make sure you didn't suffer any more losses, that it was up to him to watch out for you."

"Humph!" Angel held her head high. "I'll make sure he understands that I don't need him to watch out for me. I can do that very well indeed."

Wynema shook her head and proceeded to rearrange things in the tidy cabin to allow for Angel's hampered condition. As Angel watched her friend, she relaxed.

That's when the fear she'd fought every second of every day since the attack struck again. Her chest tightened. A red haze hovered over her vision. Her hands trembled. She went cold despite the extreme summer heat.

What if . . . ?

No! She couldn't give in. She had to fight the fear. She couldn't let anyone see weakness. Otherwise, they'd surely overcome her—she'd fail.

"Lord Jesus," she prayed under her breath, "be with me. I need you. Every minute of every hour of every day, Father, I do need you."

Alone, she'd lose. With God, no matter what happened, she'd already won, ranch or no ranch, hard though that might be to consider. She had to keep that in mind regardless of what came her way.

10

Two days later, as Angel prepared to head to town for Pastor Stone's funeral service, a knock came at her front door—to which Sunny responded with wild enthusiasm.

"Stop it!" she told the dog. "You'll knock me to the floor if you limp in my way. Now sit."

When the dog's rump touched down, Angel clumped to the door. She found Jeremy on her porch.

His black suit and tie, white shirt, polished black boots, and new-looking black hat—a hat he pulled off his blond head the moment he saw her—gave him an unfamiliar air. But before she could ask him why he'd come, he gestured toward the buggy and pair of horses he'd tied to the hitching rail by the barn.

"I reckoned it'd be better for your leg if I took you into town for the funeral. I'm headed that way, and it's no trouble to stop and fetch you."

While Angel stared into the cowboy's clear blue eyes, Sunny crept over to greet him. Angel wanted to see if even a hint of devious intent lurked there, but no matter how hard she looked, she found nothing. Nothing but sky-colored eyes fixed on her.

She remembered how often she'd assumed the worst of Jeremy, and again fought her tendency to suspect him.

"Thank you," she said. "I did wonder how I would manage

to prepare Nelly and the wagon. I didn't even want to think how I'd climb up once I did."

Jeremy straightened from scratching Sunny's head. "Like I said, it's no trouble, and I knew you'd want to be at that service."

"I do." She took a deep breath, asked the Lord for wisdom, and then gestured Jeremy inside. "I'll only be a moment."

"Won't be a bother."

Sunny dragged herself behind him to the armchair by the fireplace.

On her way to the bedroom, Angel shook her head at her traitorous dog. She gathered her hat and gloves from atop the bureau, then paused before the mirror, still struck by the similarity to her mother when she dressed in the clothes Phoebe had provided. She'd fought quite a battle to pin up her braids the same way her friend had, but with infinite patience, and many, many pauses to rest her arm, she'd succeeded.

"Lord God," she whispered. "Mama was a quiet, gentle lady, but she knew her mind and your Word. She'd never have backed down from what she knew was right. Help me stand strong, but also help me know when I'm in the wrong."

Back in the sitting room, she retrieved her cane. "I'm ready, Mr. Johnstone—"

"I'd be right appreciative if you called me by my given name. I thought we'd agreed to that."

She lowered her gaze. "I guess I still think of you as Mr. Johnstone, and it might take me a bit of doing to change that. But I'll try."

When she looked up again, she noticed his pleasant smile. He was a nice-looking man. Not that it mattered one bit to her.

"As I was saying, Jeremy," she went on in a rush to cover her momentary fluster, "we should be on our way."

Soon enough Angel realized she wouldn't have made it into town had Jeremy not come for her. It took a lot out of her to get into the buggy even though he bore the brunt of the effort.

Once the horses took up their pace, she said, "Thank you again."

"You're welcome. It's a small thing."

"It means a great deal to me." She took a deep breath. "And I also owe you a debt of gratitude. Everything was in excellent condition when I returned. You didn't even have to do it. I'd been very rude."

From the corner of her eye, she saw his cheek muscles clench and his jaw square. "I did indeed have to do it. It was the least I could do."

His voice rang with conviction, but something else roughened it. Angel had no idea what it all meant, but she figured it wasn't her place to pry.

The trip into town continued in silence until they reached the outermost limit of Main Street. At the sight of the people on the boardwalks on both sides of the street, Angel remembered her last entry into Hartville.

"I hope you don't feel too awkward when everyone stares," she said.

He shot her a questioning look.

She sat up straight. "I've raised an eyebrow or two, since I'd rather wear trousers than skirts. Most folks have a problem with a woman who does that."

"That's for you and them to settle, not me."

She wondered what he thought of her usual garments, and whether he'd been as surprised as everyone else when she appeared at the manse in these feminine things. But she didn't ask.

Instead, she said, "These aren't the most proper colors to wear to a funeral, but they're better than my work clothes."

With a sure hand Jeremy guided the horses into Amos's livery. "You're covered all proper-like, and I reckon that's all as should matter. A funeral's to honor the life of the one who's gone on, not a time to look on what folks might wear."

"That's a fair way to look at it."

A moment later, with David, Amos's stable hand, on one side and Jeremy on the other, Angel disembarked the buggy. She ignored her leg's complaint and again refused to yield to weakness.

Jeremy's arm and the cane made it possible for her to walk to Silver Creek Church not more than a block and a half from the livery. She soon felt the pointed looks of those on their way to the funeral.

She held her head high and thought only to conquer the steps that rose from the street.

"Lean on me," Jeremy said, his voice as firm as the arm she held. "Go ahead. I won't let you down."

Angel thought she heard him whisper "Again," but since it made no sense, she let the comment pass. Instead, she put more weight on Jeremy's arm, and when they reached a pew in the middle of the church, she spotted Wynema at its farthest end.

"Thank goodness," she said as she took her seat.

"What do you mean?" the photographer asked.

"I found you straightaway. I don't know many in town."

Wynema scoured the room. "And they're all studying you."

When Angel nodded, Wynema gave a dismissive wave. "Don't pay them any mind. They'd look whether you'd been here from the start or whether you'd walked in on your hands instead of your feet, never mind if you somehow grew wings and flew."

Angel smiled. One could always count on Wynema's view of life to lighten just about any moment. And the present moment did indeed need the leavening. The junior pastor, Barry Bloom, who by virtue of Pastor Stone's death had become the only pastor, droned for what seemed like hours. He went on and on about heavenly hosts, pearly gates, angelic choirs, harps, flutes, cherubs, and hymns, yet he never once remembered the town's late pastor. Behind Angel, someone responded with resonant snores.

Jeremy, who'd taken a seat at Angel's left side, did not look amused by the tailored little man at the pulpit. Angel sympathized. She'd never met the newcomer or his wife, but now she felt sure she hadn't missed much.

Across the aisle, she caught sight of the rosy splotches on the apples of Letty's cheeks, while at her side Eric had his brow drawn into a severe frown. At the center of the choir, Phoebe looked troubled, and Angel saw her shrug. When she followed the direction of her friend's gaze, she noticed Adrian, Phoebe's husband and the mining company's owner, narrow his eyes and shake his head.

After an eternity, Pastor Bloom said, "Let us pray."

Hymnbooks fell from laps where they'd lain forgotten. The long-lulled congregation stumbled to its feet. A baby whimpered, and more than one parent shushed a fussy child.

The peculiarly silent parishioners headed for the door, shook the reverend's limp hand, and then hastened away. No one lingered to chat as they'd done with Pastor Stone. None of the women said more than a simple "Morning" to the paper-pale, white eyelet-and-lace-bedecked fashion plate at his side.

If Angel had felt uncomfortable under the scrutiny of the townsfolk, she now realized she'd not been subjected to quite so much after all. This awkward silence did not suggest a happy tenure for the new shepherd of Silver Creek Church's flock.

Angel and Wynema approached Letty, Phoebe, and Miranda Carlson, the wife of the town's lawyer, a fellow redhead and the lady doctor's closest friend.

"Well!"

Wynema's outburst drew the others' attention.

"That was dreadful," she said. "I'm so sorry for Mrs. Stone. To have to endure that bushel of babble right after she's lost her dear husband."

Phoebe smiled. "We can always trust you to get right to the point, Wynema."

"Why not?" the photographer asked. "It's what's on everyone's mind, isn't it? And besides, it's true."

Randy, as everyone called Miranda Carlson, switched her sweet baby girl from one arm to the other. "Does anyone know how he wound up here?"

"Pastor Stone wrote to the seminary where he studied," Phoebe said. "They sent us Barry Bloom."

Wynema glanced back at the man in the church doorway, alone save for his wife. "Whatever were they thinking? You'd figure they could do better than that."

Angel smothered a chuckle.

Randy averted her green eyes, and Letty bit down on her lip.

"It's true!" the photographer repeated, this time with greater emphasis. "It's just that everyone else is too polite—too scared, really—to say so. Even you."

She folded her arms over her chest and pointed her uptilted nose skyward. When no one said a word, she tapped her foot against the ground and then jerked her chin in the direction of the couple in question. "Just look at them. Try to tell me they belong here."

As the women watched, the Blooms made their way down to the churchyard. The pastor held his delicate wife's elbow. Just as she came off the last step, she faltered despite her husband's grip, flailed her arms, squealed, and tumbled to the dusty ground.

"Oh!" she cried. "Oh, oh, oh, oh, oh! Help me up from this . . . this horrid, dirty mess, Barry Bloom."

The fastidious man of the cloth extended his hand to his bride and tugged. He had no success.

Mrs. Bloom oh-oh-oh-ed some more.

He yanked again.

Jeremy approached the pair. "For goodness' sake."

The reverend stepped aside now that help had arrived. Jeremy knelt by Mrs. Bloom, slid one arm across her back to brace her, and then brought her up to a sitting position. He rose to a crouch, grasped her forearms, and heaved her upright.

"Oof!" The whoosh escaped the too-pale woman's lips, and she tottered. "Oh my . . . the vapors . . ."

Jeremy caught her midswoon. "Where do you want her, Reverend?"

Pastor Bloom looked stumped. Then he pulled himself to his unimpressive height, straightened the stiff lapels of his coat, clapped away nonexistent dust from his hands, and said in an imperious voice, "The hotel."

As Jeremy strode off with his questionable trophy, Angel caught his muttered commentary. "Who'd stick a fool spike on their heel, call it a shoe, and try to walk on the blasted thing? No wonder she fell flat on her lacy behind . . ."

Wynema cut loose with a hearty laugh. "The Blooms'll never last here."

Although Angel didn't speak, she had to agree. The women around her did as well. They watched the well-dressed cowboy as he made his way down Main Street until Dahlia joined their group.

"Don't you all plumb love our new inspiring pastor and his darling little wife?"

The brunette paid no mind to the stunned expressions around her but instead watched Jeremy press on. "I do declare. They're what this backward little town of ours needs, now, don't y'all think? They'll likely uplift everyone and become assets to my little old efforts at the academy. You know I aim to civilize this place, don't you?"

Letty frowned.

Phoebe pursed her lips.

Randy's cheeks blazed.

Wynema sputtered like a teakettle.

Angel stepped toward her brash friend, but before Wynema got a word out, Dahlia cooed.

"Ladies, ladies," she said. "Isn't that lovely, lovely Mr. Johnstone just the finest figure of a man y'all have ever seen in your born days?"

None of the women mustered a response.

"Indeedy so," Dahlia added, fanning her face with her gloved hand. "I think I've just gone and lost my little old heart to that manly man of the West."

❦

A week after Pastor Stone's funeral, Jeremy headed for Silver Creek Church after supper at the Silver Belle. The group of ranchers most grievously affected by the drought had decided to meet again.

"Doubt much of anything different'll come of tonight," he muttered under his breath at the entrance to the church's fellowship hall.

Before long, his temper again hit a boil. The ranchers had gathered to rail against Angel instead of to talk of things that might improve their circumstances. Each time he tried to object to their extraordinary complaints, one of them yelled him down.

After an hour and a half, the unpleasant new pastor arrived. "Well, brothers," he said with a superior smile. "And what have we resolved thus far?"

We? The fellow hadn't even been among them. Jeremy slouched down into his chair and crossed his outstretched legs at the ankle. This ought to prove interesting.

"Our problem's that uppity Rogers girl," Albert Pringle yelled. "She's got herself all that there water, and she ain't about to help her fellow ranchers. Not very Christian of her, I'd say."

Jeremy had never liked the weaselly man. He'd heard Pringle rationed feed to his animals even when times weren't so lean. Something about the fellow's eyes also suggested a fair amount of cruelty.

Pastor Bloom frowned. "What does a child have to do with water?"

Pringle leaped to his feet. "She ain't rightly a child no more, but she sure don't behave like any God-fearing woman should."

132

A chorus of assent sang out.

With an expansive wave, Pringle continued. "She's the most unnatural critter you ever seen, Reverend. Why, she decks herself out in a man's trousers, and she's even taken to the notion of running her late father's ranch."

"Oh my," the new pastor said, distaste on his thin face. "Sounds to me as though the young lady needs a man of discernment to guide her along."

"What she needs is a husband to tame her," a rangy, dark-haired rancher called from the far side of the room.

Another rancher stood, and on his way to the door, said, "Some fellow oughta fill her belly with a passel of babies to keep her in her right place."

"Can't let that mad mountain woman rile the decent, God-fearing ladies of Hartville," a third put in.

As the men gave their frustration free rein, Jeremy's concern grew. Angel lived by herself on the ranch, and in his heart he knew her attacker sat somewhere in this outraged crowd.

He hoped the pastor would remind them of the Lord's command to treat their neighbor as they'd like to be treated themselves.

"Gentlemen, gentlemen," Pastor Bloom called out. "Allow me to offer my services in this matter. Surely, I can do some good here. I suspect this . . . girl will have some respect for me. Women are quite disposed to listen to a man of God."

Relieved sighs echoed in the room.

Pastor Bloom ran a hand over his well-oiled hair. "I'll talk sense into her, fellows. She doesn't belong in a man's place, certainly not when we have an abundance of ranchers ordained by our Lord to . . . well, the most delicate way to put it is to say that men are ordained to be men."

More discussion broke out. Some men didn't want the pastor to take over their fight. Another group figured it was worth a try. Jeremy didn't think Bloom would get anywhere with the stubborn Angel Rogers, and he'd had enough of the nasty complaints.

He prayed for help to contain his anger and stood. "Excuse me. Does that ordaining give a man the right to kill a couple head of Miss Rogers's sheep? To break her dog's legs? To stab her near to death?"

Silence crashed down. The men who had stood to rail against Angel settled back into their chairs and clamped their mouths tight. Jeremy stayed on his feet to scour the faces of those who'd argued loudest. He hoped to find a hint, anything that might give away a killer's guilt.

"At least you all will agree," he went on, "that the one who hurt her is right here, in this very room, and likely hopes someone else will go finish what he didn't."

Outrage broke out. At first the ranchers turned to each other, their voices stormy, their expressions colored with the offense they'd taken at Jeremy's words. Then one erupted.

"Who d'you think you are, Johnstone? Judge and jury and all in one?"

The throng of yeses made the rancher smile—an unpleasant smile.

From behind Jeremy, a man leaned over and smacked his shoulder. "You've a load of nerve there, boy. How d'you figger one of us went and hit the girl?"

"Nah," argued a man from the left side of the room. "Reckon he's here to throw suspicion on us so's no one thinks he's the one what's done it."

"You're right."

"Yeah, he done it, all right."

"He even offered to buy her out—"

"Listen up!" Jeremy yelled. "I didn't do a thing to that girl but offer her a fair price for her land. I'm not so stupid as to then go and attack her, since everyone knows I want to buy her place. I told Sheriff Herman that. Now I'm telling all of you, and I'll tell anyone else who wants to know."

"Gentlemen, gentlemen," Pastor Bloom said with a grimace.

"It doesn't do to fight amongst yourselves. It seems quite obvious that the problem here is this peculiar, unnatural woman."

A few dispirited claps made the pastor smile. He nodded and continued. "I'd say, from my vantage point, that Miss Rogers has reaped the consequences of her behavior, her disobedience."

Jeremy ground his teeth. He worked to contain his anger. By contrast, the fellow behind him pounded his shoulder again.

"Ya hear that?" he bellowed in Jeremy's ear.

Pastor Bloom puffed up his meager chest and studied the men with an air of superiority. "God's rules are quite clear, and a woman's not to take over in a man's stead. Not even when the man's dead. She must follow in Ruth's footsteps, follow the man's family's lead. Where are her male relatives?"

Some shrugged. Others looked around. None could answer.

"She doesn't know of any," Jeremy said. "I asked her when I went to try to buy her ranch."

"Oh." The pastor seemed displeased that his sermon had nowhere to go. "Well, then I suppose the thing to do is for me to face her, show her the error in her ways, and then maybe the sheriff can hold an open sale for the place."

That cheered more than a few. And where it should have pleased Jeremy as well, something in the pompous little pastor's plan to get Angel off her land didn't sit well with him. He'd had enough. He couldn't stomach another insult leveled against an innocent woman.

He marched out, then headed for the livery. It was well past time to head back to his ranch, where he belonged. He rode in silence and thought of Angel—as if he could keep much else in mind since her attack, much less after that disgraceful excuse for a meeting. He knew she hadn't changed her ornery mind. She wasn't about to either. Still, he now had more proof than he needed.

Angel was in danger, real, true danger.

Her attacker hadn't chased her off the ranch, or even killed her, as Jeremy knew had been the initial intent. As long as she owned the land Rogers Creek crossed, she'd be the target of those ranchers' rage.

"Pigheaded woman," he muttered.

Yes, he needed water and pasture for his herd, but he'd come to a decision. Since it didn't look likely that she'd ever sell, and seeing as he couldn't bring himself to take part in the thievery the new pastor suggested, he saw no way to survive but to try the drive to greener pastures—if it wasn't already too late.

It would take all his cash to hire men and do the job, but he couldn't just let all those animals die. Not even if it meant they'd still be too lean by market time to make enough to carry him through the winter. He'd rather invest those dollars in Rogers Ranch, where the creek and rich pasture would let him raise herds for years to come. But that wasn't about to happen.

And yet he couldn't see his way clear to leave the area . . . to leave Angel unprotected. She really did need a man, a husband to watch out for her. He wasn't the man to wed her. At least, he sure didn't think so. But he couldn't argue against what Pastor Stone, Eric, Douglas, Amos even, for goodness' sake, all felt. He was the one who'd have to approach her.

But only to help her, to offer her what protection he could give. For a wife, he needed a real lady, one who'd take over the care of him and his home, who'd bear him a passel of youngsters to inherit his land. Dahlia came right to mind.

At the same time, the memory of Angel in her skirt and blouse stole into his thoughts. He couldn't deny how pretty she'd looked at the manse and on the day of the late pastor's funeral. Surely some decent fellow would soon notice and ask for her hand.

In the meantime, perhaps it would be wise if Jeremy at least tried to befriend her, if for no other reason than that he owed her his protection. True, if there was any way he could convince her to share that water and pasture of hers, he'd jump right to it.

But he had to make up for his ham-handed offer a while back. He'd failed to reach out a hand in friendship that day.

Then, when the more reasonable men of Hartville had come to him with what struck him as a rattleheaded notion, he'd refused to listen. Not that he'd ever think of Angel as wife material. Nothing wrong in that.

Where he'd failed was when he hadn't offered to help her. Because of that, someone had managed to hurt her. The least he could do now was to make sure no one got to her again. And seeing as how Aunt Gertie always said that the gift of a pie made it easier to make friends, he was ready to try a different approach.

He wasn't about to bake a pie—he'd likely poison the woman if he did, and he didn't rightly mean to do that—but he had to think of Angel as an unbroken filly. He would try to tame her with kind words and a gentle approach.

And he'd start tomorrow. The meeting he'd just left told him he dared not waste even a minute more.

Angel needed him, and she needed him straightaway.

11

When Angel took aim and pulled the trigger, Papa's old shotgun kicked back like an angry mule. Although her injury was to her left shoulder and she'd shot from her right, the effort to hold the heavy weapon steady and then shoot was more than she was ready to endure.

"Looks like Doc Letty does know what she's about when it comes to doctoring," she told Sunny, who'd limped along at her side. "She said the blade stabbed right into the bone and that it would take as long to heal as my broken leg."

Sunny paused, most of her weight on her healthy legs, and shook her head. Then she stretched her neck and responded with well-articulated yowls.

"Now, don't you join the rest of them and lecture me," Angel argued back. "I'm the one in charge at Rogers Ranch, and don't you forget that."

Indignant yowls followed. Then, when she saw her mistress step toward the cabin, the dog hobbled on. Although it pained Angel to watch Sunny's labored gait, the dog refused to stay put. She had stayed with her mistress every minute since Wynema had brought her back to Rogers Ranch.

The dog's love humbled Angel. It also reminded her to turn to the Lord each time she noticed that generous affection. Now, as the sun glinted pure gold off the animal's silky coat, and her tail, with its long, thick fringe, waved like a plume in the hot, still air, Angel again thanked her heavenly Father for her constant canine companion.

At the cabin, Angel opened the back door to let Sunny go ahead of her, then clumped her way inside. "You know," she said, "there's not much I can do around here yet."

Inactivity didn't suit her, and complaints to the dog didn't help one bit. An idea broke through her irritation.

"Very well, Sunny girl. I'll head to the loft. I know it's hot, but since I doubt it'll change for days and days yet, I don't see a reason to wait for that break. I might not be able to do much else, but I can pedal my loom with one foot and ply the shuttle with my good arm."

Angel sat on the bottom step of the split-log stairs and made her way up on her rump. When she mastered one step, she took up the gun and moved it to the next. Something told her she'd be wise to take to heart the many warnings she'd received.

She figured the gun might give a scoundrel pause. She wasn't about to tell anyone she couldn't shoot worth spit yet, much less that it hurt too much for her to fire at will.

At the top of the stairs, she leaned back against the wall. Her climb had worn her out. But the sight of the large loom and the cream-colored wool blanket she'd started that winter made her smile. She loved the comfort of a weaver's rhythm, and it gratified her to watch a piece grow yarn by yarn.

It took her a while to set up a new pace, one that took her injuries into account, but soon the familiar peace surrounded her once more. "Thank you, Father, for this gift, too."

Not much later, from where she'd collapsed in resigned defeat at the foot of the treacherous stairs, Sunny gave a little woof and twitched her ears. A mad battery of joyful barks followed, and then she hobbled to the kitchen door.

Angel figured Jeremy had arrived.

He'd taken over her daily chores. She had to wonder who'd taken care of his, but the Double J was a larger operation than Rogers Ranch, and he would have to have a number of hands to run such a spread. She didn't think he'd neglect his herd to protect her flock—especially since he didn't hide his dislike of sheep.

"Morning," he called from the doorway.

"Hello there."

"Everything all right?"

"Of course."

"Well, then I reckon I'll head to the barn. I'll come back in later on today to let you know how I find things."

To his credit, Jeremy always made a point to let Angel know he saw her as the owner of Rogers Ranch. He'd yet to overstep the bounds of helpful neighbor, and he hadn't tried to push his views on her. She had to respect his upright attitude.

Angel lost track of time as she plied the shuttle. She felt closest to her mother when she wove. Mama began to teach her the art back when Angel's fingers became strong enough to shoot the shuttle through the warp threads. She still remembered the long-awaited day when her legs reached the pedal.

She heard Jeremy at the back door. "May I come in?"

"Of course."

His strong, sure steps approached; then he stopped. "Where are you?"

"In the loft."

"Of all the fool things a body would do!" He clomped upstairs, and Angel braced herself for the lecture he was about to deliver. But Jeremy had an uncanny ability to surprise her. At the top of the steps, he again stopped.

She never broke her rhythm. "How did you find things today?"

"Fine, fine."

His distracted answer made her glance at him. He seemed

quite taken with her work at the loom, as though he'd never seen anyone weave before. Many folks hadn't.

"It was Mama's," she said. "She taught me when I was little."

"That's right remarkable, Angel. I reckon it must take a great deal of practice."

"I don't know that I'd call it practice. You just start to weave, and while at first what you make does look awful, in time, if you keep it up, your results get better and better. And you always look for ways to make your finished cloth better."

"What is that you're making?"

"A wool blanket. From last summer's shearing."

He leaned back against the wall and crossed his arms over his chest and his legs at the ankle. "So you cut the wool, make that yarn, and turn it into blankets yourself."

She chuckled. "See the big wheel in the corner over there?"

"Mm-hmm."

"That's where I spin the wool into yarn. I wind the yarn into these big hanks." She gestured toward the basket where she'd piled masses of cream, brown, and black yarn. "And they're what I use to weave."

"I'm impressed."

Angel looked him over but saw only the admiration he'd expressed. "Thank you. It's something I enjoy."

"I can see that." He straightened, and Angel felt the change. "But I've less enjoyable things to talk about now."

She sighed and set the shuttle on the smooth piece of woven cloth. "I suppose it has to do with the ranch."

"Indeed."

She turned to face him. But before she could speak, she heard him muffle an exclamation of . . . dismay? Anger? Both?

"If that isn't the darndest thing," he said. "Angel Rogers, you're the most unusual, contrary critter I've ever met. Even mules are right helpful compared to you. What are you doing with a shotgun on your lap while you sit and make cloth?"

She took her time to rise to her feet, but she also took care to keep the gun in her hand. "I would think you'd approve. You did warn me about those who'd come to offer for the ranch and refuse to be put off."

He shook his head in apparent disbelief. "Do you have any idea how peculiar you look? You're a woman in men's clothes, doing a lady's job, and holding a man's weapon on your lap."

Angel narrowed her eyes. "That should show you I can indeed do whatever I need to do."

"Do you even know how to use the thing?"

"I assume you mean Papa's gun."

"What else? A blind fool could see you're a pretty good hand at that loom thing."

"Well, then perhaps you ought to keep right on assuming. Rest assured I'm familiar with this gun." She hadn't really lied. She'd seen Papa with it over the years. That counted as familiarity, didn't it?

"You might be familiar with the thing, but are you ready to fire it? At someone else, that is. Don't you know, if a man comes to challenge you and you aim that at him, why, he might just pull out a revolver, shoot you dead, and count himself justified since you were armed?"

"Who's to say I wouldn't shoot first?"

Jeremy didn't answer but kept his direct blue gaze on her face. Angel's cheeks warmed, and to break the tension, she hobbled to the top step.

"Would you care to join me for a bite to eat?"

He wavered, then reached a decision. "If it won't put you out."

She waved away his concern. "It won't be a bother. I always make more than enough for me, since Wynema stops by for about one meal every day, sometimes two, now that I'm home again. I figure she won't be here for this one, since it's later than she usually comes. I have enough for two."

Angel lowered herself to a sitting position on the top step, ready to descend.

Jeremy snorted. "Here. Let me help you before you fall and break your stubborn neck as well as your leg."

He scooped her up in his arms and sailed downstairs. Angel caught her breath. This was the craziest thing.

She didn't know whether to scold him for his forward behavior or thank him for his help. In the end, she chose to ignore the entire thing. She had to catch her breath, however, when he put her back on her feet again.

Why couldn't she slow down her pulse or even take regular, deep breaths? After all, he was the one who'd exerted himself. True enough, Jeremy was a fine figure of a man, as Dahlia had said after Pastor Stone's funeral. It took a sturdy sort to pick up a woman as tall and strong as Angel and then descend Papa's steep stairs as though he'd done nothing at all.

Oh my. Angel turned toward her cane to hide her blush.

"I'll only be a moment," she said, dismayed by her breathlessness. "I mixed roast chicken with a boiled sauce and diced vegetables. It's in the icebox with the last little bit of ice Mr. North delivered. I cooked the chicken this morning, since I couldn't bear the thought of a lit stove in the heat of the day, much less to eat a hot meal."

She knew she was babbling, and her missish behavior mortified her, but those moments in Jeremy's arms had indeed flustered her. After all, she was a normal woman, and he was a very nice-looking man.

"That sounds mighty good," he said, an odd note in his voice as well. She turned to try to read his face but found him by the front window, where he now stared out toward the drive that led to the nearest road.

How odd.

But it was none of her business, right? She forced herself to put aside her peculiar awareness of her visitor. The only thing that mattered right then was that she put out a decent meal.

"I hope you don't mind plain old bread from the bakery," she said. "It's been too hot to bake any myself—that chicken was likely the last thing I'll cook inside until the weather breaks. I don't reckon you want me to stoke the oven for biscuits right now any more than I do. It's hot in here as it is."

The look he shot her made her catch her breath. He'd narrowed his eyes, and his cheeks wore a strange, ruddy tint. "I'd say it's become far, far too hot."

The intensity of those blue eyes stunned her, and she blushed again. She'd spoken only of the endless summer heat. Jeremy's comment seemed to refer to something altogether different from the weather.

What had happened? What did he mean?

Despite her discomfort and confusion, Angel couldn't tear her gaze from his. The moment stretched. Time seemed heavy, slow. Something told her she'd never forget these edgy minutes, that this was a turning point in her life.

She didn't know whether the turn would be for the better or for the worse. She just knew she'd never be quite the same again.

To her dismay, she realized the tension between them left her more alert, more alive, than she'd felt minutes before.

Jeremy Johnstone was a dangerous man indeed.

❦

What had just happened?

Jeremy wished he could wash the charged moment away with the soap and water he used on his hands in Angel's kitchen. But even though he'd turned his back to her, he was now aware of her every movement, of every breath she drew.

He'd never thought himself a sappy fellow, but when he'd taken Angel in his arms to haul her down those hazardous steps, something had shifted inside him.

Perhaps it had all started when he found her at the loom. He'd noticed, for the first time, her graceful hands, the delicate curve of her neck, how feminine she was despite the men's clothes.

Then, when he held her warm, supple body against his chest, something inside him came alive. He saw Angel as a lovely woman for the first time.

He hadn't wanted to put her down.

When she stepped away from his side, he'd also recognized her vulnerability. She was a woman alone, one who, although different from the women he'd met before, had more determination and courage than most men but still didn't realize how great a danger she faced. More than ever he needed to protect her. He'd never live with himself if he failed her again.

At the table, she asked him to offer the blessing, which he did. He also offered a private, silent prayer—one for wisdom at this moment of so much confusion.

What should he do about Angel? How could he best protect her? How would he counter Pastor Bloom's smug sermon when it came? Had the men who'd suggested he court her been right?

Could he do it for the sake of her land? Her safety?

". . . Mrs. Bloom injured?"

Angel's question caught Jeremy off guard. He had pondered matters too deep for mealtime at her home.

"If you want my opinion," he said, "then I'd say she only turned her ankle. But I reckon it was all her own fault. Those fussy boots with their buttons and high, thin heels might be right for a fancy parlor back east, but they sure make no good sense in Colorado."

"But she fainted. A turned ankle wouldn't do that, would it?"

He took a drink of cool, sweet milk. "No, the ankle didn't do that. It was her—"

Jeremy stopped short when he realized what he'd been about to mention. A lady's undergarments—as peculiar and unreasonable as he considered boned corsets—weren't a topic for proper conversation in mixed company.

"Well . . . ?"

His cheeks blazed, but he figured if she was that curious, then she deserved to share the embarrassment he felt.

"Her silly, too-tight whalebone corset got in the way of her breathing. She swooned on account of her not filling her lungs proper-like."

Angel shook her head and gave a gentle tsk-tsk. "Mama had no patience with that kind of thing. Can't say I've ever wanted to try one."

Would she ever stop surprising him? He doubted it.

"Seems silly to me, too," he said. "But then I reckon she'd never get that fluffy dress on without those bones to squeeze her all up."

"I'd never want a dress like that any more than the corset. All that lace just gathers up dust. And the white?" She rolled her eyes. "I'd much rather wear denim trousers than fight the dirt stains come laundry day."

Jeremy laughed. He couldn't help himself. Angel's simple practicality struck him as unusual, but it was also refreshing. "I don't reckon Mrs. Bloom's done much laundry in her days."

Angel thought a moment, then chuckled, too. "I suspect you're right. Wonder what will happen once they move from the hotel to the manse and she has to run the house."

"I reckon Naomi Miller will have herself another customer for her washing and pressing business."

They fell silent toward the end of the meal. When Angel set down her fork, he looked up.

"How is your herd?" she asked.

"Hungry. Thirsty. No better than the first time I stopped by."

She caught her bottom lip between her teeth, then said, "How much pasture would satisfy them?"

"If I mixed other feed . . ." He took a deep breath. "I'll tell it to you straight. I wouldn't be in this sorry plight if I owned this place instead of you."

She studied her hands, and he saw her fingers twisted tight around each other, the knuckles lily white. "If . . ."

Angel glanced up, and in his heart Jeremy knew what she was about to say. He could hardly believe it. He prayed he wouldn't ruin his chances with some dumb thing that might pop out his mouth without thought. He bit his tongue to stop himself.

"If it doesn't take away from what my flock needs," she said, "would your animals get enough to eat from my land?"

He nodded slowly. "I think so."

She closed her eyes for a moment, then met his gaze. "I've prayed a great deal about this, and I've thought long on what the Lord would do if He were me. Pastor Stone always said we needed to walk in our neighbors' shoes to know how they fared, and after Maggie was . . ."

Her bottom lip quivered, and she swallowed hard. "After I lost Maggie, I found it hard to think of your cattle dying, too. Especially seeing as how you saved my life."

She seemed to wait for his response, but Jeremy didn't dare speak, not yet, not until she offered what he thought she would, what he hoped—prayed—she would.

"I guess it'd be fine if you watered some of your herd here on Rogers Ranch. They can pasture, too. You'll bring the worst off ones first, won't you?"

Thank you, Lord. "I'm right honored by your offer. I promise to keep your flock from hurting on account of your kindness to my herd."

"I thought you might say something like that," she said. "Pastor Stone thought highly of you. That counts a lot with me."

She looked away again. Then, with a shuddery breath, she met his gaze, and Jeremy saw the gleam of tears in her eyes. "I miss Pastor Stone."

"I do, too. Everyone does."

"Do you think the Blooms will stay in Hartville?"

He tried to relax now that she'd given him such a great gift. "I don't know them well enough to judge. But unless they mean to learn our ways out here, I don't think they'll last long."

"I agree."

He thought back to last night's meeting, how he'd come inside earlier to warn her, and how even the pastor felt Angel needed protection, no matter that his plan was a foul one. "Perhaps he has a few good ideas for guiding his flock."

"Has he told you any?"

Lord? Is this your way of telling me I should tell her their plans? Although God stayed silent, Jeremy decided to plunge ahead. "Well, he agrees with me on one account."

"And that is?"

"That you need protection if you mean to stay here by yourself. There are many who are ready to do near anything to keep from going under."

Green sparked bright in her eyes. She pushed back her chair and stood. "I thought you finally understood that I'm not going anywhere and that I can take care of myself."

"I know you believe that—"

When she went to object, he raised a hand to stop her. "Please hear me out. You think you can protect yourself with your shotgun and your determination, but you nearly died a few weeks ago. If I hadn't come, you'd be with Pastor Stone and the Lord by now."

"You can't be sure of that."

He stood and took advantage of his greater height. He knew he'd made his point when she took a step back. "You couldn't prevent the attack."

"But I fought him off and didn't let him kill me."

"No one said you're not a feisty one, but there's only one of you on this real good tract of land. You can't watch over all of it all of the time."

"Tell me where I've failed to maintain my ranch."

"You haven't. You have a right fine garden full of what looks to me like a grand harvest coming up. Your buildings are solid—thanks to your pa's smarts, I reckon. And you keep everything in fine shape. That's why you're in danger. Anyone can see what a good bet Rogers Ranch is."

"I think it's time for you to head on home."

"At least let me protect you as much as I can. You've offered to help me, and I can pay you back that way. Or do you want cash for the privilege of water and food for my stock?"

"Keep your money. I don't need it—don't want it. I have all I need right here." She fell silent, studied him for long moments. "I was afraid it'd be a mistake to help you. Now you figure you can come here, tell me what's what, and take over when you please. That wasn't what I meant at all."

"I never thought it was—"

"You sure sound that way." Her chin rose. "I can't take back my offer. It wouldn't be right, and I can't punish your animals because of you. So my offer stands."

"So does mine."

"Don't go doing anything behind my back."

Jeremy ran his hand through his hair. Every time he tried to talk sense to her, no matter how calm he kept himself, no matter how gentle his voice, she still sent him away. That only left her more open to another attack, even to the one he figured would come from a sermon full of pious words.

At the counter by the kitchen door, he picked up his hat. "I can see I'm done here for today. Just be ready. More offers and arguments are coming your way. And don't do anything silly."

"I'm not a silly woman. I weigh matters carefully and even measure them against God's Word."

"Then perhaps you ought to remember that the Father tells us to listen to wise counsel." He opened the door and waited to see what she would say.

She picked up the Bible she kept on the kitchen table and hugged it close. "Who's to say, Jeremy Johnstone, that your counsel's any wiser than mine?"

He crammed the hat on his head and stepped off the back stoop. "Pigheaded is what you are," he called.

This time he didn't wait for her reply.

12

On his way back to the Double J, Jeremy knew he'd pushed too hard. He should have taken Angel's offer of help, thanked her, and headed on home. To remind her of the attack had not been wise.

Angel was a strong woman, stronger than most. And she was no weaker even after she'd been hurt. She knew herself well, and she wanted what was hers.

He'd be happy to keep what was his, too. All he wanted was enough water and grass for his cattle, and she'd offered that.

Even though he figured other women worked just as hard as Angel did, he'd never seen another get the same results she did. She'd run the ranch through the whole winter, and on her own. Why, she'd done what the average hardworking rancher did. Her efforts showed in every corner of Rogers Ranch. Her animals— those blasted sheep of hers, her cows, her bull, her chickens, and good old Sunny—were all healthy and strong. She kept her buildings clean and tidy, and even her yard was neat as a pin, in spite of the chickens that wandered all over the property.

He'd found her tools in excellent condition, no sign of rust or carelessness there. And the cabin always pleased him. With its plain, sturdy furniture, it was the kind of place where a man could find peace after a long day's work.

Angel deserved better than she was likely to get from the angry ranchers back in town. And that Pastor Bloom fellow . . . Jeremy didn't know quite what to make of him.

Would the new pastor come and tell Angel she didn't belong on her property on account of her being a woman?

That was pure stupid.

Jeremy's conscience was struck with a load of guilt. He'd thought pretty near the same when he first came to offer to buy the ranch. He'd thought a girl as young as Angel didn't belong at Rogers Ranch.

He no longer thought that way. He just thought a woman—any woman, and Angel in particular—didn't belong there without protection from the dangers that came with the promise of prosperity in these parts. She did need a man at her side now that her pa wasn't there to watch out for her.

And seeing as how he was her nearest neighbor, and how she'd gone so far as to offer to help him with his herd, the very least Jeremy could do was to make right sure she didn't suffer again. She'd already seen enough misery because of the last time he dragged his heels.

Whether she wanted it or not, Angel would have all the protection he could provide without riling her up again. He could leave his ranch for the most part in Esteban's good hands, and Jeremy could keep on with the chores Angel still couldn't do on account of her leg.

She couldn't stop him from watching over her while he helped out at Rogers Ranch.

It was the least he could do and face the Lord each new day.

၆

A short while after daybreak, Jeremy headed over to Rogers Ranch. He got there in time to see Angel's chickens busy pecking at the corn she'd scattered all around her barnyard.

"Morning." He didn't know if she'd answer, seeing as how she'd been angrier than a rattler when he left the day before.

Her polite nod came with a plain "Good morning."

Seemed she wasn't over her anger and didn't care to talk. That was fine with him. He had work to do, and he meant to finish it before Esteban and a ranch hand arrived with a part of his herd.

In the barn, he milked her cows, mucked out her horse's stall, made sure the animals had water and as much feed as they needed. Then he went outside. Did she need firewood for the stove? If she did, she'd have a bad time of it with the ax, what with that shoulder and that leg of hers not quite healed yet.

True, she'd said she had no interest in firing up the iron monster as long as the heat raged on, but she did have to eat, and most food needed cooking.

Resigned to another spat, he headed for the cabin, less than half ready to approach her. On his way there, he heard a horse approach. He did expect his men and some stock, but not in the tidy black buggy that made its way up the lane.

Marcus Sutton disembarked from the vehicle. The banker looked no less taken aback to see Jeremy than Jeremy did to see Dahlia's father on Rogers land.

"Can't say I expected to find you here, Jeremy."

"I've been helping Miss Rogers with the chores she can't do since she was hurt."

"Ah, yes. I did hear about that. Nasty business."

"Begging your pardon, sir, but nasty can't describe what happened here."

Sutton frowned. "Have you bought her out, then?"

Jeremy took off his hat and wiped the sweat off his forehead. It was still early morning, but the day burned as hot as any so far this year. "No. I decided it's wasted time to try to argue with her any more."

"Wrong as she may be, she knows her mind—"

"Yes, I do know my mind."

The men turned toward Angel, who stood on the front step.

The banker removed his bowler. "Good morning."

Angel tilted her head and narrowed her eyes. "I guess I'll decide how good it is once you tell me why you've come."

Sutton blinked. "Well! I'd hoped for a friendlier welcome, Miss Rogers, but I can see you're hardly so inclined. Could we perhaps go inside so I can explain why I've come to be so ill received?"

"It's awful hot in here, but if that's what you want, you're welcome to come with me."

Jeremy followed up the steps, not ready to miss a second of the meeting—that is, if Angel didn't chase him away before anyone chose a seat inside.

"Would you care for a glass of water?" she asked. "I've no ice, since I haven't been able to ride up the mountain to fetch any after I was hurt, and Mr. North hasn't been by in days. But the water does come cold from the pump."

"That'll do."

"Jeremy?"

He hung his hat from a peg on the kitchen wall. "I'd be right appreciative about now."

Angel nodded, then limped outside, a pitcher in hand. Jeremy hurried to help her, since the full vessel would pose a challenge. She still needed the cane to get around.

He took the pitcher when it was full.

"Thank you," she said, her eyes staring through him as though he wasn't there.

He bit off a smart remark. "Welcome."

Back inside, she brought down enameled cups from the shelf above her storage cupboard and plunked them on the table. She poured the water, pulled out a chair, and sat.

After long, silent moments, she said, "Well? To what do I owe your unexpected visit?"

Sutton choked on his drink. Evidently, he wasn't used to a woman as direct as Angel. Jeremy figured few men were.

"Miss Rogers . . . I . . . ah . . ." The banker floundered for words but then shook himself and tugged on the lapels of his seersucker coat. "I come to represent an investment interest."

She narrowed her eyes.

"I've been . . . er . . . entrusted with a substantial sum of money and come to make you an offer—quite a good one, I might add."

"An offer . . . another offer."

Jeremy smothered a chuckle at the green sparks in Angel's eyes.

"Indeed," the banker said, warming to his subject. "Surely, after you were so brutally attacked, you've come to realize you can't possibly continue to live out here all alone."

"Have I, now?"

"Why, it's the only logical conclusion a woman, even a man, would come to, wouldn't you say, Mr. Johnstone?"

"It's none of my business, Mr. Sutton."

Sutton glowered. "I suppose that is quite true, Mr. Johnstone." He turned back to Angel and charged ahead even without the support he'd wanted. "Now, this interest, Miss Rogers—a fine enterprise indeed—has pooled its money and wants to offer you an outstanding opportunity to realize the true value of your land. That way you'll be able to advance yourself to the comfortable life any lady aspires to."

This time Jeremy nearly choked on his water. The laughter was hard to control.

Angel rose to a dignified stance despite her injuries. "I'm not interested, sir, and you can say so to your investors . . . your interest or enterprise, whatever you mean by that."

Sutton surged to his feet. "Now, wait a minute there, missy. You haven't even heard my offer."

Jeremy laughed. "That's what I said when she turned my offer down a while back. Haven't managed to convince her since then either."

The banker came at Jeremy, wagged a finger under his nose,

and glared in obvious offense. "This is no laughing matter, Jeremy Johnstone. A woman has no business running a ranch, especially when there's money to be made from—"

The banker cut off his argument right about when Jeremy thought it promised to get good. What was Sutton up to?

"What I mean to say," the banker went on, "is that a good number of decent family men are going through awful times trying to do right by their loved ones."

Jeremy's humor vanished. "Same hard times as I face."

A canny light brightened Sutton's gaze, and Jeremy felt awkward under the nosy stare. "Perhaps you'd care to join the enterprise," the banker said. "I'm sure there's room for one more party at this table."

Angel turned frightened eyes on Jeremy.

Her fear made his gut churn. "Sorry. Can't do it. But I'll take my hat off to you if you can get her to take your money and leave the place."

Angel crossed to the front door. "I won't leave, Mr. Sutton, but I figure it's about time for you to do so."

The banker's eyes bulged so far out of their sockets that Jeremy feared the man might just have himself an apoplexy on the spot.

"You can't just dismiss me," Sutton argued. "Don't you know who I am?"

"Yes," she said. "You're another man who can't abide the sight of a woman on her own ranch. I believe I heard say you own the bank in Hartville, so yes, I do know who you are."

Her lack of awe at his importance didn't sit well with Sutton. "You're just an ill-mannered, uneducated child. You'd do well to take my offer and buy yourself some polish. Why, my darling daughter, Dahlia, has just the school for you."

Still robed in quiet dignity, Angel opened the door. "My late mother was my teacher, and since her passing I've had the best teacher of all. The Lord's guided me through Scripture and life, and I prefer to take my lessons from Him."

"Oh, don't start with that churchy nonsense, girl," the banker said in disgust. "Just take your money, for goodness' sake. Help yourself out of this predicament. I doubt anyone else can."

"The Lord is my help in time of trouble," she said. "It's time for you to leave."

Sutton grabbed his hat. "I'll leave now. But I've not finished my negotiations. I can see why you've disturbed everyone hereabouts. You're quite . . . you're a . . . oh, I can't describe the kind of oddity a woman like you is."

Angel just stared at him, and the banker hurried outside. Jeremy didn't care for the way the man had spoken to Angel, so he followed Sutton to the hitching rail by the barn.

"I don't think insults will work for you," he said.

Sutton untied the reins and shook his head. "I didn't even begin to insult her. And is it an insult when a man tells the truth?"

Jeremy hooked his thumbs in his belt loops, legs wide apart, and stared right back at the peeved banker.

He outlasted the older man.

"I'll tell you, son," Sutton said, "that's the most unnatural thing I've ever seen—and that's saying plenty, what with that doctoring woman and that Wynema Howard taking everyone's likeness in our town. But this one . . . This one doesn't even look like a woman, doesn't talk like a woman, doesn't listen to reason like a woman does . . . or should. She's different, not like a woman should be at all. Not like the rest of us regular folks."

"On account of she won't do your bidding?"

"Don't try to tell me you didn't try to get her to sell, because you said you did."

"But I didn't mock her or call her insulting things."

A nasty look crept onto Sutton's face. "If my recollection's right, you called her a stubborn, pitchfork-toting, sheep-loving, redheaded mountain madwoman—or some such thing like that. Do you deny it?"

Jeremy remembered the night he'd said that, and shame burned up his face. "You're right. I did call her those things. I've come to regret it, and I reckon I owe her an apology."

"So you no longer think like that?"

Jeremy took his time to consider the question. "I'll never think she's anything if not stubborn. She loves her sheep, has lots of red hair, owns a mean-looking pitchfork, and lives in the foothills of these great mountains."

His words made Sutton sputter, but Jeremy no longer feared the fit the man would likely pitch any minute now. "I don't think she's mad," he added. "Not really. So I guess that's all's I have to ask forgiveness for. For calling her a madwoman. That leaves you a passel more to beg her pardon for."

The banker put on a lofty look. "I regret nothing I said. I spoke the truth. A woman's meant to be a gentle soul, obedient, respectful, and submissive to a man's greater wisdom. God's Book says so. That redheaded mule is more man than woman—unnatural, I say. Not fit for decent folks to keep around."

Jeremy remembered how Angel had felt in his arms. Nothing could be farther from the truth than the banker's opinion—somewhat hypocritical opinion, since Sutton invoked God when it suited his purpose but chastised Angel when the invocation didn't suit him so well.

"She may look different from those ladies you know," he said. "But I'd wager that underneath she's no different from . . . oh, your daughter, I reckon. Besides, it doesn't rightly matter what you think of Miss Rogers. This is her land, and if she doesn't mean to sell, why, then she doesn't mean to sell."

"I don't doubt you've good reason to defend her. You probably figure that after this she'll be so grateful, she'll do your bidding. Then again, maybe you've changed your mind and are ready to marry her, like I told you before. Have you figured that if you give her a bellyful of kid and keep her busy with those things she ought to do, you can sell water access to the others around these parts?"

A cloud of dust rose up from Double J way. Esteban and the cattle were about to arrive. He had to send Sutton packing or else the man would come up with more wrongheaded ideas as to what was happening at Rogers Ranch.

"Thought never crossed my mind, Mr. Sutton. Now, I think I recollect Miss Rogers asking you to leave her spread."

"Oh, I'm leaving all right. But don't think you and that man-woman have seen the last of me. I haven't come this far in life by giving up. This is business, and nobody gets the better of Marcus Sutton. No sirree."

The banker's buggy rolled off toward Hartville, and Jeremy took a deep breath. Had he struck Angel as puffed-up as Sutton struck him? He hoped not.

More to the point, he'd defended Angel's right to her land. Had he really meant it?

For a moment he examined his feelings.

Yes, he'd meant it. Every last word he'd said had come from a well of conviction. He no longer felt Angel should leave. He only thought she needed help, protection and help.

The question was, had he defended her for the sake of what was right? Or had he done so for his own benefit? Did he have hidden hopes as to what it might mean for him if Angel stayed on the land now that she'd given him access to the water?

He couldn't be sure. And he didn't like what the uncertainty said about him.

"Jeremy?" Angel called from the doorway.

He turned and looked her over with great care. What motive lay behind his defense?

He didn't know, but he'd better figure it out soon. Otherwise, he might not be able to face the Lord. Not with a clear conscience, at any rate.

Angel glared at Wynema. "I already said I'm not going." She crossed her arms and sank deeper into the armchair.

Wynema glared back. "Why not?"

"Because I have no desire to be the subject of sideways looks and whispered gossip all evening long."

"What difference does it make if the biddies gossip?"

"None, but it's unpleasant regardless."

"Then I'll just have to round up reinforcements. Doc Letty, Phoebe, Randy, Mrs. Stone, even Daisy and Mim—do you know them?"

Angel shook her head.

"Well, let me tell you," Wynema said, triumph on her face, "if anyone has reason to avoid a gathering, it's those two. They're Doc's protégées. The town's so-called good and upright sorts abandoned them in their time of need, and then others with no conscience took advantage of them."

Wynema's half story piqued Angel's interest, but she knew better than to encourage her friend. "I'm sure Doc Letty did something wonderful for them, but that has nothing to do with me."

"Of course it does. Most folks mistreated them and spoke even worse about them and the doc, but they didn't let that stop them. See how well Doc Letty's doing?"

When Angel didn't answer, Wynema rolled on. "And Daisy's now promised to marry Mr. Wagner's other reporter—the other one besides her, you understand. They'll be at tonight's social, and you can meet them. He's a fine young man."

Angel's prolonged silence seemed to give Wynema even more fuel. "Besides, the social's at the church fellowship hall." An impish light brightened her brown eyes. "Not too much can go wrong there, since Mrs. Stone will be there. She won't let it."

"Mrs. Stone is no longer the pastor's wife, Wynema. She has no authority these days. Mrs. Bloom holds that position now."

"That pile of fluff and lace? Hah! I doubt anyone will pay her any mind—if she lasts any time at all, what with that stupid corset to squeeze the life out of her and the like."

"I do not intend to make a fool of myself for others' delight."

Wynema met Angel's gaze. "I'm an outcast, too. I'm going because I won't stop doing things or meeting folks because someone might think or say something disagreeable."

Wynema twisted her fingers, and Angel got a rare glimpse into a very private side of her friend. The vulnerability she found surprised her.

But the photographer didn't give her a chance to comment. She elaborated her argument with ever more nervous zest. "They'd best get used to women like me. And you. Goodness knows, there must be more than one photographer who also happens to be a woman."

"That has nothing to do with me."

"Sure it does. Surely, there's more than one rancher who happens to be a woman, too. I'd wager any number of widows take over their husbands' work. It's only reasonable for folks to accept it."

Angel tried to find a way to counter her friend's argument, but Wynema fixed her with another of her penetrating stares. She wavered under its strength.

Wynema pounced on her hesitation. "You can't spend the rest of your life afraid that someone'll come and take your ranch while you're not looking."

Angel drew in a sharp breath. She should have turned away, walked off, done something—anything—to keep Wynema from seeing so much. But it was too late now. She couldn't deny her basic fear.

But she could try to keep her friend from seeing her other, newer and greater one. She didn't want to die, not yet, and not for some water and pasture land. "Fine," she said. "I'll go with you. But I'll find a quiet corner to sit and watch the event. Perhaps I'll take a book . . . or some needlework."

Wynema's smile could have lit the town of Hartville for a month. "Splendid! Take whatever you want. What matters is not to cower out here and deny yourself life's simple pleasures. Let's get you ready."

Angel asked the Lord to bless her with strength and courage for the upcoming ordeal. She limped to her room, and at the armoire she paused. Although she did like the skirt and blouse Phoebe had given her, they weren't her clothes. Not really. And she didn't feel quite right in them. Tonight would be difficult enough without fretting over her garments.

She squared her shoulders, patted the satiny oak piece, and then turned away. She was who she was. Different clothes would never change her. And if she was about to go to a church social, why, then she would do so on her own terms.

"If you'll take my sewing basket," Angel called out to Wynema, "I'll get my hat and cane, and we can be on our way."

Lord, have mercy on us, please.

❦

Jeremy was late. There'd been no way around it. Esteban had found another dead calf, the second in a week. Neither one had died from the heat, hunger, or lack of water. Both had as much meat on their bones as any of his herd did, and they'd been part of the group that had just come back from Rogers Ranch.

Besides, there was no denying someone had poisoned them. Their corpses told the story right clear.

He and Esteban searched the area where they'd found the two animals but saw nothing to show who'd lured them from the others. They found nothing unusual, for that matter.

Now he was late for the church social. He hoped Dahlia hadn't hooked up with some other fellow in the meantime. Just because Angel had agreed to let his cattle share her water didn't mean he'd given up his plan.

He meant to marry that wonderful young lady. Then he meant to fill his ranch house with heirs to their wealth.

He left his horse at Amos's livery and practically ran the two blocks to the church. At the door to the fellowship hall, he stopped to catch his breath, took off his hat, and then strode inside.

The town band sat in the far corner of the huge room and offered a lively piece by which folks could visit with each other. Jeremy looked around for a beautiful figure and a mass of black curls, listened for the tinkly laugh of the woman he meant to marry.

"Hello, there, Johnstone."

Jeremy returned Eric's greeting.

The newspaperman said, "I hear you had the good fortune to persuade Miss Rogers to let your animals share her water."

"I didn't think anyone knew."

"I doubt anyone does—other than Miss Rogers's closest friends, that is."

"Ah . . . your wife."

"Indeed. Letty has been to the ranch to check on her patient. They were friendly before the attack, but since then they've become very close."

"Is there any way you could see your way clear to not . . . could you perhaps not—" Jeremy stopped short. Why did everything that had to do with Angel come coated with complication? He tried again. "I'd be much obliged if you—"

"Rest assured," Eric said, "there'll be no gossip coming from the ones who know. We've all been its victim at one time or other."

"It's hardly the gossip that concerns me," Jeremy said, relieved nonetheless.

Wise brown eyes studied him. "Just what does concern you?"

"Two things. First, someone's out there who doesn't care about things that really matter. He's too ready to kill to get what he wants."

Eric nodded but didn't speak.

"Then there's the matter of my two calves."

"What do you mean?"

Jeremy smacked his thigh with his hat, clamped his lips, and shook his head. "Two days ago my foreman found a dead calf right about a mile away from where it should've been. And today I found another one near to where that one was."

"Surely, you've had other animals die in this drought. That's hardly a matter for concern—on Angel Rogers's account, that is. I'm sure the loss of even one animal is troublesome to you."

"Begging you pardon, sir—"

"Call me Eric. Please."

Jeremy nodded. "There is reason to worry, Eric. I've rotated my herd so as not to overgraze Angel's pasture. These two came from the group that just spent a couple of days out there. And they were poisoned."

"Poisoned? Are you sure?"

"Oh, I reckon there's always a chance that a fellow gets something wrong, but I'd trust Esteban, my foreman, with anything he has to say about cattle. Man knows just about all's there is to know about them. Besides, I had a couple of head die on account of the drought. The bodies sure didn't look anything like these two."

"And they're part of the group that came back from Angel's property?"

"Yes—"

"What about the group that came back from my ranch?"

The two men turned toward the new arrival. Angel glared at them, one hand on her cane, the other at her hip, her expression more mulelike than ever.

Jeremy glanced at Eric, who barely shook his head. He agreed.

It wouldn't do to tell Angel what had happened. Not until he learned more about the incident.

"Ah . . . nothing much. Just that I'm real thankful that you let them go and share in the bounty of your property. I just told Mr. Wagner here that I send the cattle in groups so's not to overgraze the land."

Angel's eyes narrowed, suspicion in their depths. She looked from Jeremy to Eric. When she studied him again, Jeremy felt the guilt spread from his head to his toes.

He didn't make a habit of lying, and it didn't sit any better with him knowing that she couldn't yet deal with the whole truth and that all he'd done was not say everything he knew.

Jeremy made himself hold her gaze, even though it was one of the hardest things he'd ever done. Then, just when he felt he couldn't do it one second longer, she turned and headed into the crowd, clumping the cane ahead of her and dragging the splinted leg behind.

Moments later a shrill cry rose over the music.

Something told him to hurry.

He found a much-annoyed Dahlia holding Angel by the shoulders and keeping her at arm's length.

"Why don't you watch where you're going with that plumb ugly stick?" Dahlia said. "And whyever would you come here tonight in your condition? It just isn't ladylike to expose yourself to the public at such a time. It simply isn't done. And in those dreadful clothes."

Jeremy stepped toward them but paused when Angel spoke.

"I have a broken leg," she said in a quiet voice. "I don't think that will keep me from enjoying the evening."

"You don't ever, *ever* talk of—" Dahlia dropped her shrill voice to a loud whisper. "—body parts in public." She tossed her mass of curls. "I do declare." She waved a shiny fan at Angel. "No lady should let anyone see her like . . . like that."

"How?" Angel asked, again in that soft, gentle voice. "With a leg I broke while fighting the man who killed two of my sheep? Or do you mean the trousers I fixed so they would cover my broken leg?"

The brunette gasped. She blinked again and again. Her cheeks reddened, and she waved her dainty white fan before her face. "Why, I never . . ." She glanced around and took note of their audience. She went on as she'd started. "I've never met a single solitary body with such frightful, awful manners. Where is your mama? Or your papa? Surely they must do something about . . . about your disgraceful . . ."

Dahlia's voice trailed off as Angel stepped back. Angel drew up to her full height, firmed the straight line of her shoulders, and held her head high. "My mother and father are with the Lord these days, but when they were here, they taught me a great deal. I'd rather be struck dumb than offend another, much less do so in a public place."

Wrapped in the simple dignity Jeremy had noticed before, Angel limped to a table in a corner of the room. The crowd parted before her, much like he imagined the Red Sea had parted before Moses.

He felt a wave of pride rise in him. Pride in Angel.

To his dismay, he also felt shame—for Dahlia.

13

The awkward silence continued even after Angel found a chair in the far corner of the fellowship hall. She made herself take long, deep breaths and prayed for the Lord's sustenance. She'd told Wynema something like this would happen. She never should have let her friend persuade her to come.

Whispers soon took over, and a chorus of coughs and ahems followed. Moments later, the Hartville Memorial Band launched into a cheerful piece, their music colored with forced jollity.

Wynema dropped to her knees at Angel's side. "I'm sorry. I should have listened to you."

"It's not your fault," Angel said. "I knew better than to come. I chose to believe that things could change. I'm not ashamed of who I am, so I shouldn't let these episodes fluster me."

The photographer shook her head, a gesture that sent a hank of stick-straight brown hair down onto her forehead. "I persuaded you to come, and I'm responsible for that. You did nothing to deserve Dahlia's unpleasant words, but still, if I hadn't insisted you come, you wouldn't have had to endure them."

"I hold Dahlia responsible for her words. You only wanted to share an enjoyable event with me. Please don't let what happened here spoil your time on my account."

"Bah!" Wynema rose and began to pace. "Some folks in this town do all the spoiling—mighty few, true, but they still do it."

Anxious to change the topic, Angel asked, "Are you here to work?"

The photographer stopped. "I'm always a professional. Mr. Wagner hired me to record the evening for the *Hartville Day*."

Relieved by the results of her conversational diversion, Angel added, "I didn't see your contraptions when you drove me in your buggy."

"I'd already brought them here."

"Ah . . . well prepared."

"As I said, I'm a professional. And I'd best go about my duties before I fall down in that regard. Would you like some punch? I can have one of the little Wagners fetch you a cup."

"Not right now, but thank you."

Her response earned a penetrating look from Wynema. "Fine. But don't plan to sit here and fade away. No one has the right to make another feel that bad."

Angel fought to control the rush of heat to her face, but she knew that her fair, redhead's complexion concealed nothing. She had indeed hoped to become inconspicuous for the rest of the social.

Although flashes from Wynema's camera showed how busy her assignment kept her, a steady stream of young Wagners trotted to Angel with food, drink, and charming chatter. Eventually, their mama also showed up in search of the chance to rest her feet.

Angel gave Letty a sideways look. "You're the tiniest lady in town, Letty, so I doubt there's much weight on those feet. Did you walk especially far today?"

The doctor plopped into the chair she'd dragged to Angel's right. "You'd be surprised how these feet feel at the end of a long day. Lately I've been so busy that by early afternoon, it's all I can do to keep going. I'm just exhausted."

"Are you unwell?"

Letty gave a weak wave. "No. I'd have diagnosed an illness. I suspect I've taken on a mite more than is wise, what with preparations for the auction in Rockton when they hold the livestock sales. The missionary society plans to sell a quilt there. I've never run a medical practice, mothered a brood of five, and run a church committee at the same time."

"That does seem demanding. You're the most energetic woman I know, but I suppose everyone runs down sooner or later."

"That's how I've felt these last few weeks."

"Then it's good you've come to rest awhile."

"In good company, of course."

"I don't know how good a company I make. Many will likely shun you if you stay with me too long."

Letty's eyes narrowed. "I'm no stranger to controversy, Angel. I've been criticized, ostracized, and vilified by just about everyone in town. But by our Lord's abundant mercy, I found peace in doing His will, not by seeking folk's approval."

"I'm trying to do just that."

"It's not easy, is it?"

Angel shrugged.

Letty reached out to take Angel's hand. "Please don't pay the biddies or brats like Dahlia Sutton any mind. They've nothing better to do with their tongues than to savage others."

Angel looked up at the approach of fine, rustly fabric and saw a grim-faced Phoebe. "Who's been wagging their tongue now?" she asked.

Letty tsk-tsked. "Dahlia doesn't have enough to keep busy."

Phoebe knelt into the cloud of her sky-blue silk skirt. "I don't care to speak ill of others, but I've had to accept that idle minds and hands lead to busy, harmful tongues. That must grieve the Father a great deal."

Angel looked at the needlework in her lap. "I hate to put myself in situations that encourage that kind of talk."

Phoebe took hold of Angel's cold hands. "Nay, you didn't do that."

The lovely blonde's use of the Shaker word made Angel smile. She went to object, but Phoebe didn't let her. "You did nothing wrong. You're a member of this congregation and have every reason to be here. Dahlia's wrong. God calls His people to speak love, not death."

Angel shuddered. "There are many ways of killing, aren't there?"

"And so far," Wynema said, her return up to now unnoticed, "Angel's been the victim of two. If I were some in this town, I'd be awful worried. God's wrath is nothing to trifle with."

"Goodness, Wynema," Letty said. "I don't know if I'd put it in those terms."

The eccentric photographer clapped her fists onto her slender hips. "And how would you put what happened to scads of disobedient, sinful Israelites in the Old Testament?"

Angel chuckled for the first time since she'd arrived at the hall. "I reckon that's as good a way to see things as any."

Wynema stuck out her delicate chin. "Not *as good*, I assure you. It's the only way."

Phoebe stood and smoothed her skirt at the waist. "Yea, dear, you do indeed have a point." She pulled up a chair to Angel's left. "These days I prefer to sit more than ever. Although you warned me, Letty, I never realized how great a toll a growing child in the womb could take on a woman."

From there on, the women chatted, and now and again spouses and other friends also joined in. The time flew by. Before Angel knew it, folks began to exchange farewells.

"Are you ready?" Wynema asked.

"Indeed," Angel said, then caught her bottom lip between her teeth. "I do so appreciate your offer to drive me home, but I hate to put you to so much trouble on my behalf."

Wynema slung the strap to her camera over her head and

across her chest. "Don't mention it. I made you come tonight, and it's up to me to take you back." She hoisted her unwieldy tripod, paused and, tripod in hand, gestured toward the door. "I'll stow these in the buggy so I can help you out."

"Oh, please, don't. I can walk well enough with my cane."

Wynema scowled but marched off without an argument.

A moment later, the clasp of a large, warm hand on her shoulder took Angel by surprise.

"Jeremy!" she said. "I didn't realize you were still here."

"I didn't mean to startle you." His blue eyes revealed an odd emotion, turmoil perhaps. "I came to offer you a ride home."

"I see." She didn't, but Angel didn't know what else to say.

The blond cowboy's cheeks grew red. "I'm headed that way, and I reckon it'd be no trouble to take you home."

"I'm much obliged, and your kind offer would keep me from imposing on my friend."

"Your friend?"

Angel gathered her needlework bag. "Wynema, she brought me tonight and wants to drive back. But you have a point. It makes sense for you to take me—at least more sense than for her to."

Relief played over his handsome features—more than her acceptance warranted, or so it seemed to Angel. But she made no comment.

"See? We can agree." His smile didn't reach his eyes. He held out an arm. "Let me help you."

Angel held her head high. "I appreciate your offer, but I'd much rather leave on my own steam."

His lips thinned, but he said nothing.

Angel took note of his respectful farewells to Mrs. Stone, Letty, and the Gables. She smiled when he ruffled Steven Patterson Wagner's tousled hair. And she voiced her gratitude as he held the door for her to make her way outside.

Jeremy was a gentleman . . . a gentleman cowboy.

Once they reached Wynema's buggy, they faced the immutable force that was Hartville's lady photographer.

"I will drive Angel to the ranch," Wynema said, a mulish cast to her face. "I brought her, and I can just as well get her home again."

Equal determination blazed in Jeremy's eyes. "It's right simple for me to stop by her spread, while you'd still have to drive back to town, ma'am. It's not safe for a lady out there at night."

Indignation overtook Wynema's obstinacy. "I can take care of myself—and Angel, too." She dove into the buggy and popped back out, a pearl-handled revolver in her hand. "I mean business, sir, and I don't mean to give in to any fool who doubts me."

"Wynema!" Angel cried. "Put that thing down. It's dangerous to wave a gun around."

"I'm not waving, Angel. I'm making a point."

Jeremy nodded. "And you've made it right well. Still and all, ma'am—"

"Oh, don't call me that," Wynema muttered. "I'm not hardly old enough to be a ma'am."

A smile quirked up a corner of Jeremy's mouth. "My aunt Gertie would've tore a strip off me if I didn't use the manners she taught me, Miss Howard. Even though she's been with the Lord for years now, I don't forget my lessons."

Against her better judgment, Angel found herself charmed. "Don't argue, Wynema. I can make up my own mind, you know." She gave her friend a gentle smile. "You're the nicest, most generous soul I know, but Jeremy is right. You shouldn't have to ride out to my ranch and then back to town when you don't have to. I've accepted his offer."

Wynema's jaw jutted again. "Jeremy, is it?"

Angel blushed but nodded.

Her friend persisted. "Are you sure? It's not that long since you called him presumptuous and arrogant, what with that offer for your land and his not thinking you could do a thing for yourself."

Angel blushed again at Jeremy's arched brow and amused expression. "Ah . . . well," she said, "there is such a thing as a practical decision. And I've made one right now. Besides, the ride offers me a chance to change his opinion about me and my ranch."

Jeremy turned serious. "I already have."

"Oh?"

"Indeed. I was wrong to say all's I said. You belong at Rogers Ranch. Not just because your pa left it to you, but I reckon with all the work you've put into it, you've earned the place all right."

Angel didn't know what to say.

Wynema didn't have that problem. "Don't take his word for it. He's a man, and besides, I'd wager he's up to something. None of it too good either."

"No, Miss Howard," Jeremy said without malice. "I'm not up to anything. I just had a change of heart."

"More like a change of tactic," the photographer muttered. "I figure there'll be a passel of others with changed hearts who'll come at her before long."

He shrugged. "They already have, as you likely know if you're as good a friend as Angel says. Difference is, I'm a man of faith, and when I give my word, why, I reckon it means something before God."

Wynema's eyes widened.

Respect filled Angel. Jeremy's words rang with conviction.

He went on in the sudden silence. "Besides, I've a debt to pay, and I mean to do so regardless."

"A debt?" Angel asked.

"I reckon I owe the Lord for those stripes He took on my behalf." He shrugged. "And there's others who've suffered on account of my mistakes. A man's wrong to shirk his duty."

To Angel's surprise, Wynema didn't retort with her usual sass, but instead murmured a good evening and headed down Main

Street toward home. As Angel followed Jeremy toward Amos's livery, she couldn't shake the feeling that there was more to Jeremy's mention of debts and duties than there seemed.

She wondered if he saw her as a duty and a debt to pay.

⚘

The Monday after the dismal church social, Angel felt well enough to limp to the creek without her cane. A much improved, if still lame, Sunny hobbled at her side, overjoyed to leave the barn stall where Jeremy had kept her for her own protection, and where Angel now put her from time to time.

"Easy now," Angel called when the golden-yellow dog picked up her pace and barked at every grass or leaf that moved. "You don't want to hurt yourself again, girl. You'll wind up in the barn for longer than before. I know you don't much like it there."

Not that she herself liked to be housebound for so long. Angel detested idleness. She relished the accomplishment of a job well done. These past few weeks, she'd chafed each time Jeremy or one of his men had come to do chores for her. It felt wrong to hand over her responsibilities to someone else.

"I'm better now," she said, pleased with the sound of her voice underscored by the ripple of creek water over rock. "All thanks to you, Father God."

At the water's edge, she gave up her efforts to control Sunny. The dog hopped into the chilly water and splashed with abandon. Envious of the animal's complete freedom, Angel sat on a boulder in the shallows and removed her boots and socks. A cautious dip of her toes sent shivers through her, but the chill also refreshed her more than anything had in ages.

"Aah . . ."

At peace there in God's creation, she let herself think back over the ugly confrontation with the banker's daughter. She figured there was truth in the old phrase 'like father, like son'—or, in this case, daughter. She'd heard Marcus Sutton's opinion, and his child had echoed it not much later.

The thought of the kind women who'd kept her company nudged out the painful memory. "Thank you, Lord, for the friends you've provided. I haven't known them long or valued them enough, but now that you've shown me the nasty side of others, I treasure Letty, Wynema, Phoebe, and Mrs. Stone much more."

She plucked a dandelion to the left of her perch. The humble yellow blossom wore a simple beauty, showed the kind of honesty in its vibrant color that made her more determined to avoid the airs and false front that some seemed to expect.

She owed only obedience to God.

The breeze, although dry and hot, felt good against her damp shirt, and she let down her guard. Here on her land, alone with her Lord and her dog, she didn't have to brace against criticism. She could simply enjoy His grace.

Calm enfolded her. She glanced up at the sky and counted the dozen wispy clouds that waltzed across the vast blue canopy. To her right, Rogers Ranch spread out far and green, its rich meadow grass dotted here and there with a rainbow of flowers. Purple, blue, and pink nodded against the emerald background with each windy sigh. Elsewhere, bunches of dark red clover drew the attention of busy bees. Somewhere up in the branches of the willow a short distance to her left, she heard cheery birds, the rush of creek water a sweet echo of their song.

She smiled and thought she could feel that echo ring right through her and down to her toes. Her heart swelled with joy, and life throbbed through her veins. She was home, where the Lord had placed her. Surely this was as close to paradise as one could get while here on earth.

Then a sound startled her. She thought it might be from nearby cattle. Was Jeremy on his way with a new group of animals?

But she didn't see a dust cloud when she glanced every which way, and as dry as the ground still was, any cow or horse would kick up a mess. "Hmm . . ."

Moments later she heard it again, and this time it sounded more like thunder. The past few days, dark clouds had hovered a time or two atop the mountain peaks, and Angel had felt a surge of hope. Thunderclaps had followed, but not a drop fell.

Today, however, nothing more than misty scarves of white graced the sky. And yet again, she heard the noise. She stood, her boots and socks in hand.

A rifle cracked and shattered the bark of a nearby tree.

She ducked. "Dear God, help!"

Someone had just shot at her. Hadn't it been enough to stab and beat her, kill her sheep, and maim her dog? Someone out there meant to get rid of her. That rifle meant business.

She crept toward the taller grasses in search of cover. "Sunny," she called in a hoarse whisper. "Come here. Now!"

Her heart pounded, its beat loud in her ears. The rush of fear in her body made her queasy, and Angel worried that she might vomit. But she couldn't falter now. She had to get home, barricade herself inside the house, and pray for God's mercy and protection from those who'd set their sights on her land.

Sunny crept up to her, ears low, teeth bared but more silent than Angel had ever seen the dog. It seemed her too-friendly pet had learned a bitter lesson. Angel prayed neither of them had another one to learn in the immediate future.

Eerie silence reigned as she and Sunny made their way back home with stealthy, smooth, and slow movements. Nothing stirred; not even the songbirds shared their tunes anymore. The silver-bell sound of the water's rush no longer charmed her. It now babbled to inspire men's greed. That moisture mattered more to someone out there than a woman's life.

When she came about a dozen yards from her back door, the dust cloud Angel had expected billowed up. This one, however, surged from the opposite direction of the shots. A carriage soon broke through the dry, gold haze, but she didn't recognize it even when it drew near.

She hurried to the cabin, her gut knotted. She had no reason to suspect the shots and the carriage had a common source, but it wouldn't hurt to be careful. She'd greet the driver from the door and keep Sunny behind her. For good measure, Angel grabbed Papa's shotgun and swallowed her distaste for the weapon.

"What do you want?" she called out when the rig pulled up.

Soon the new pastor and his fashion-plate wife disembarked. The moment they laid eyes on her, they did nothing to disguise their repugnance.

"Miss Rogers!" the reverend said. "You don't need a firearm."

Mrs. Bloom pursed her lips and sniffed. "That's no way for a lady to greet guests."

"Not welcome ones, I agree."

"Surely, you cannot object to a visit from your pastor."

The couple's condemning looks didn't offer Angel much comfort. "I reckon it depends on the reason for the visit."

The well-pressed and well-dressed man tugged on his lapels and straightened his formal black coat. Angel didn't know how he could bear the heavy thing in the heat.

"Ahem."

She feared his false cough didn't bode well for her.

Pastor Bloom rocked back on his heels and said, "It's been brought to my attention—"

"And mine, Mr. Bloom," his wife cut in.

The reverend turned his stern gaze on his wife. "Indeed, my dear, yours as well." His black stare flew back at Angel. "It's been brought to *our* attention that your actions aren't what they should be."

"Indeed," Angel said, her grip tight on the gun. "How so?"

Husband and wife exchanged looks.

"A woman," Mrs. Bloom began, "is called by God to be sweet, gentle, demure, and submissive—to her menfolks, you understand."

Angel stared.

The husband then took the lead. "And when there are no male relatives, then the church must take their place."

"I see . . ." Far more than they hoped she would, she'd wager.

"Splendid!" He beamed at the women. "I knew you'd understand once a man of the cloth approached you. I've always found ladies especially responsive to one of my calling."

He thought her responsive? "Hmm . . ."

"And so, Miss Rogers," he blundered on, "it's to my great delight to see that you're amenable to my counsel."

"And that would be . . . ?"

"Why, that you must face reality," he declared. "A woman alone out here goes against all godly doctrine. You must put yourself under the headship of the church, if not one of the gentlemen who've offered you marriage. And you must do so with no further waste of time."

"I've no intention of wedding."

Mrs. Bloom's expression soured even more. "An advantageous match is always a lady's greatest aspiration. And that would be the wisest choice for you, you know."

"I trust the Lord to reveal His wisdom at His own best time."

"And that," Pastor Bloom said, "is why I'm here today. As a man of the cloth, I can counsel you as to which path would be the most godly one for a woman in your circumstances."

Angel narrowed her eyes. "And would that most godly path lead to giving my ranch to Silver Creek Church's newly appointed shepherd?"

Husband and wife looked around. "Dear me, no," the reverend replied. His words echoed the scorn on his face. "This is not the sort of thing we care for."

Mrs. Bloom added, "I'll have you know, I'm a proper Bostonian. Were it not for my husband's appointment, I would never have set foot outside that great city's perimeter." She tipped up her nose to a prideful height. "I was raised right. I know my place. As you'll notice, I've no desire to usurp my husband's leadership, even if that has brought us to this forsaken corner of the world."

She looked at her once-white kid gloves and grimaced. "If there's anything to hold on to, I can certainly thank the dear Lord that you're the only woman we've found so determined to be . . . to look like . . . why, to pretend she's a man!"

The woman's disgusted blue glare stung Angel like a slap. Although she longed to retort in anger, she prayed for gentle words to deflect the attack.

"Trousers make more sense on a ranch than skirts and petticoats, Mrs. Bloom. There's a lot of work to do out here, and I don't need skirts or flimsy shoes to trip on. A rancher needs sturdy stuff to do the honest and decent hard work that must be done."

Red dots blazed on the woman's cheeks. "Why, you're as rude as you are unwomanly, accusing me of sloth and deceit. I declare, you are indeed an abomination in the Lord's eyes."

Angel sucked in a breath. "I reckon you should take your leave of me, then. Surely, you wouldn't want to spend time in the presence of an abomination."

The pastor shot her an angry look. "Do you mean to defy my decision as your authority in God's eyes? Will you continue to turn your back on the Lord's call on you as a woman?"

"I only wish to spare you from the hint of a smirch on your witness through association with the likes of me."

"Oh!" Mrs. Bloom cried out. "Oh-oh-oh-oh-oh! She's awful wicked!"

A hand in its smudged kid glove waved as though its owner might again succumb to a swoon. "Evil," she cried. "Dear me, Mr. Bloom. Surely, you can see she's demon possessed. Please, husband. We must leave. I want nothing more to do with this creature . . . or any of the other dolts we've met here. I want to go home. Boston's the only civilized city in the world."

She spun on her spike heels and rushed to the carriage, the bustled fabric of her white skirt swishing briskly from side to side.

The pastor approached Angel. "Your insistence is in direct rebellion to our righteous God, young lady. He ordained men to be men, leaders and owners, and to run His world. He also ordained women to be submissive wives and daughters and sisters."

When he halted for a breath, he waggled a finger under Angel's nose. "Mark my words, Miss Rogers, nothing good can come of your sinful stance. It's a perversion, I tell you. It says so in the first chapter of Romans when it talks of women who change their natural use into that which is unnatural. Your desire to be the man you're not is surely included in that condemning verse."

"I'll take up my sins with the Lord, Reverend." Angel fought the shivers that threatened. "Do tell. Is this sinner no longer welcome to worship on Sundays? Do the trousers and the ownership of a ranch make me worse than the woman Jesus met at the well?"

The pastor gaped; he snapped his mouth shut. He tried to speak but stammered instead. He again clamped his thin lips, and then, with as much dignity as Angel presumed he could muster, he turned toward the carriage and his wife's plaintive call.

On his way there, he called back, "I'll have to pray on that, and I suggest you confess your multitude of sins. Pray! Pray for the Lord's merciful forgiveness."

The carriage left in another flurry of dust, and Angel stared until it disappeared from sight, her thoughts in turmoil, her heart heavy and sore.

Had she reacted in a too-human urge to strike at those who'd hurt her? Or had she spoken the truth? Was that truth valid, or was it what she wanted to see, how she wanted things to be? Could she honestly say she'd spoken in love as God commanded?

And just what had she done that needed the Father's forgiveness? Wear trousers? Treasure the ranch her father had left her?

Did the truth lie in the Blooms' assertions?

She'd been shot at twice today, once with lead bullets and the second time with hateful words. Had she brought it all on herself?

Perhaps the reverend was right, if in only one thing: she did indeed need to seek the Lord in prayer.

14

Rebellious . . . sinful . . . unnatural . . .

Was she all those things? Was she any of them?

Angel spent a sleepless night. She sought the Father in His Word by the light of her lantern; she sought Him in prayer perched on the edge of her bed.

"Help me, please," she cried out. "I don't know which way is yours. Am I headstrong? Willful? Disobedient and sinful?"

As usual, the Lord kept His peace. The night stayed silent, perhaps too much so. Its quiet gave Angel many hours to revisit the memory of the shots by the creek. It also let her mull over, time and again, the awful things the pastor and his wife had said to her.

Even Sunny's raucous snores did nothing to distract her, since they started only when the first rosy hint of dawn crested the eastern horizon and Angel gave up hope of sleep.

She rose, stripped off her soft muslin nightgown, washed up, and then donned her red-and-black buffalo-check cotton shirt and her practical, if much maligned, denim trousers. Although it was early, she rolled up her long sleeves. The day was already too warm for comfort.

She unraveled her braids, brushed the waist-long mass of red hair, and then wove the six thick strands back into their usual ropes. Because of the heat, she took the extra time to coil and pin the braids into a roll on her crown just as Phoebe had.

She stepped to the kitchen without the cane to test her leg, as she often did these days. Without a word to Letty, she'd removed the splint and felt no worse for it.

As she cut a slice off a loaf of bakery bread, Angel looked out the back window toward the source of Rogers Creek. Why should it matter to anyone what she wore, what she owned? Did she hurt anyone by living life her way?

There wasn't much she could do about other folk's opinions. It would be foolish to even try.

She put down her knife and sighed. She'd continue to seek the Lord, obey every commandment she knew as best as she could, and try to love anyone she encountered as Christ once had.

She prayed others would honor their Savior in the same way.

❦

In the dead of a pitch-black night, a group of men met at the outskirts of Hartville, their identities shielded thanks to the moonless sky. They formed a tight circle, and of his own volition, one took his place in the middle.

"Since there's been no way to talk sense to that fool girl," he said in a quiet, harsh voice, "then I'd say it's time to take matters into our own hands."

"Someone's beat you to it with a sharp knife."

A murmur made the rounds.

The man in the middle called for silence. "I don't want to know about it, even though I'm sure someone here is to blame for that."

Hot denials shot at him.

"Hold on!" he cried in the loudest voice he dared use. "I said I didn't want to know, and I meant it. All I want is that woman gone and that creek free from any claim."

He got some yeses and fewer amens in response.

"There's more at stake here than just water for thirsty cattle," the leader went on. "I can't let on all I know. You'll just have to trust me on that account."

"I don't care what all else you have up your sleeve," a squat fellow said. "I only want to keep my herd alive and kicking. That water and meadow's all's I need to do it."

"Hear, hear!" someone cheered.

Another clapped and added, "Indeed."

Yet a third said, "Of course, and that's all's any one of us here wants. We don't give no never mind about the girl or any other scheme you've cooked up for yourself."

That satisfied the one in the center. "Well, then we'll just have to see about getting that selfish little—"

"Watch what you call her," someone else warned. "She's only a girl, you know."

The leader nodded. "That *selfish biddy* will just have to see things our way. And I'll say it again. We have to take the doing into our own hands."

A tall fellow who'd kept himself a bit apart from the others stepped forward. "How do you mean to change her mind when no one else has, not even with a knife, and the land is rightly hers?"

"Don't you worry—there are ways to get folks to do what's right for the betterment of most. Here we're talking about a whole bunch of folks who'll benefit once she's gone."

"Gone?" the squat fellow asked. "How gone d'you mean? I want no part of hurting her. What happened was bad enough."

"You won't have any part of anything like that," the self-appointed leader said. "There are ways. And it won't be long now before it's done."

The men exchanged farewells, then dispersed.

※

Jeremy hadn't seen Angel in days. The display Dahlia had put on at the church social that Saturday night still troubled him.

184

He'd sent Esteban to help at Rogers Ranch since then, and when the foreman couldn't get away from his regular chores, a hand or two went in his stead.

Jeremy didn't want to explain himself, didn't know if he could.

He'd told Angel how he'd changed his mind since they first met, but he sure wasn't ready to share his thoughts or the reasons for the change.

Still, his conscience nagged him, and he didn't like to think himself some kind of coward. He had to face Angel again.

At Rogers Ranch he made straight for the barn. When his eyes adjusted to the dim light inside, he blinked a couple of times, peered around, and then shut his eyes hard. He didn't dare trust what he thought he'd seen. But he came closer, so close that he couldn't deny what stood before him.

To the tune of "Onward Christian Soldiers," Angel heaved pitchfork after pitchfork full of sodden straw out from a cow's stall, her motions timed to the music. She didn't move as smoothly as she probably had before the attack.

"Are you crazy?" he blurted out.

She stopped midheave, her back to him, the large implement in the air, its smelly load ready to tip. "There's some as think just that," she said. "I figure you'll make up your mind on your own."

He heard no spite in her voice. Still, something in the way Angel held herself, the way she gave her answer, alarmed Jeremy. "What's wrong?"

She shrugged and followed through with the fork. The wad of rank bedding landed atop the pile she'd already cleared out, and Jeremy wondered if she'd fought the temptation to toss it at him instead.

He gave her a measuring look. "I don't reckon Doc Letty's been by lately, has she?"

No answer.

185

"Did you tell her you've taken to mucking out stalls as a remedy for a broken leg and a knife stab?"

She ignored him again.

It didn't sit well with him.

"Doubt your lost splint would please the good doc," he said. "I reckon you could do yourself some harm, and of the kind she might not be able to fix. No serious rancher would risk a bum leg that'd drag around behind him . . . or her—"

"Did you come here to nettle me?" she asked, the tines of her pitchfork planted in the dirt floor. "Don't you have better things to do back on your own spread?"

"I've plenty to do back home," he replied at length, "and I know what it takes to run a ranch. You had too much to tackle on your own in the best of times, and it'd seem to me you aren't near your best just yet. You won't be for quite a while either."

Her chin went up. "I can't abide laziness, and I'm plumb sick and tired of lying about. I can walk and I can use my arm, so I'm taking back my responsibilities. I'm much obliged for all the help you've given—you and your men—but I can handle the ranch now."

She turned back to the soiled hay, but she did so with too much force, and her injured leg didn't respond as she'd probably hoped. She stumbled, flailed the pitchfork, moaned in pain, and if Jeremy hadn't rushed forward, she would have fallen in the muck and likely hurt herself again in the bargain.

"Fool woman," he said, his arms tight around her. "You ought to still be inside, and I reckon you know it, too. Besides, that splint should've never come off your leg."

"I make my own decisions, you know."

"Of course you do, but if you make dumb ones, you have to pay a price for them. This time it's a right high one, since you'll ruin Doc Letty's good work and make the time Esteban, my men, and I spent here count for nothing."

"Oh, so you begrudge me the time those obliged to you wound up . . . 'wasting' on me. I never asked for your help."

"That's a dim-witted twist to my words, and you know it."

"Telling me what to do in my barn, on my ranch, and to my leg is sillier still."

"Not if you maim yourself on account of your cantankerous streak."

"I'm not cantankerous."

"Ornery then."

"I'm not."

He snorted. "Of course you are."

"I'm a strong, principled, and able woman."

"Doesn't matter if you're a woman or not . . ."

But it did. It mattered a great deal. Especially now as she lay sprawled across his lap, his arms around her, on the floor of the barn, where the force of her fall had pushed them. As he had that other time he'd held her close, Jeremy took in the soft scent of her copper-penny hair, the satin glow of her skin, the bright gleam in her eyes, the soft curves in his arms.

"Let me go," she said with little strength.

He nodded, but his arms refused to obey. They didn't move, didn't ease their hold on the warm woman cradled near to his heart.

"Please . . . ," she whispered, unease on her pretty face.

Again Jeremy nodded, but this time, without a real decision, his head went lower down, closer to her, and then his lips touched hers. Her warmth welcomed him, and he pressed a bit more.

Soft.

Sweet.

Long moments passed.

Jeremy pulled away to savor what they'd just shared.

She sighed, and her warm breath brushed his cheek. He dipped his head again, and this time took a real kiss from her mouth.

Angel didn't fight him, but her obvious inexperience soon made him pull back.

She was an innocent. Even though Jeremy was no ladies' man, and he prided himself on treating those women he knew right, Angel was different. She merited the greatest care and respect. Even if her stubborn nature made him want to scream and shout and stomp and—

"I . . . ," she started, then stopped.

Jeremy looked down and saw confusion in her eyes, a blush on her cheeks. He bit his tongue before a curse could escape the bounds he'd set for his speech.

"Ah . . ." He cleared his throat. "Do you reckon you can stand?"

She nodded. "My leg doesn't hurt . . . much."

"Are you ready to head back indoors and stay put until you're well and healed?"

Angel's dignity took over, and she freed herself in a smooth move. He planted his fists at his sides so as to not up and clasp her close again. He hadn't expected to miss her warmth, her weight, her nearness that much or that soon.

Now he knew the real crazy one in the barn.

She took a cautious step, then gave him a radiant smile. "See? No harm done."

No harm? Ha!

Jeremy's wits had just suffered their most serious blow. He'd kissed Old Man Rogers's daughter—not once, but twice. If that wasn't even crazier than his distaste for Dahlia since the tantrum at the church social, then he sure didn't know crazy at all.

"Ah . . . er . . ." He shook his head, dismayed by his tied tongue. "I reckon your sheep out yonder on that hill might be hungry for some salt right about now. I'll be on my way, and you just take care you don't go and do anything foolish again while I'm off and can't help put you to rights."

Blast it all! That kind of blither suited some kind of youngster better than a full-grown man. He crammed his hat back on, touched the brim in farewell, and hurried toward the barn door. Before he got to the opening and freedom, a sudden report rang out.

He stopped.

Another blast followed. Then a third.

Gunfire. And it hadn't come from too far off.

"Angel," he called in a rough whisper.

When she didn't answer, he turned and felt the bottom drop out of his stomach at what he saw. She'd gone pale. She shivered. Her eyes had opened to impossible widths. She looked just like she had the day he'd found her in the stall, stabbed, shocked, surrounded by her dead and wounded beasts.

He ran to her side and wrapped her in his arms again, this time his only thought that of protection. He wanted nothing more than to shield her from harm, to melt the fear from her eyes.

A tremor wracked her. She shut her eyes tight. "He's back."

"Who is?"

With obvious effort, she pulled away. "I don't know. But it's not the first gunfire in the last few days."

Jeremy clenched his fists. "Did you tell the sheriff? Did you see who it was?"

She shook her head, wiped her hands on her trousers, then squared her shoulders and headed outside. She paused in the doorway, reached to her left and picked up something he couldn't quite make out. "I intend to do so this time."

What had she grabbed?

"Wait!" he called. "You can't go out there all angry-like. You don't know what's waiting for you."

She didn't slow down. "What I can't do is go on like this. If I'm bound home to the Lord right about now, then I'm ready. If I'm not, then the Father will surely see me through. But I'm good and tired of someone using me for a pincushion or target practice."

Angel's determination and courage made Jeremy's opinion of her soar. As it did his fear. "What do you mean to do when you meet up with him? Tell him to shop for pincushions and targets at Adrian Gable's general store?"

"I intend to acquaint him with this." She waved a shotgun.

He swallowed another curse and asked the Lord's forgiveness. "What are you doing with that thing? Last I knew, you'd no idea what to do with it."

"I learned," she said, her words sharp with raw emotion. "I was forced to go against my convictions."

Cruelty had changed Angel. And it had happened on account of nothing more than a stream of water and long blades of green grass.

Again his admiration for this fine, rare woman grew. At no time did she falter in her progress, but instead, she made straight for the western border of her land, the direction from where the shots had come.

Jeremy loped up to her. "Let me take the gun. I've used one a time or two."

She didn't respond to his irony, but instead shook her head and kept going, her eyes on what now looked like a man and a horse up ahead of them. She broke into an unsteady trot, and Jeremy didn't have it in him to hold her back. Instead, he picked up his own pace and ran beside her, their goal in his sight.

As they approached, Jeremy recognized the rider. "Pringle! What's the reason for your visit?"

"Theft. And dead stock."

Jeremy didn't wait for Angel's response. He ran full tilt ahead, his gut full of dread. He pulled up short when he saw a pair of calves and a horse on the ground.

"What's all this?" he asked, his breath tight.

Pringle doffed his hat and swiped the sweat from his bulging brow. "I told you. Them's mine, and they're dead. Someone's stole and kilt 'em."

Jeremy didn't like the man's angry glare at Angel. He leaned forward, clasped his thighs above the knee, and made himself drag in full, deep breaths. "You sure they're yours?"

"You blind or something? I sure ain't." Pringle pointed to the horse's flank. "That's my brand there, an *A* an' a *P* a-sharing a leg."

Jeremy's breath came easier now, so he went up to the dead animals. They bore the same mark. "I see."

Angel ran up. "What did you do to them?"

Pringle glowered.

Jeremy tried to catch her attention and warn her against speaking her mind, but to no avail. Angel wasn't a woman easily swayed from her intent.

She asked again.

"You know too well what happened to these here beasts," Pringle replied. "You ain't one to share, so when them poor things, hungry and thirsty for days in this cussed heat, smelt water and came to help theirselves, you took care of 'em."

Angel's eyes flashed. "I did no such thing. I wouldn't hurt a living creature."

"You sure would," Pringle countered, his face livid. "You do it each and every day, what with your selfish hold on all that there water."

"I'm not selfish. It's my land, and my flock needs water and pasture. Besides, I have shared—"

"Angel didn't shoot your stock," Jeremy said to keep her from digging herself a deeper hole. "She doesn't know how to use a rifle and likely couldn't hit the broad side of her own barn back a ways over there."

Pringle slanted him a look. "She's mighty comfy with that there shotgun, I'd say. Especially them shots she takes at empty tins."

Angel's eyes widened. She studied the shotgun, then Pringle, and finally looked toward her cabin's backyard.

"The gun was her pa's," Jeremy said. "I reckon she's held it for him a time or two, and she's maybe decided to learn how to use it. If you recollect, someone did do her harm. She's got a right to protect herself."

Pringle aimed a blob of spittle at a clump of lush grass. "That's not my never mind, Johnstone. My animals are dead, and she's holding a gun. That's pretty good for me."

From the corner of his eye, Jeremy saw Angel flinch.

"I can vouch for her," he said. "I was with her when we both heard the shots. We were on our way to see what happened when you rode up. She didn't shoot anything."

Pringle jabbed out his chin. "I'm supposed to take your word for this?"

Jeremy nodded.

Angel kept quiet—for once.

The rancher waved in disgust. "I'm not the fool you think I am. I know what's what. You're defending your best interest. It ain't good for you if another herd gets to share her water. I been watching the goings-on hereabouts. Don't think I don't know you been grazing and watering your stock at Rogers Creek. Of course you'd say she didn't shoot these critters to keep the water and pasture to yourself."

"I'm a man of my word," Jeremy said through clamped jaws. "And you know it. She didn't do this."

When Angel's accuser didn't yield, Jeremy added, "If you're so all-fired sure you know what happened here, then go fetch Sheriff Herman. He'll want to look into it, see what tracks the killer left, investigate for himself, that kind of thing."

"I think I'll do me just that." Pringle turned on Angel. "You owe me, lady. And you'd best pay up. Those there were good, valuable animals. Now I can't get nothing for them, and times ain't as good for some as for others."

He spun on his heel, mounted his horse, and rode off, his spurs digging at the animal's sides.

Jeremy couldn't keep his gut from twisting. He glanced at her in time to see her crumple into a wretched mound on the much-desired meadow.

Had she swooned?

He started toward her. She'd again been hurt, and he hadn't been able to prevent it. It was cold comfort to know that, if nothing else, he'd been at her side when the animals were killed. Then, too, she hadn't had to face Pringle on her own. He'd heard the shots that took down the horse and the calves, and Angel had done nothing wrong.

It would be hard to make others believe him. Pringle had given him a right clear look into what others would think when he defended Angel. But Jeremy wouldn't back down. He wouldn't let someone's misguided notion do her any more harm.

They did, after all, live in Colorado. They hung horse thieves and rustlers here.

Jeremy saw Angel's shoulders heave. It did something to a man to watch the tears of a good woman. It made him more determined to make sure they didn't fall for no good cause. Something inside him wept with her, too.

They had a tough fight ahead of them. He prayed he'd be up to the challenge they'd soon face.

Pringle wouldn't be the only one to press that challenge. Too many others wanted what Angel had, what she'd shared with him. He couldn't let such goodness of heart be seen as anything other than what it was.

Lord God, he begged, *let me bear as good a witness of your love as she already has.*

❧

Letty stepped inside the long, low ranch house she shared with her beloved husband and their five youngsters, and her relief went beyond gratitude for God's abundant blessings. She was drained, sleepy, and not one bit hungry for whatever Mrs. Sauder had prepared for supper.

It smelled good, but Letty couldn't appreciate it. Her day had brought a full roster of sick and needy folks, and although she treasured her ability to serve, the work had tired her. After the last patient left, she'd taken inventory of her supplies, a constant need in a busy practice like hers. Later on, she'd hurried to yet another missionary society meeting at Silver Creek Church, one that dragged far longer than it should have.

She'd rather head to bed than eat.

"Is that you?" Eric called out.

"I'm finally home," she said. She dropped her medical bag next to the hall tree that still bore a harvest of coats, now useless in the summer's relentless heat.

Eric joined her. "Finally? You're early, and by quite a bit."

"It doesn't feel early." Letty leaned against her husband's broad chest and breathed in his distinctive male scent underscored with the tang of bay rum. She was blessed, richly so, to be this man's wife. She murmured, "I love you."

He curved a long finger under her chin and tipped up her face. His lips came down on hers in a long, tender kiss. As always, Letty's heart brimmed with joy, and she returned the caress with every bit of her love. Long, delightful moments later, Eric pulled back.

"I love you, too, Mrs. Wagner. But now you'll take yourself to bed, where it'll be my pleasure to bring your supper."

"Don't bother, dearest. I'm too tired to eat. If Mrs. Sauder sets something aside for me, though, I'm sure I'll be hungry sometime later on."

She started down the hallway toward their bedroom, then noticed the unusual quiet in the house. Five children made a great deal of noise. "Where's our brood?"

"They should be back any minute now. Daisy and Mim offered to take them to the wading hole on Silver Creek. You should have heard Steven's whoop of joy."

"If I weren't so tired, I'd go meet them. The cold water sounds awfully appealing, even though this miserable drought has left precious little of it in the creek. But I'm afraid our bed is calling more loudly right now."

"Go ahead. I'm sure the girls, Mrs. Sauder, and I can manage to feed, bathe, and ship our crew to bed without you for this one night. You do work too hard, you know."

"Don't, please. Not now that I'm so worn—"

A rap on the door cut her off. She drew her brows together. "Did you expect someone?"

Eric crossed to the door. "No. I would have told you if I did." He pressed on the latch and drew back. "Mrs. Stone! What brings you out at this time? And Adrian . . . Phoebe, too?"

Letty's curiosity overcame her exhaustion, even though she knew she'd pay for it later on. "Oh dear. What's happened? Who's hurt?"

"May we come in?" Mrs. Stone asked.

"I'm sorry." Eric waved toward the large parlor. "I forgot my manners in my surprise. Please make yourselves comfortable. How can we help?"

The unexpected guests filed in, Douglas and Randy Carlson in the rear. Letty bustled to the kitchen to ask Mrs. Sauder for a pot of coffee and a kettle of water for tea. She then returned to the parlor and sat by Eric on the settee. He took her hand in his.

"Now that everyone's settled," he said, "please tell us what's happened."

Douglas went to the vast stone fireplace. "We've a problem. Someone shot some of Albert Pringle's calves and one of his horses. He's out for blood."

Letty looked at her husband. He shrugged, then turned to the town's attorney. "I don't understand why that brought you here."

"We decided you both should know," Douglas said. "After all, Letty's her friend, and you might want to put something in the paper."

"Whose friend?" Letty asked.

Douglas removed his spectacles and rubbed the bridge of his nose. "Pringle's beasts were at the edge of Angel Rogers's property. He says she met him with a gun, and he filed a complaint with Max Herman. He claims that because she hoards her water, she begrudged his stock a drink and simply killed them."

"Bah!" Letty exclaimed. "That's silly. Don't give it another thought. Angel did no such thing. She wouldn't. She doesn't even know how to handle her father's old shotgun."

Adrian shook his head. "It seems that since her attack she's taken up arms. She's taken up practice on some tins, and Pringle says he's seen her."

Letty's exhaustion returned. This was too much to take in. "When did the cattle die?"

"Earlier today."

"Was she alone? Didn't Wynema stop by? Were any of Jeremy Johnstone's men helping today?"

"That's the worst part," Douglas said. "Jeremy was with her. They both heard the shots."

Letty stood and smiled. "Well, there you have it. He can vouch for her."

Douglas looked away. "It's not that simple, Letty. Pringle says Jeremy will vouch for Angel to protect the access she's given him to the water. Not only did Pringle see Angel practice with the gun, but he also saw Jeremy and his foreman lead a dozen head to Rogers Creek."

Eric sighed. "That sounds like trouble."

Adrian added, "Albert Pringle wants her jailed."

Letty swooned.

15

Despite the frustration of ranchers still thwarted by the drought, preparations for the stock sale took up everyone's attention for the next few weeks. Many worried about the outcome of the auction. How much they'd make would determine how they'd fare through the winter, and if they could raise a herd for next year.

Angel understood their concerns. It wasn't that she didn't care. She did, and not just because their troubles had spilled over and affected her. She didn't want anyone to suffer, not even an innocent beast. But their troubles weren't her fault.

Everyone was on edge.

The few times she'd gone into town since Pringle found his dead stock, she'd faced the anger of those he'd turned against her. Even at church she'd felt unwelcome. Pringle had worked hard to spread his suspicion.

Her handful of friends had urged her to ignore the others. She'd tried, but Angel no longer found it worth her while to put herself through the painful effort each Sunday morning. She could worship Christ far better on her own than in the company of hate-filled strangers. Once the animosity died down, she'd return.

Even the quilt auction to benefit the missionary fund at Silver Creek Church failed to entice her from the ranch. Phoebe and Letty had organized the event. The town's quilting circle, under Mrs. Stone's direction, had done the exquisite work. Angel would have liked to participate, especially since the work was for a worthy cause.

She doubted the women there would stomach her company these days. Many saw her as the reason their livelihood was now in question. Few wanted to accept the drought, not something they could blame on another, as responsible for the failure of their herds.

The night before she was to head to Rockton, Angel knelt by her bed, her Bible open, her head bowed. "Father God, I'm about to step into a lion's den of sorts tomorrow. I don't have the strength to bear up on my own, so I'll have to lean on your strength again. It will be sufficient for me."

That thought in mind, Angel went to bed, rose the next morning, and with Sunny's help, herded her sheep to market. She prayed every step of the way.

§

"Good evening."

Jeremy looked up from his supper to find Eric at his side. He stood, and they shook hands.

"Will you join me?" he asked the newspaperman.

"I was hoping you'd ask." Eric hooked his hat on the ladder-back chair's finial and then sat so as not to dislodge it. "I've something to discuss with you, and I'm free for a while. Letty and the ladies from the missionary society are at some auction. They put together a quilt to raise money for a pet project of theirs."

"Care for supper?" Jeremy asked.

"I could use a bite."

They ate and spoke of the crowds, the town, the heat—nothing that would've made Eric seek him out.

The young lady who served their meal topped their coffees,

but before they took another sip, Eric stood. He waved to Adrian, who'd just entered the hotel's dining room. "We're here."

Jeremy stood, uneasy. "Pleasure to see you, Mr. Gable."

"Call me Adrian, please." The mine owner turned to Eric and said, "It took me longer than I thought to finish the purchase of a better quality cot for the store. Then I took Phoebe to the quilt sale. Douglas was there with Randy, and he said he'd be here in a moment."

No sooner had the three taken their seats, than the attorney joined them. Jeremy's dinner turned to lead in his gut. Something wasn't right.

"I might just be a plain old cowboy," he began, "but I sure am not blind. What's all this about?"

Douglas and Adrian turned to Eric, who took a deep breath. "You know I'm here to write up the fair and the auctions, right?"

Jeremy nodded.

The newspaperman smoothed his thick mustache with the thumb and index finger of his right hand. It surprised Jeremy that someone who had such a way with words could at times find himself without any ready at hand.

"Well," Eric finally said, "sometimes it's all a man can do to just write and not speak. This time I've decided to speak. There's trouble brewing, and I'm afraid Angel Rogers is in for a bad time."

"What kind of trouble?" Jeremy asked.

Douglas shrugged. "The same as before. Albert Pringle couldn't sell his bony cattle. He blames Angel for his troubles, and he's after his pound of flesh, so to speak."

"He's been after her for a good while now," Jeremy said. "He called the sheriff on her back when he found those dead calves and the horse a couple, three weeks ago. I don't reckon this is news."

Eric tapped the tabletop. "It's not news, but if Pringle continues to feed his anger, his actions could lead to news—bad news."

Jeremy looked from man to man. "You figure he'll hurt her?"

"Someone already did," Douglas replied. "And Pringle has hounded Sheriff Herman. He insists she's responsible for the animals' deaths."

"I know that. I heard him that very day. Did Herman find anything to tie Angel to the killings?"

"Thankfully not." Douglas removed his spectacles and wiped them with a clean linen napkin. He pointed at Jeremy with a wire temple. "You know it wouldn't be hard to pin them on her. He says she met him shotgun in hand."

"She did have her father's gun, but I'd gone to help her earlier, and we both heard the shots. We were in the barn right then, and I know she didn't shoot."

Adrian made a rough noise deep in his throat. "There are those who'll believe the worst of anyone. They'll blame an innocent person on just enough truth to make it look possible. That happened to me."

Jeremy nodded. He remembered the trouble the mine owner had gone through not so long ago. "That does happen. Has something new made Pringle crazier than before?"

Douglas donned his spectacles. "Now that his animals didn't sell, he must be close to broke. And I've heard that Angel's flock went for a pretty penny. The wool she sheared in the spring brought her good money, too. That just added to Pringle's anger."

"Resentment and jealousy are often enough," Eric said. "They're strong feelings, and with everyone as anxious as they've been for so long, who knows what it would take to start trouble."

Jeremy sighed. "Is there something you reckon I ought to do?"

Adrian flattened his palms on the table and leaned forward. "That's why we came. You've looked out for Angel since the attack, and our wives would have our heads if we let anything else happen to her. We figured the four of us could come up with an idea . . . some plan to protect her."

"I failed her the first time you told me I ought to help her," Jeremy said. "I couldn't live with myself if I failed a second time."

"What do you suggest?" Eric asked.

"I don't rightly know." Jeremy rubbed his chin. "She's a stubborn one, I'll give her that. She won't likely look too kindly on any one of us sticking by her all the time."

The others exchanged looks and laughed.

"We all have experience with stubborn women," Douglas said. "Whatever we decide must not be obvious to Angel. But we can't just let a wild accusation grow into something worse."

Eric slanted a look at Jeremy. "You'll have to take the lead, you know. We've got our wives to deal with."

"I figured as much. I'm right honored that you'd all trust me with something this serious, especially since I didn't do so well the other time."

Adrian clapped a hand on Jeremy's shoulder. "You proved yourself after the attack. No one asked you to step in and help. You just took over. If the women hadn't told us what you were up to, no one would have been the wiser."

"You're a good man," Eric added.

Jeremy's face burned at the undeserved praise. "I've a righteous God to face each day. Angel got hurt on account of my failure. I couldn't face the Lord if I don't do all's I rightly should this time."

"I don't follow your logic," Douglas said, "but we can leave that for another time. Right now we need to decide what to do next."

"She's staying with Wynema over at Miss Moore's rooming house," Jeremy said. "Even though I'm at the Range Hotel on this side of town, I don't see why I can't head on over to Miss Moore's and ask if she's got an empty room."

Eric frowned. "I doubt anything's vacant. The town's bursting with visitors."

Jeremy pushed back his chair. "Then if that's that, I reckon I'd best be on my way to find me a spot under Miss Moore's porch or in her back shed. If things are so bad as to send you all to hunt me down, why, then I don't need me a feather bed to sleep on."

Adrian opened his mouth, but before he could speak, Jeremy held out his hand.

"I know it sounds crazy to swap a bed for a shed," he said, "but Angel's not about to be alone one minute of her time in Rockton. Well, excepting the time my stock's up for sale. If one of you could take over my place with her then, I'd be much obliged."

"I don't see why I can't do that," Adrian said. "Phoebe would love to spend time with Angel. They're both partial to needlework."

Jeremy held out his hand to the mine's owner. "My first steer's up right around ten tomorrow morning. I'll look for you then."

"We can all meet again in the afternoon," Adrian added.

Eric stood and straightened his brown suit coat. "I'll keep my ears open. Who knows what I might learn from a good question here and there."

Douglas reached for his leather portfolio, then pushed his spectacles up his nose. "I've a number of clients to meet yet. I might learn something, too. All it will take is one slip of the tongue, and we'll know who killed Pringle's stock."

Although his concern for Angel hadn't shrunk any, Jeremy felt better with others on his side—her side. "It won't hurt none if we all do a good deal of praying, too."

The others nodded.

"First though," Jeremy said at length, "I'd best confess that I'm as guilty as those who want to hurt her. I was the first to try and buy her out. I didn't look farther than the end of my fool nose and saw her like I wanted to see her."

Eric smiled. "We've all been guilty of that at one time or another—not necessarily about Angel either. I did the same when Letty came to town."

"And I didn't give Phoebe enough credit when I first met her," Adrian admitted. "I thought she was too delicate and innocent, so I didn't tell her the truth about my past. That nearly cost me the greatest gift the Lord's given me."

"Oh, I don't know about gifts or anything like that," Jeremy hurried to say. "I just know Angel's no little girl who can't do a day's honest work on that ranch as well as anyone else, man or not. I reckon she's earned that spread, and her pa wanted her to have it." Jeremy shook his head, his earlier closed mind not something he was proud of. "Doesn't seem right anymore to say she ought to leave on account of my land being dryer than hers."

Eric stepped toward the door. "I spoke the truth when I said you're a good man, Jeremy. It takes courage to admit when one's wrong—I know."

"I'll say it again. I've a great God to face. If I'm not honest before Him, I'm not worth anything much. He knows what's what."

Adrian nodded. "He does, and He sees those we find so different as worthy as anyone else He created. Phoebe has suffered snubs and insults because of the time she spent with the Shakers. And I know there are those who make more than they should of Angel's clothes and her reserved way."

Jeremy chuckled. "Oh, she's different all right. But that doesn't give anyone else the right to say she's not entitled to what's hers. And I'm not about to let anyone use her to make themselves feel better." He clapped his hat on his head. "I'll be somewhere around Miss Moore's place if you need me."

To Adrian he added, "I'll look for you at the auction barn tomorrow."

"I'll be there."

"Perhaps I can persuade Randy to spend time with Angel—to keep her company while Wynema's busy with her camera," Douglas offered.

Eric raised his hands in surrender. "Fine, fine. I'll do what I can with Letty. If there's any way about it, she'll be there as well. We can't just sit and wait until something happens and then act."

The four men left the restaurant in different directions. Even though things looked murky, Jeremy felt comforted. His confession had been sincere, and the others had accepted it. He knew God forgave him, and he reckoned the men forgave him, too.

Now he just had to forgive himself. He'd never do that if anything else happened to Angel.

♔

Jeremy walked into the auction barn at ten o'clock but found it crammed with an angry mob. Shouts of outrage rang out, and more than one face looked ready to burst into flames.

Foul language ripped from somewhere toward the center of the structure. Although the voice sounded familiar, Jeremy couldn't quite place it. The rage behind the oaths roughened and lowered it to where it pretty near hurt to hear it.

To his right stood a man he'd never met, a frown on his face but no fire in his eyes and no red in his features.

"Excuse me," Jeremy said.

The man turned toward him. "Yes?"

"I just got here on account of my herd was supposed to be sold right about now, but I walked into this. What's the problem?"

"That man." The fellow spoke with a Spanish accent. "He say that his cattle have been . . . how you say? Venomed?"

"Venomed? That doesn't seem right—unless a rattler got at them. Snakes?"

"Sorry. I no speak well. The cattle, they eat, drink bad stuff. It kill them."

"Is it poison you're thinking?"

Relief dawned on the man's face. "Yes! Poisoned. He say somebody poisoned his cattle. He very mad."

"Can't say I rightly blame him. I had some of my herd poisoned not too long ago. It's just pure meanness, and I hated to

204

know those poor critters had suffered on account of someone's spite."

"Spite—good word."

"Good word for a bad thing."

The uproar reached a peak, and the mob surged toward the door. Jeremy shook his head. This looked awfully bad. Someone was likely to get hurt.

Over the din, he heard, "She ain't gonna get away with it this time!"

This time he identified the enraged man. With nothing more than that one blurted threat, Jeremy knew just who Pringle aimed to hurt.

He slipped outside between two fellows on their way inside in a hurry to not miss a thing. At the corner of the barn, he broke into a trot but came up short when he spotted Adrian about ten yards away.

"That trouble we all talked about last night?" Jeremy said.

Adrian frowned. "Is it here already?"

"Just about to explode."

"What happened?"

"I'm not rightly sure, but I hear say someone poisoned Pringle's stock overnight. He just yelled out that *she's* not going to get away with it."

"I'll just have to see if I can get him to see reason."

"Doubt you'll get anywhere with him. He's blind mad right now."

"I can't do nothing," the mine owner said. "I have to try to stop the madness."

"Tell you what," Jeremy said. "I'll head on over to the sheriff's office. I reckon Rockton's law can't be wanting this kind of thing in the streets any more than we want it in Hartville."

Adrian rose on his toes and craned his neck to look between the open doors of the barn. Evidently, he saw what he was looking for. "Keep me in your prayers, brother," he said. "Pringle's in the middle of that bunch over there. I'll head toward him—oh, and if you come across Eric or Douglas, send them along. I can use their help."

Jeremy took off at a lope toward the center of Rockton, his steps spurred by many prayers. To his dismay, the sheriff's office was locked tight. A sign said the man had gone to the train station to see that a prisoner made the 10:15 to Denver.

His gut tightened into that knot that had become so familiar since he met Angel. He'd never been the kind to worry before, but something about that woman, the trouble she seemed to draw her way, had changed him. Her safety was now always on his mind.

"Hey there!"

Jeremy turned at the shout. "Eric! We need to hurry to the auction barn. There's been trouble, and it's headed for Angel."

Eric broke into a trot.

"Do you know where Douglas is?" Jeremy asked.

"On his way to the sale, as far as I know. At least, that's where he told me we should meet."

"We can sure use his help. I left Adrian alone at the barn . . . I don't rightly know if I did the right thing."

"How do you mean?"

Jeremy sucked in air and continued. "I came after the sheriff, and he's gone to the train station. Adrian's alone with a herd of angry ranchers."

Eric stopped. "I can see that now."

A wave of dusty, distressed men came at them, Pringle in the lead. At his side, Adrian gestured and argued but seemed to get nowhere for his efforts.

Eric took a small black notebook and a lead pencil from his jacket pocket. "Let me give it a try." He ran up to Pringle and asked, "What's happened?"

"I'll tell you what's happened, Mr. *Hartville Day*," Pringle mocked. "That there—"

"Now you watch what you call Miss Rogers," Adrian warned. "You don't want to put yourself in the wrong, do you?"

The rancher looked startled, but if nothing else, Adrian's question pierced his rage. He shook his head. "I guess not. But that don't mean I ain't gonna make right sure she gets what's coming to her."

"Who?" Eric asked, his voice even and quiet. "And what has she—whoever she might be—got coming? And why?"

Pringle smirked. "That's right. You put it all down good and straight. That Angel Rogers—more like a she devil, that one is—she's gone and poisoned my cattle. It weren't enough that she's too selfish to share a bit of water and grass with 'em in the first place. They were near dying anyway, and now she's gone and poisoned the lot."

Jeremy held his breath.

Eric looked Pringle straight on. "Did you see her do it?"

"Nah. Didn't have to. I know she's the one. Why, she shot two calves and a horse when they were wanting nothing more'n a drink at her place a couple weeks ago. You must've heard."

"I understand Sheriff Herman investigated but found that Miss Rogers's gun hadn't been shot in quite some time."

"That's what he said, but I know better'n that," Pringle countered. "She's selfish and greedy. Look at all that money she made with her cussed sheep."

"Did anyone see Angel near your cattle? Anyone see anything at all that might lead you to believe she did anything to harm them?"

"No, but—"

"Why, then you don't really know what happened," Eric said. "Do you?"

Jeremy began to breathe again.

Pringle jutted his chin. "I didn't *see* nothing, but I *know* she's the one."

"You *suspect* she's the one," Adrian said.

"But you don't rightly know," Jeremy added. "It's not like you saw or heard her do anything."

"Well, no . . . but—"

"Then I reckon," Jeremy went on, "it's in everyone's favor if we head on down to the sheriff and see what he says. It's his town, and he's likely to be some particular as to what goes on here."

Pringle wavered. "Maybe . . ."

"That makes sense," Eric said. "I'd like to know how the local arm of the law will handle this type of thing. I'm sure he'll want to investigate and then take appropriate action."

"Action," Pringle said. "That's what I'm ready for. Some action against that critter-killing woman—"

"Hey, Albert," one of the other ranchers cut in. "You did say you didn't see her do anything. Maybe Wagner here has a point. Go get the sheriff."

Pastor Bloom stepped forward. "It's just as I always contend," he said. "Greed is at the root of all sin. When a person covets something, that unholy desire leads to sin. And sin always begets chaos."

He looked around and seemed satisfied with the attention he'd drawn. His expression darkened and his voice deepened. "Anyone with eyes to see will surely agree that chaos, utter and complete chaos, has taken over this fine town. When, I ask you, when has chaos ever led to anything but crime?"

Jeremy narrowed his eyes and went to object, but Eric shook his head. He bit down on his tongue and bided his time.

The reverend continued. "We are the creation of a just and righteous God!" A vein throbbed in his forehead. "A God that cannot tolerate anything but goodness and virtue and, above all else, justice."

Mutters of agreement rose from the mob.

That set the reverend off again. "Let us go forth and seek justice for this fine fellow. And let the sinner pay the price of sin!"

Jeremy's eyes widened. He met Eric's horror-filled brown eyes and then Adrian's dark blue ones. They'd been right to fear trouble. It had just caught up with them all.

The rabble had found a new leader, one with the cloak of righteousness. A man of the cloth led their angry rampage.

Jeremy's chest felt as though someone had grabbed his heart and squeezed tight. Despite his anxiety, he murmured, "Let's pray."

The three men took a moment to call their Lord into their midst, and then, certain of His presence among them, they hurried off. An innocent was about to be declared guilty of a crime she didn't commit.

❦

Hours after the crowd burst into the sheriff's office, Jeremy, Adrian, Eric, and Douglas decided there wasn't much more they could do.

"At least we got Sheriff Dowd to agree to look at the pens where the animals died," Adrian said.

Jeremy turned to Douglas. "You did a right fine job arguing down that crowd. They didn't like the sheriff's measured approach, but you made them stop and temper their anger."

The lawyer chuckled. "My father will be happy to hear all those years of schooling amounted to something after all."

"I just hope we don't need them for more," Eric said. "Albert Pringle is a hard man, and he's lost everything. He doesn't have enough for taxes or interest, and Marcus Sutton will call in his loan in a very short time."

"We gained time," Adrian said. "That's something. Now Jeremy should head back to Miss Moore's and see how he can keep Angel in sight."

Anxious to see her again, Jeremy nodded. "I'll meet you tomorrow for coffee at nine."

The four shook hands and parted ways. Ten minutes later

Jeremy knocked on the door of the rooming house. Tall, gray-haired Miss Moore greeted him.

"How can I help you?" she asked.

"Is Miss Rogers in?"

"I don't cotton to unmarried men and ladies consorting in my home," Miss Moore said, "so you'll just have to have your say with her out on the porch."

"That's right fine, ma'am, Miss Moore. We can sit on these chairs you've kindly provided."

The lady sniffed and then closed the door. Her heels rapped against the floor and then faded off. Jeremy waited, the seconds longer than he reckoned they ought to be. After what felt like a whole night went by, a different set of footsteps approached.

Angel opened the door. "Jeremy! I didn't expect you."

"I hear say your woolly critters did fine at the sale," he said with a smile. "I came to congratulate you."

"Why, thank you. That's very kind."

"It's only right. You worked hard, and it brought you success."

"How did you fare?"

"Not as well as I would have liked, but I'll make it through the winter."

"I'm glad. You've done the work of two, what with helping me when I—"

"There she is!" someone yelled.

"Miss Angela Rogers?" a gaunt, silver-haired man asked.

Fear crossed Angel's face, but she paused, took a breath—likely prayed—and said, "I'm Angela Rogers."

"I'm Sheriff Dowd. I have something to show you."

She clasped her hands behind her back. "What is it?"

The lawman took from his pocket what looked to Jeremy like a scrap of cloth.

"Have you ever seen this?" the sheriff asked.

Angel took the scrap and turned it over. Jeremy stretched to see what it was but couldn't quite make it out.

"It looks like some of the things I have," she said. "But I don't think any of my shirts has a hole."

Dowd pointed at the scrap. "You do have a shirt like this?"

"Yes."

"Then I'm afraid I'm going to have to arrest you. This was in the stall where Albert Pringle's cattle died."

Angel stumbled backward. Her hand went to her chest; she fisted the bit of shirt, and only then did Jeremy see what Dowd had given her.

Against her blue chambray work shirt, the large red-and-black checks of buffalo plaid looked harsh. They couldn't have been more damning.

Everyone knew Angel wore that kind of shirt. Jeremy didn't remember when he'd seen anyone else with anything like it.

Angel shook her head. "I didn't do it."

"That remains to be seen," the sheriff said. "For now, you must come with me. There's a jail cell all ready for you."

Jeremy thought she'd faint, she went so pale. But then, with poise and dignity, she held her head high and said, "My Father in heaven is my witness. I have nothing to fear. He is my defender. I'll trust in Him. He'll set me free."

16

Angel's heart pounded hard. "How could this happen to me, Mr. Carlson? I live a quiet life, I mind my business and make sure I offend no one."

The lawyer, who'd offered to represent her without charge, shook his head. "It's beyond me. Why don't you tell me what you do remember?"

"Last night when the sheriff showed up, I was sure everything would be cleared up in no time. But then he sent Miss Moore to look through my things. She found my red and black shirt in pieces."

"Did it tear when you last wore it?"

"I wouldn't pack a torn shirt to bring to Rockton," she answered. "And I haven't worn it here."

"So someone entered your room and ruined the shirt."

"It would seem so." Angel drew a shuddery breath. "But who? Who hates me so much? And why?"

Douglas took off his spectacles and polished them with his handkerchief. He set them on the table and rubbed the bridge of his nose. "Albert Pringle says you killed his calves and horse. But Sheriff Herman found nothing that pointed your way, especially when he saw you hadn't fired your father's shotgun recently."

"That's right. Now he's filed a complaint that says I poisoned his animals. Why would he think I'd go out of my way to hurt them? Why me?"

"Let's look at something else, shall we?" At her nod, he went on. "How well do you know this Pringle fellow? Did you have words sometime in the past? How about your father? Did they get along?"

"Papa didn't deal with many folks," Angel replied. "And I can't imagine how he would know Mr. Pringle. So all I can think is that he's still sore that I sent him on his way when he came to the ranch with some story about my need for help—his help."

The lawyer's eyebrows shot up, and he put his spectacles back on. "Could it perhaps be a matter of the heart?"

Angel laughed. "Only if his heart is in his wallet. All he wants is my ranch and Rogers Creek."

"So we're back to the drought and his herd."

"I can't think of anything else."

"And you haven't gone into the cattle stalls since you arrived in Rockton?"

"I had no reason to. The gentleman I saw when I came to the auction barn said I should keep my flock in that little pen a ways out back. I never went in the barn again until the sale."

Douglas took a few more notes on his notebook, then closed it and stood. "It's clear you're innocent, and I'm fairly certain I can show the judge how silly Pringle's accusation is."

"Fairly . . ." Angel said. "Now that's a good word. I just pray that's how I'm judged."

"We will all pray. You're not alone, and we've lifted you up to the Father regularly."

Angel shook his hand. "It's His mercy I'm counting on," she said. "It's the best I can hope for."

"Let's hope it's not the least you receive." He put on his hat and rattled the bars to Angel's cell. "We'll need His wisdom and His justice to prevail."

The auction barn was the only structure in Rockton large enough to hold the crowd that came to Angel's trial two days later. To sit before the curious eyes was bad enough, but when Pringle swore on a leather-bound black Bible to tell the truth, Angel felt more alone, more abandoned than she ever had. She hadn't felt so bad even after Papa died.

From then on, matters worsened. Pringle played on the onlookers' sympathy.

He waved the scrap of fabric the judge gave him. "I tell you, there ain't nothing more to see than her tore-up shirt and this here piece what was stuck in my steer's stall."

"Mr. Pringle, that wasn't the question," Judge Gordon said. "I asked if you know for a fact that this is the piece of cloth that was in your animal's stall."

"'S what I said, ain't it?"

The judge stared at the balding rancher. "Did you *see* this in the stall?"

The judge's question caught the smirking Pringle off guard. "Ah . . . er . . . sure. That's where the sheriff found it."

The questioning then went to the sheriff, who described how he found the piece of plaid fabric.

Then the judge asked about Angel's shirt. "It was where?"

"I don't know precisely where it was," the sheriff said. "I sent Miss Moore up to Miss Rogers's room—on account of their both being ladies, you see."

"You may take your seat again, Mr. Dowd." The judge scanned the audience. "Miss Patience Moore, please."

The owner of the rooming house stepped forward, took her oath on the Bible, and then faced the same questions as those who'd come before her.

The judge passed the garment in question to Miss Moore. "Please tell us where you found this."

"I went to the room, sir, and saw Miss Rogers's things all neat in the bureau. It didn't take but a minute to see that nothing like the rag Sheriff Dowd showed me was in the drawers. So I had to go into her valise—it didn't feel right to do all this to someone else's belongings, you know."

"I understand, madam," the judge said. "But we must know precisely where you found the evidence and in what condition."

"Oh, dear me! It was dreadfully torn, just like this—" she shook the red and black cotton, and a gasp arose from the audience—"not at all like the rest of Miss Rogers's things."

"Where did you say you found it?" the judge asked one more time.

"In Miss Rogers's valise, but I don't think she's the sort who'd pack something like this to travel. True, her manner of dress is . . ." She darted a look at Angel, and an apologetic expression spread on her plain face. "She dresses in an odd manner for a lady, but her things are in good repair. Not like this at all."

"So it was torn and in Miss Rogers's valise."

"Yes, but—"

"Thank you, Miss Moore." The judge turned to Douglas. "I yield to you."

Douglas called Pringle, and Angel's knotted stomach eased a fraction. When her advocate pinned her accuser with regard to the finding of the evidence, she began to relax.

"Well, I wasn't right there over the sheriff when he did find the cloth," Pringle answered, his demeanor defensive and argumentative. "But I know he found it in my steer's stall on account of I was there."

"Did you, Mr. Pringle, see the evidence in the stall when you first found the dead animal?"

"What do you mean?"

"Did you see the fabric in the stall when you first found the dead steer?"

Out came Pringle's chin. "Who'd look to see if he could find some piece of rag when someone's done gone and kilt his steer?"

"Again, sir. Did you see the red and black fabric in the stall when you first found the dead steer?"

The rancher pursed his lips, his chin still out. "What are you trying to do here? I tell you, the sheriff found the fabric there, and it's from Old Man Rogers's kid's shirt."

"Did you see it or not?"

Pringle huffed and waved his arms. "No, all right? I didn't see nothing but my dead steer. I felt like a pile of cash just up and burnt on me. No one in his right mind would be looking for some piece of rag or nothing. That's for the law to do. And it did."

"So you didn't see it when you first arrived." Douglas took off his spectacles, nibbled on one of the wire stems, and then used it to point at the rancher. "Could it be possible—now, I'm not saying this is what happened here—but could someone with a grudge against Miss Rogers have put it in the stall while you went to find the sheriff?"

A gasp ricocheted around the barn. Pringle blanched. Angel took her first deep breath since her arrest.

"Ah . . ." Pringle studied his dusty boots. He looked up at the rafters overhead. He glanced at various members of the audience and finally swallowed hard. "I reckon someone coulda put it in there, but who'd bother? There's lots of folks in there, and someone would've seen someone messing with my stock. No one's fool enough to risk that."

A couple of yeses rang out, and Angel counted more than a few nods. Her stomach cramped again, and her breathing stuck on a boulderlike knot in her chest.

From that moment on, no amount of logic brought Pringle around. He refused to budge. It was Angel's shirt, found in his stall, and so she was the one.

When the judge looked ready to doze off over the same questions Douglas had asked a dozen times or more, he gave a sharp nod and picked up his gavel. He rapped the thing hard against the podium from which the auctioneer had called out bids, and Angel stiffened with fear.

"I believe our jury has heard enough. I'll now turn the matter over to them and wait for their verdict. We can adjourn until they let me know they've reached it."

Angel's heart pounded the seconds until she'd learn her fate.

๖

"Before we proceed any further," Judge Gordon said, "I must commend the folks of Rockton. I have presided over many such cases, and I've rarely witnessed a more proper trial. Everyone listened to the evidence and the questioning with interest and respect. And now I request a bit more of your forbearance. We'll soon know the verdict."

Angel found it hard to breathe. During the recess she'd knelt and cried out to God, tears on her cheeks. It wasn't that she didn't trust the Lord, she just didn't trust the crowd . . . or the jurors.

One of the jurors stood, his white beard quivered, and his bushy brows met over his nose. "We didn't take too long to see what was before our noses," he said. "We found her guilty of shooting Albert's calves and horse, and guilty of poisoning his steer."

Angel's head swam and she fought for air. This couldn't be happening. It just couldn't.

"And her sentence . . . ?" the judge asked.

"We hang rustlers, your honor."

Deadly silence filled the barn. Desperation filled Angel. Objections rose to her lips, but she fought them, certain they would only do her more harm. *Lord God, where are you?*

She heard voices to one side, triumph threaded through them.

Then the audience parted. "That's crazy!" a man cried.

Jabbing his elbows out on either side, Jeremy broke through.

"He said he didn't see that rag when he found his steer. Didn't any of you hear him?"

"Order," the judge said with a bang of his gavel. "Order in this court!"

Douglas ran to Jeremy, and they exchanged whispers. Then Douglas stepped toward the judge. "Your Honor," he said. "I wish to appeal the verdict."

"Very well, you may do so in the proper fashion, but right now I must conclude these proceedings. One cannot object to the trial itself. There was no madness about it, no brashness, no lack of representation for the accused. The jury of her peers has spoken."

He rapped the gavel again. "Angela Rogers, you are found guilty of cattle rustling and killing—as charged. You have been deemed a danger to the community and shall hang for your offenses. Court is adjourned."

The last thing Angel heard was the crack of wood against wood.

She went numb.

A vise crushed her chest.

The barn and the crowd spun to black.

When Angel fell, Jeremy rushed to her side, but Sheriff Dowd blocked his way. "My deputy will see to her, son. She's a prisoner."

Jeremy fought the urge to retch. "How can they do this?"

Douglas, lips tight and white around the edge, led him away. "Man's cruelty has no limit," the lawyer said. "I can't let this stand."

Over his shoulder, Jeremy saw the sheriff's deputy carry Angel out in his arms. His heart tightened again. The fellow looked gentle enough, and the look of pity on his broad face gave Jeremy enough peace to stay put and gather his wits.

"Oh, I do declare," he heard Dahlia say at his side. "It's my dear Mr. Jeremy Johnstone as I live and breathe."

The banker's daughter, a vision in a yellow and white dress with bits of black tossed in as well, sidled up to him. He should have been pleased that she'd come to him, but the memory of Angel on the dirt floor of the barn left no room in his thoughts for Dahlia.

"Morning," he answered.

She took the brief greeting as an invitation. "Why, I was just telling my daddy that I hadn't seen you since way back at that church social all that time ago. It's a pure delight to see you, sugar."

His memory of the church social couldn't have a thing in common with hers. And a delight to see her?

Jeremy looked the spoiled young woman over from head to toe. "You look right nice, Miss Sutton—"

"Now, sugar," she cut in, "we agreed a while back that you'd call me Dahlia. I'd be tickled if you would, you know."

He caught Douglas's amused look out of the corner of his eye. This was no time for humor. Angel had swooned, these madmen had her locked up in a cell, and Dahlia had a death grip on his arm.

A glare didn't faze the lawyer.

"Miss Dahlia," Jeremy said, "I'm afraid you've caught me at a right bad spot. I've a duty to see after Miss Rogers. I'm sure you'll agree this whole fool thing needs to be put to rights—and straightaway."

"Fool thing?" she asked, her fan fluttery as always. "Why, that dreadful Angel Rogers is just where a thief should be. I'll have you know, I never did stand for that nonsense of wearing men's clothes and acting like a man. She's just not one of us, now, is she?"

Bile burned in Jeremy's throat. "I reckon what's on the outside's not what matters most. It's a person's heart the Lord looks at."

"Oh, that's just church stuff," she said with a superior smile. "What counts is whether a lady's a lady. Or not."

"And what would you say makes a lady a lady, Miss Dahlia?" he asked through clenched jaws. He watched Marcus Sutton come their way.

"Hello, there, Johnstone," the banker said. "And Dahlia—quite a surprise to find you here. An auction barn isn't the kind of place that usually catches your fancy."

With her right hand, Dahlia flicked her luxurious black curls over her shoulder. "I wouldn't have missed watching justice, Papa. I do declare, it's plumb scandalous what some people do to get their way."

"I'd say you need to find your mama and leave serious matters to us men. No need to trouble yourself, you know."

She pouted. "Oh, all right, Papa. I'll go back to the hotel." She turned to Jeremy. "Now don't keep making yourself so scarce, sugar."

He nodded, his gaze on Douglas, who'd worn a questioning look from the moment Marcus Sutton arrived.

"Mr. Sutton," Jeremy said. He still remembered how the banker had insulted Angel. "Were you looking for me?"

The banker stared, and Jeremy wondered if the man had decided to measure him for a suit—he couldn't have missed the slightest point. Sutton nodded and said, "I've a proposition for you—"

"Marcus!" a man called.

Jeremy looked in the direction of the call and saw Pastor Bloom avoid a particularly large piece of "evidence" left by a steer. Jeremy couldn't stop the smile.

"Reverend," the banker said. "A pleasure to have you join us."

"Us?" Jeremy asked, suspicious.

Sutton nodded. "As I began to say, I have a proposition for you. One that I think will solve your money problems and provide a tidy profit for me—and the pastor here, too."

The pastor involved in a business venture? Jeremy had known

Pastor Stone for years, and the good man had been careful with his pennies, but he'd never given the impression that he thought of much beyond his flock's well-being.

Douglas's discreet cough reminded him that the lawyer still stood not ten feet away, his ear cocked in their direction. When Jeremy opened his mouth to invite him over, the attorney shook his head and gestured for Jeremy to continue his conversation with the men.

"So," he said, "what kind of proposition is it, Mr. Sutton?"

With a broad smile, Sutton dropped a heavy arm onto Jeremy's shoulders. "Have you heard of the railroad's plans for a new line to join our spur to Hartville?"

"Can't say as I have. I don't reckon it has anything to do with me."

"That's not so," Sutton said, his face growing more animated by the moment. "Now that the Rogers girl is behind bars and headed for the noose, you ought to be able to buy that land—and at a good price."

Jeremy recoiled as though the man had slapped him across the face. "I don't intend to let a woman hang without objection."

Sutton pursed his lips and shook his head. "Don't waste your time on her kind. Justice was served."

The pastor cleared his throat. "I daresay the Lord's rejoicing that a sinner has again faced the consequences of her sin—or is about to. Outright rebellion against God's decrees leads to crime. An unnatural woman runs against all the Lord's design for women, the gentler ones, as you surely know."

Jeremy prayed for patience. "What is this proposition of yours?"

His abrupt question made Sutton narrow his eyes. The banker looked at the pastor, and both shrugged. "It's about selling the land to the railroad. They'll pay well, and you'll have the money you need for your stock. I hear say you didn't sell as well as you'd hoped."

"Nobody did. But I've enough to make it through the winter."

"It'd be so much better if you had a tidy sum to fall back on."

"Kept at your bank, I reckon."

"Safest place in town."

"Just how do you figure I'm going to get that land? Angel won't sell."

"She's going to hang," the pastor said, and Jeremy detected a hint of relish in his voice. "Surely, you can find a way to talk sense to her now."

"She's innocent," Jeremy said. "And I mean to help her prove it. It's plain wrong for someone to hang for something they didn't do."

"Do I detect . . . affection for that creature?" the banker asked. "Here I thought . . . I mean, Dahlia led me to believe you were interested in courting her."

Jeremy couldn't believe what he'd just heard. Hadn't this same man warned him against courting his daughter not so long ago? "I thought you didn't think I was good enough for Miss Dahlia."

"I never said such a thing," Sutton said with much bluster. "And besides, you've proved yourself an able rancher. Then, too, my little girl seems to have her heart set on you."

Jeremy hooked his thumbs in his belt loops. "You mean to say I can court Miss Dahlia *and* take part in your scheme—business deal?"

Sutton smiled. "Sounds about right to me."

"I do think I hear the silver ring of wedding bells," the pastor said.

Jeremy's stomach tightened. Here was what he'd wanted not so long ago. But at what cost did it come? Was the promise of money to ensure his ranch's future worth leaving Angel to her unfair fate? And what was fair for him? He had worked awfully hard for an awfully long time.

"I'll have to think on that," he said. Was he really about to make his dreams come true?

"Don't take too long, now," the banker warned. "They'll be hanging the Rogers girl any day now. The judge won't be in town for long, and I'm sure he'll want to see justice served."

Half of him wanted to give in to the budding excitement in his gut; the other half couldn't forget Angel, bloodied and beaten, crumpled on the dirt floor of the barn, warm and sweet in his arms, her lips pink from his kiss.

"I won't take long." He held out a hand and shook with the banker and the pastor. As he went to the door, he remembered Douglas.

He turned, and the lawyer's look of disgust brought him up short. He went to speak, but Douglas turned and left without a word.

Something inside him began to itch. Jeremy feared it was his conscience. This wasn't the time for it to make its presence known. He had a decision to make. One that would determine the rest of his life.

It could determine Angel's, too, an irksome voice said. *She needs help more than you need what Sutton offered.*

His cheeks heated, but he wasn't about to let his opportunity slip by. Jeremy shoved thoughts of Angel to the very back of his mind. He had his future to consider. And he wasn't about to sacrifice it for the sake of a crazy, redheaded, ornery mountain woman who didn't mean a thing to him.

He'd done his duty by her.

He didn't owe Angel Rogers one blasted thing.

What about the Lord? the voice asked. *What do you owe the One who died for you?*

ༀ

Jeremy wiped up the last streak of gravy from his plate with a scrap of tender biscuit. He'd enjoyed every bite. The steak, for a change, had been better than leather, the vegetables were fresh, and the hotel dining room's cook sure knew how to bake biscuits to suit a man.

The fleeting memory of a meal with Angel and Sunny, and the biscuits they'd shared, made him force his thoughts from the past to his future—his bright, hope-filled future.

His ranch secure. A lovely lady at his side—even if Dahlia was a mite spoiled.

Images of what might be overtook the images of Angel, and Jeremy didn't realize he was no longer alone until Eric called his name from across the table.

Jeremy blinked. "Sorry. I've a lot on my mind."

"So I hear," the newspaperman said, his expression blank. "And I've come to serve you another dish of food for thought."

"Oh?"

"Douglas had no success with the judge. Gordon doesn't want to put off the hanging, since he's due back in Denver for a big case. They've scheduled that travesty for tomorrow morning."

"Tomorrow!" Jeremy's dinner no longer seemed as good.

"Yes, and if you meant what you said earlier, then you must help us stop this madness before it goes any farther. Before they kill an innocent woman."

"What can I do?"

"Douglas has looked into the law, and there's a provision that might interest you. It seems you could save Angel's life."

"What do I have to do?"

"You can assume her debts, pay them off . . . once you become her husband."

Jeremy surged to his feet. "Have you lost your wits? Me marry Angel Rogers? Why does everyone think that's the solution to all what ails around here?"

"It's the best we have."

"I'll tell you now what I've said before. I do not intend to marry Angel Rogers. I'm practically betrothed to Dahlia Sutton."

Eric also stood. "I thought you were a man of more substance than that. And one who would stand up for what's right. It seems I was wrong."

224

Jeremy stared back into Eric's piercing brown eyes.

Eric went on. "I'd urge you to spend time on your knees. If you can face the Lord after these madmen kill Angel when you know you could have saved her, then do what you will."

"I know my mind," Jeremy said. "I don't need anyone to tell me what they reckon I should do."

"You don't. But you claim to serve a just and righteous God. Listen to Him before Angel's blood is on your hands."

Eric spun on his heel and left. Jeremy watched him go.

He knew what he wanted. Didn't he?

He wanted his ranch, a proper wife, a family, a place in Hartville's life.

A soul-deep sigh escaped him. Was that what God wanted? And could he turn his back on the Lord?

Eric was right on one account. Jeremy had hours ahead of him on his knees before the Almighty. He just didn't want to go through what would likely be a night in cleansing fire. He didn't know what he'd learn through that private trial.

He also knew that God wouldn't give up. The God of Abraham and Jacob and Joseph would pursue him until he met Him face-to-face. On his knees. Stripped bare of all pretenses, wants, and claims.

He had to face his Savior, the One who hung on the Cross for his sake. And Jeremy feared the Father wanted him to surrender his life to save one of His own.

He feared the Father wanted his dreams to die so that Angel might live.

17

Angel didn't sleep all night. The narrow cot and dingy blanket didn't offer rest, and that was before she took into account the turmoil in her heart. Her jailer had balked when she asked for a Bible, but to her relief, when Douglas came by he'd agreed to fetch one for her.

Alone with the Lord and His Word, she'd prayed and sought comfort—comfort that didn't come—but she did achieve a measure of peace. If this was the Father's will, then she would accept it. Even if she didn't believe He'd let such abuses of justice stand.

Still, she knew He awaited her, as did Mama and Papa. She'd say her farewells to those who'd been so kind to her: Letty, Eric, and their children; Douglas and Randy and their sweet little girl, Emma Letitia; Adrian and Phoebe; Mrs. Stone; dear Wynema; and of course, Jeremy.

Although at first she'd thought him arrogant and rude, his actions after her attack had proven him a kind and generous man. He'd helped when others resented her, when perhaps in private they cheered on the man who'd tried to kill her.

And then his kisses . . .

Angel still didn't know quite what to make of them. They revealed an attraction and surely some kind of affection for her.

And she had to confess that over time she'd come to appreciate Jeremy as a man, a decent, hardworking, godly man. Handsome, too.

His caresses had thrilled her to the core of her feminine heart.

Regret for what might have been now filled her. She'd never know the joy of falling in love, perhaps with Jeremy. And children? It hurt too much to think she would miss that joy.

Oh, how she wished she didn't have to miss any of it. She wished she could look forward to the day when she and . . . Jeremy—there, she'd said it—pledged themselves to one another. To know the blessed joy of a family, to watch babies grow into decent, God-honoring men and women. To have grandchildren, even.

That hurt the most. Not the actual death at the hands of a foolish, blind crowd. Death simply meant she'd see Jesus face-to-face a lot sooner than she'd expected. Not knowing the life the Lord had planned for her—that hurt.

Tears poured down her cheeks. "Where are you, Father?" she asked in a whisper. "I need to see you, to feel you with me when I go through this final trial. I need your comfort, this final gift of your mercy and goodness."

Keys rattled nearby. *Dear God, has the time come?*

Angel wiped her face and smoothed her hair. She tucked her shirt into the waist of her trousers. She set her features in a neutral expression, faced forward, and prayed she'd be ready for whatever came next.

"Jeremy!"

The blond cowboy passed in front of the sheriff's deputy, who said, "You only have thirty minutes with the prisoner, you hear?"

"Loud and clear," Jeremy answered, his voice raw and hoarse.

Jeremy looked dreadful. His tanned skin had an off tint to it; dark smudges circled his reddened eyes; his handsome features were now drawn with tight, tense lines. He looked haggard. She'd never seen him this way.

"What's wrong?" she asked.

"What's wrong?" He waved. "You're here, and you shouldn't be. It's wrong, all of this."

Tears threatened again, but Angel swallowed and blinked hard. "I . . . I'm ready for whatever happens. The Lord will be with me."

Jeremy yanked off his hat and raked a hand through his pale hair. "I . . . you must know how sorry I am about this, sorrier'n I've ever been about anything before—except maybe when that beast killed your sheep and cut you up."

"I know."

He looked her over, winced, then averted his gaze, as though it pained him to see her. Angel covered his hand with hers.

"Don't do this to yourself," she said in an effort to return the comfort his visit had brought her. "The Lord is with me—"

"Don't." He reared back. "Don't say it again. It feels more like He's left you to fend for yourself against a pack of hungry coyotes. I can't stand all this."

Angel wrapped her arms around herself. "Please go home. You have to see to your ranch, and if you wouldn't object, I'd appreciate if you'd look after my sheep once I'm . . . after they—"

"Stop. You don't have to go through with this. There is a way to get you out of this place, out of their grasp."

Her heart gave a little hop. "There is?"

He again raked his hair but refused to meet her gaze. "I'm here to offer you that way out." He shot her a split-second glance, then studied his boots. "I can assume all your debts right off and make restitution. The judge can clear the matter, but you have to . . ."

Turmoil burned in his blue eyes. "We have to marry right away."

Angel gasped. Only moments earlier she'd lamented the missed opportunity with this man. Now he stood before her to extend an offer of marriage. But it came with a price. And for a different reason than the one she'd envisioned.

"Why?" she asked.

His expression turned incredulous. "Why? You have to ask why?" He shook his head in disbelief. "To save you, that's why. I can't let these madmen kill you on account of Pringle's blasted pride and greed. I'd be as guilty as them if I stood by and did nothing to stop this stupid, wrongheaded craziness that's taken over everybody here."

"I see . . ." She bit her lower lip. "It's all about duty, I reckon."

"Yes . . . well, no. Not just duty." Confusion seemed to derail his thoughts. "It's what's right that counts. Before the Lord, I mean. It's wrong for them to take your land, and much worse for them to take your life."

"Ah . . . so it's about the ranch."

That brought him up short. "I never gave the ranch a thought. Not yesterday or today. But it does strike me as even more wrong for them to cut it up among themselves and profit after they do away with you."

Angel turned away, not ready to have him see her pain. She hadn't expected to hurt so much when she'd asked about his reason for the proposal. A part of her had hoped he'd offered on account of those kisses they'd shared, because he cared for her. But no. It was all about her land.

"Thank you, Jeremy, but no."

"No?"

"I can't marry you for the sake of a plot of land. That's not what God intended for marriage. And even though I never planned to wed, now that you've offered, I realize that I can't do it this way. I'd rather go home to the Father than make a mockery of what He designed."

"You can't mean that. You must be mad!"

She gave him a sad smile. "No. I think I'm the most lucid and sane I've ever been."

He sputtered, muttered bits and pieces she didn't catch, frowned, glared.

"Go home," she said gently. "And thank you for your dutiful effort. I reckon the Lord knows your heart is in the right place. Thank you very much for all you've done for me."

He spun away with a last angry look. He banged on the door with a fist, and she heard him mutter again. When the deputy had let him out, she went to the cot, fell face first on its unyielding surface, and let the tears fall. Hard sobs wracked her.

Bitterness began its slow burn. "Why?" she cried. "Why now, Lord? And why like this?"

Why had she been given a glimpse of what could have been at the last moment of life? This last temptation had come with a cruel twist.

Should she marry Jeremy to save herself and yet lose her land? It would be his after they married, as the law decreed. Should she marry Jeremy even if his feelings didn't match the ones she'd finally acknowledged? Should she give up on Papa's dream? Her dream? And for what? To achieve a mockery of her own deep and secret desires?

She could never sell herself to a man. And that's what wedding Jeremy would be. Angel was no prostitute. She'd walk to the gallows later today, head held high.

❦

Hours later, Angel suffered the humiliation of shackles on her wrists. But she didn't complain. She only allowed herself to think of the God of her childhood, the one who'd loved her and always stayed by her side, not this one who left her at the mercy of men.

She prayed to that God, thought of meeting Mama and Papa again soon, wondered if she'd meet Maggie in heaven.

"It's time to head on out, Miss Rogers," Sheriff Dowd said, pity in his voice.

His pity made her stand tall, call on all the dignity she could muster. "I'm ready, sir."

He took her upper arm, his touch gentle, much more so than it had been since he'd arrested her the other night. It seemed he wasn't without compassion after all. She wondered where that virtue had gone during the mockery of a trial, if it had abandoned all those present.

Angel walked out onto the boardwalk, where the crowd's jeers greeted her. She stumbled, and the mob cheered.

A deep breath gave her the courage to straighten her spine and square her shoulders. She looked neither to the right nor to the left but thought only of Jesus on His way to Calvary and the Cross.

He'd suffered much worse than she would, and He'd done so of His own choice. For her sake and that of all those who surrounded her.

She could do this.

At the end of Silver Lode Street, Rockton's main road, the sheriff helped her make the turn. They went to the right, onto cleared, if straggly, ground, toward a tall cottonwood about a hundred yards away. Angel saw a table under it and the rope that swung from a thick, sturdy branch.

Her stomach sank.

Fear gripped her.

The urge to break from the sheriff, to run, to escape from what now was too real to bear, overtook her. Perspiration soaked her clothes. She went cold as ice. Thoughts tumbled through her head, making it impossible to follow any to its end.

The sheriff made certain she walked in a straight line. Her body shook, and she knew he felt it, but she couldn't bear to see more pity in his eyes. She stared at the noose and thought of God and God alone.

231

Angel prayed for strength enough to walk those final steps, and she received it. When they reached the table, the sheriff asked her to stay right there. A wild, panicky moment made her dart looks in all directions. She found no escape; there was nowhere to turn.

The mob that had followed them from the jail surrounded the makeshift gallows, making escape impossible. The number of ladies who'd turned out shocked Angel; their faces wore the look of avid curiosity. None looked familiar or friendly or the least bit saddened.

"Miss Rogers," the judge said.

She faced him.

"Since your own pastor is in Rockton and has agreed to serve you at this time, I'll leave you to a private moment with him."

Pastor Bloom stepped up to her, his thin face lugubrious but his eyes bright with some emotion Angel couldn't identify.

"Are you ready to confess and repent of all your sins? Your disobedience, your rebellious nature, your disdain for what God called you to as a Christian woman?" He glared at her. "Do you confess and repent of your thieving ways?"

Angel's shoulders slumped, and she lowered her head. "I have nothing to confess. I didn't steal or kill those animals. Scripture doesn't say what clothes I should wear, only that I dress modestly, and I reckon everything is covered."

"Unrepentant to the end," he said to the sheriff.

From a corner of her heart, Angel dragged a final bit of strength. "I do confess my love for Christ, my Savior and my Lord."

The crowd gasped.

The sheriff took her elbow to help her onto the tabletop.

"Stop!"

Everyone turned, even Angel. Jeremy plowed through the audience, his hand tight on the wrist of a small, rotund man in long black robes.

"Counselor Carlson told me some law somewhere says a man

can take on the debts of his lawful wedded wife and pay back what's owed to spare her. I'm here on account of I want to do just that."

The gasps sounded more like a windstorm on its way down the hills. The onlookers whispered among themselves, and the sheriff turned to the judge.

"Is that so?" he asked.

The judge scratched his head and nodded. "There is such a law, but I've never had to deal with it."

"There's always a first time," Jeremy said. He propelled the priest to the front. "I reckon I know well enough how Pastor Bloom feels about Miss Rogers, so I went ahead and fetched us Father Pedro, who'll do the marrying, all legal and all that. He's the only ordained minister in this town."

Jeremy looked to Angel, his blue eyes pleading for her consent. She met his gaze without clear thought. She glanced at the noose as it swung from the fat branch where it had been placed, the slipknot her fate.

Unless she accepted Jeremy's proposal.

Dear God, what should I do?

Her panicked prayer didn't bring a heavenly answer, just greater dread of dying like this. She looked at the man who'd offered, in a sense, to give his life, his freedom, that she might live out her days. That was when she knew she wasn't ready to let the mob take her life in payment for someone else's crime.

She didn't think she was ready to marry Jeremy either, certainly not under these circumstances, but at the moment, what other choice did she have?

"Well, Miss Rogers?" the sheriff asked.

Angel gave the noose a final look. She peered at Jeremy and again wished he'd offered marriage in a different way. She didn't want it to happen like this.

She was a woman. And she realized she wanted this man's love, not just his pity or duty-inspired sacrifice.

Tears burned her eyes, the back of her throat. *Dear God, the alternative—*

"Angel, please," a woman said nearby. She saw Letty, Phoebe, Randy, Mrs. Stone.

Letty stepped closer. "Please. Jeremy's a good man. Don't let these people do this. It's wrong, I'd say murder in God's eyes."

Mrs. Stone wrapped an arm around Letty, and Angel saw tears shine on the cheeks of her late pastor's widow. "Angel dear, this isn't the kind of sacrifice the Lord wants. Jeremy will make you a good husband. He's decent, honorable, kind. You'll have a good life together, I'm sure of that."

The visions she'd conjured the night before flew in and out of her thoughts. Almost without conscious effort, she nodded.

"Yes," she said in a faint voice.

"What was that?" the judge asked.

"I said yes, Your Honor. I'll marry Jeremy Johnstone."

A roar rose from the crowd, then settled into a rumble. Jeremy ran to her and stood at her side until the sheriff unlocked the handcuffs. He took her hand, which was numb from the shackles.

"I won't let you down," he said, his icy fingers tight around hers. "I know this is all right strange, but I've prayed and prayed my knees away, and I can't just let you die. I promise, Angel, I won't let anyone hurt you again."

She nodded. She knew he'd do everything possible to keep that promise. What she didn't think he knew was that he was the one most likely to hurt her from that day on.

The ceremony, held under that tree where she was to have died, went by in a blur of Spanish-accented words. Angel stood still and silent; she spoke only after Jeremy's elbow prodded her ribs.

"Say yes," he urged. "You'll be safe."

There were many kinds of safety, as Angel had begun to learn. Still, in this case, she could only see this one way out.

"Yes," she said, her voice barely audible, even to herself.

The priest continued, and moments later he said, ". . . man and wife."

Jeremy squeezed her hand. She felt rather than heard his sigh of relief. If only she could share it with him. She had just entered into a marriage with a man who thought more of her land than of her. A man who had stolen into a corner of her heart without her notice.

Angel wondered how safe her heart would be from this day forth.

She didn't have much time to ponder the matter, since the Wagners, the Gables, the Carlsons, Mrs. Stone, and Wynema soon gathered around them. A tall stranger, lean and possessed of the most piercing, dark eyes, was introduced as Robert Andrews, a friend of Adrian.

It was almost more than Angel could take in, and she stood in a silent daze. Letty came to her side. "I'm so glad you married Jeremy. I know I already said so, but he is a good man. You should have seen how distraught he was these past few days."

Angel bit her bottom lip and looked at Jeremy, her new husband. He stood among the men, listened to them, but maintained a certain reserve—something she'd never noticed before. She supposed he wouldn't relax until they'd resolved the legalities about her ranch.

"I suppose," she said at length. "I want to thank you for your faith in me."

Letty tilted her head in her characteristic way. "I've not a shadow of a doubt about your innocence. It's some folk's wits I question."

Angel shrugged, the daze returning.

"This is a reasonable solution," Letty went on. "Albert Pringle will come out ahead of where he started, since Eric says his herd's in a bad way, but I count it a small price to pay for your life. Besides, you and Jeremy have the rest of your lives to restore what you've paid."

Again Angel withheld comment.

". . . I ask you?" Pastor Bloom said, his voice more than a little strident. "What kind of man marries an unnatural woman? One who does herself up like a man? Wrong! This is all a sinful mockery of God's law."

Angel closed her eyes. She wondered if the nightmare would ever end.

Then she heard another familiar, if unfriendly, voice. "This wasn't in our agreement," Sutton said. "But it's even better, as I see it, Johnstone. Come by my office once the paperwork is done, and we'll have us a better talk."

He slapped Jeremy on the back, and her new husband paled. He shook his head slowly and with what looked like reluctance.

"There won't be any paperwork," he said. "I won't be changing anything. Oliver Rogers left the ranch to Angel, and I mean to see it stays that way."

The banker turned beet red. "You traitor! We took you into our confidence, offered you benefits no one else knew about, and this is how you repay us? You just want to keep it all to yourself, you greedy, good-for-nothing cowpoke. Not to mention, you've now broken my little girl's heart, you sly conniver, you. You've wound up with the woman, the water, and the land. I should never have sent you to woo the Rogers girl."

Angel's stomach, which had begun to settle, lurched again. What had Jeremy done?

She looked at her husband, a question in her eyes. To her horror, he refused to meet her gaze. His cheeks were red, his stance defensive.

She'd been right. This man was the one who would hurt her most from now on. She hadn't known, however, how soon the pain would start or how deep it would cut.

"What . . . ?" Letty asked in a fading voice.

Angel turned to see her friend faint dead away.

Not only had her life turned into a nightmare, painful and

bewildering, but it had also hurt those around her. She knelt to help her friend and prayed for the Lord's forgiveness.

She'd been wrong to act so selfishly. She should never have agreed to marry Jeremy. She should have faced death with courage.

❦

"It ain't right, I tell ya," Pringle said yet again. "Just because that Jeremy Johnstone's made himself a sweet deal with that Rogers girl don't mean she can just escape justice. She was tried fair 'n' square, and she was sentenced to hang. Where's the justice in her walking off on account of that sly fox marrying up with her?"

The supporters around the long counter at the Silver Nickel Saloon murmured in agreement.

"I been wronged," he lamented. "And I deserve to see justice."

Another chorus of yeses rang out.

Pringle shot back another slug of whiskey. "I aim to see that justice is done, too."

"Hear, hear."

"Yessir!"

"That girl can't just get away with killing my stock. Who knows who she'll kill next?"

Pringle grabbed his hat and crammed it on his balding head. "This ain't over. No, sir. That there judge ain't the only one around."

Heavy silence fell on the revelers. A few exchanged uncomfortable looks. A chair squeaked. A soft cough rang out.

"We have us our ways to deal with crooks in these here parts," Pringle added. "You just wait and see."

❦

Eric carried Letty up to Angel's bed at Miss Moore's place. The boarding house was closer than their hotel in the center of town.

Angel pulled back the red, blue, and gold quilt so he could set down his wife.

"I don't know what's come over me these days," Letty, propped on her elbows, said. "I've never been this tired. And here I thought I'd stopped doing quite so much after I came to Rockton a few days ago."

Mrs. Stone bustled in, an indulgent look on her round face. "You just lay yourself back down, young lady. I don't know what you young ones these days are thinking about. And you in particular."

Letty smiled. Angel marveled at how well Mrs. Stone bullied the redoubtable lady doctor into compliance.

"You always tell me I need to rest," Letty said, "but too many folks need me, starting with my children."

Mrs. Stone's nod made her silver topknot bob. "Your children do indeed need you. All of them."

"Of course they do. I don't stint any of them either."

The pastor's widow plumped up a pillow and slipped it on top of the one from which Letty had risen. "Oh my, yes. You have stinted one of them. And your neediest, youngest one, at that."

Letty bolted upright, indignation on her face. "I do not neglect William, Mrs. Stone. How could you say that?"

"Pshaw!" The older woman gave her a dismissive wave. "I don't mean Willy. He's quite well these days." She shook her head. "And you a doctor and all. Take a look at yourself, Letty. When will you diagnose yourself?"

The doctor looked puzzled. "Me? I'm fine. A mite worn out, but healthy as always."

Mrs. Stone smiled in bemusement. "You really haven't noticed, have you?"

Letty tipped up her chin. "Noticed what?"

Only then did it dawn on Angel what Mrs. Stone meant. She smiled with the first bit of joy in what felt like forever. She waited for the pastor's widow to break the news.

Mrs. Stone sat at Letty's side. "Dearest girl, you're carrying the newest member of the Wagner brood."

Eric, who up to now had stood silent and worried at the far corner of the room, rushed to the bed. Fear and joy met on his handsome face. "Letty!"

His wife cocked her head and thought a bit. "No . . ." Then she seemed to count back in her head. Before long, a mellow smile lit her pretty face with a radiance Angel had never seen.

"Do you know?" she said, her voice full of wonder. "I do believe the Lord's now given me every single last desire in my heart."

Tears poured down Angel's face. Could the Lord redeem the mess her life had become? Could He perhaps someday do for her as He had for Letty?

Could He—would He—ever give her the desires of her heart?

18

"Tell me how that's fair," a pugnacious Albert Pringle asked the men who'd met under cover of darkness. "She ain't being punished for what all she done to me, but then that there marriage of hers and Johnstone's keeps the land and the water in her hands."

A stocky man stepped up. "She has her a husband now. Man'll see things different-like. Things might could change."

Pringle shook his head. "I heard him say he'd have that Carlson fella make sure it's all legal-like for her to keep her pa's land after all."

"That ain't right," said a man to Pringle's right.

A man moved forward. "Sure ain't, and I betcha she don't let no one near her water ever, no matter what. All for them lousy sheep."

"They sure do ruin all they touch," a lean cowboy said.

A grizzled rancher cursed, then added, "Eat right down to the root, they do. Leave nothing for decent cattle."

"Told you it weren't right," Pringle crowed. "Women ain't made to run a ranch, and not no sheep ranch. She ain't one of us neither. Someone more friendly-like is what all we need."

The stocky man spat away from his cronies. "She's a strange

one all right. Can't even be sure she's a woman, way she dresses in trousers and such. Wouldn't want one of them oddities in my bed."

"Who says Johnstone's gonna bed her?" the lean cowboy asked. "All's he wants is her land for his herd. He don't have to do nothing more for it."

Obscenities burst from more than one mouth.

"Justice is all's I want," Pringle hissed. "Can't have some stranger—she don't come to town much like regular folks or behave normal—make a circus of our courts. There's more'n one way to get justice, you know."

"Sure is."

"Indeedy so."

"Count me in."

The fellow across from Pringle cleared his throat. "Is it time for our friend 'Judge Lynch' to do his job?"

"Looks that way," Pringle said with satisfaction.

A white-haired cowpoke added, "This here 'Judge Lynch' works quicker and cheaper than them what run them fool courts."

One who'd been quiet then shook his head. "Don't see no other way to clean up our town of that unnatural woman. Don't want her turning others like her."

Pringle spouted again. "I tell you, it's all about justice and serving it up."

"Jury found her guilty, fair and square. Sentenced her to hang."

"She's getting away with—"

"No she ain't!"

"Not as I live and breathe."

"It's what's best for our town."

A well-dressed gent with a powerful, dignified demeanor approached Pringle. "Are we all agreed then?"

"Oh yes."

"Can't let this mess stand."

"It's near to midnight."

"Let's go—and quiet, now!"

A few men traded pats on the shoulder, while others exchanged determined nods. The group melted into the night, crept through barely moonlit alleys, their faces now covered with dark masks. Someone produced a rope. Another gathered a hefty piece of lumber along the way.

The mob paused outside Miss Moore's rooming house. "Once we get her outta the picture," one said, "we'll bargain better with her sad and lonely widower."

Another tittered.

"Yeah," Pringle offered. "I reckon he'll be right reasonable about that water, him being a rancher hisself."

A third fellow snorted. "Won't hurt none that he'll know 'Judge Lynch' took care of his thieving wife."

"Hush!"

"Ready?"

"Let's go!"

☙

Loud banging roused Angel from her broken sleep. Fear shot through her when she heard muffled oaths. Now she wished she hadn't sent Jeremy away. She'd figured it more appropriate for them to keep to their separate arrangements. They weren't truly married, not by her reckoning—and more than likely, not by the Lord's either.

Still . . .

Wood splintered. Her heart pounded and her breath hitched. "Dear God, please be near me."

She tossed off the sheet and went to the window. The sight below redoubled her alarm. Men in dark clothes milled together just beyond the house's front porch. Their masked faces troubled her most.

Another loud crash made the house shake.

Miss Moore cried out, "Who are you? What do you want?"

She got no response, but a third battering made the loudest noise yet—the whine of yielding metal followed by that of breaking wood.

Someone thumped up the stairs. Angel darted another look out the window. Men trooped onto the porch. The footsteps inside the house drew nearer.

Perspiration drenched her nightgown. Someone beat on her door. She again glanced outside to measure the distance from the porch roof to the ground below.

A second blow shook her door. The wood creaked; metal hinges groaned. She reached for the window latch, scrabbled to undo it, fingers clumsy with fear.

Finally she pushed up the plate of glass, but behind her the door gave way. Angel hitched up handfuls of nightgown and slid a leg over the windowsill, but as she bent to slip out, arms caught her around the waist.

"Ain't no running from justice," her foul-smelling captor said.

He dragged her backward. Angel fought. Her fear grew. She lost control of her muscles, her body. The disgrace of wetting herself made her cry for mercy.

Everything blurred. Bile scoured her throat. She retched but fought against the vomit. She wouldn't give these beasts the pleasure.

Rope burned her bare forearms.

Dear God, have mercy on me!

She didn't see who took the swing, but his fist mashed into her gut. Breath left her. Sparks burst before her eyes. Pain swelled.

Brutal words struck her.

Another blow landed, this one on her head.

Angel groaned.

A slap split her lip. "You don't get to whine, you thieving, unnatural mountain woman. You ain't one of us, won't never be, all strange and different."

They threw her down. One yanked her arm. Another grabbed the other arm. They dragged her. She bounced over the roadway. She felt death nearby.

"Father," she whispered through swollen lips. "Forgive me everything . . . I love you, Lord . . ."

They shook her arms. A moan broke through.

"Shut up!"

She bit her lip . . . felt every rock, every blow . . . couldn't stop the tears.

At last the men stopped. Angel opened one eye. It hurt. She saw what she most feared.

The rope they'd meant for her all along swung from the same cottonwood tree. The table again stood in its place. This time there'd be no salvation—at least none on this earth.

"Up with you." They threw her onto the tabletop. One climbed with her and made the table shake. He yanked her to her feet, grabbed a braid, pulled her head up, and slipped the noose over her head.

Hemp scratched her cheeks and her jaw, then circled her neck.

"Get ready to meet your maker, thief!"

In the depths of her faith, Angel found the strength to say, "Father . . . God . . . I'm yours . . ."

❦

Wynema barged into the Excelsior Hotel's dining room. She glanced to the left, then to the right. At first, she saw no familiar faces. Finally, toward the back of the large room, she spotted someone she knew. Not well, true, but she had met Robert Andrews, Adrian's Pinkerton friend, before.

She smacked her palm flat on his table. "I need your help."

He caught his teetering water glass. "Do I know you?"

Wynema blew a hair off her forehead. "I'm a friend of Phoebe Gable."

His puzzled brown eyes took her measure. Then he said, "Ah . . . the photographer, right?"

"Yes, but that doesn't matter. What does matter is that something horrid's about to happen. I need help to stop it."

He didn't grasp her urgency.

"I mean it," she said, her voice full of fright. "I thought it was all about the creek, and it was, but there's more to this than anyone—or most anyone—knows."

"The creek?"

"Rogers Creek."

He frowned.

"You know, Angel's ranch has a good creek, and with this dreadful drought, more than a few ranchers have been after her to sell."

He pushed back his chair—too slowly for Wynema's comfort.

"Can't you move any faster? At this rate, she'll be dead."

"Dead?"

Wynema looked over her shoulder. "Look, this isn't the place to discuss this. Please, *please* come outside with me. We must stop the madness."

Her plea must have made an impression, because he clapped on his hat and took long, brisk steps toward the door. Wynema almost ran to keep up with him.

"Thank you, Father," she whispered as they stepped onto the boardwalk.

"We're outside now," he said. "What's this about?"

"We don't have much time. We have to stop a murder first. I'll tell you everything afterward."

He stopped. "Do you mean what I'm afraid you do?"

Wynema tugged on his coat sleeve. "Keep moving or we'll see the worst men can do. Yes, I mean just what you fear I do. And you and I might even be too late already—"

"Wynema!" Eric called out. "What are you doing to that poor fellow?"

"Thank you, Lord Jesus, and send us more help," she cried. "Oh, Mr. Wagner, you must come with us. This town's gone mad. They're out to kill her."

"Good heavens!" the newspaperman said. "Where . . . ?"

"Back by the tree. We must hurry—"

"Go fetch Jeremy Johnstone, Adrian Gable, anyone you find. Just go!"

"He's there, Papa," a boy said. "Or almost there. I got Mr. Johnstone, I told him to go. But you gotta hurry to the tree like Miss Wynema says. They hurt Miss Angel awful bad already, but that ain't—*isn't*—what all they want to do to her. They want to . . . to . . . you know." He pulled an imaginary rope over his head.

The Pinkerton nodded, then loped off toward the accursed tree. Eric glared at his oldest son. "And what are you doing out at this hour of the night, Steven?"

The boy stubbed his toe against the road, his cheeks red in the moonlight. "I . . . ah . . . I heard some things earlier, an' I couldn't sleep. Didn't think anyone'd believe me if'n I said anything 'bout it. But I couldn't let them do it. It's . . . it's a *sin*, Papa! And Miss Angel's not bad."

Wynema shifted her weight from foot to foot. "Look, Mr. Wagner, you can scold him later, but now you need to hurry. He ought to go back to the hotel, go to Letty, go to sleep even."

"Yes, he should," Eric said as he ruffled the boy's hair. "But since he's up, he might as well make himself useful." He dropped down to the boy's level. "Go fetch Mr. Gable and your uncle Douglas. We need them, too."

"Oh, I will, Papa, you can count on me. You can too, you know." The boy tapped a finger to the brim of his cap, turned, and broke into a run.

Eric turned to Wynema. "Thank you. You've done more than most. But this isn't something you should see, especially if we're too late—"

"I'm not leaving her to them." Wynema hitched up her chin and stifled a sob. "If they do their worst, well, then I . . . I need to be there. I can't leave her to them. So don't you waste another minute arguing with me. Go save Angel. Please!"

"I can only pray that we're in time."

ॐ

Jeremy hadn't wanted to accept what the boy told him. He'd run as soon as Steven alerted him. But now, the closer he came, the more he believed. The child was right.

Lynching. A filthy, foul thing.

Rage filled him. How could anyone do that? And to Angel. Who had she hurt? They'd stabbed her and killed her animals practically in her arms. Wasn't that enough?

She'd only cared for the ranch her pa had left her.

He ran as fast as his legs would go, but it wasn't nearly fast enough for him. He cursed himself. He shouldn't have listened to Angel, shouldn't have left her when he knew he ought to stay. He shouldn't want to please her so much; he shouldn't have done what she'd asked.

At the end of Silver Lode Street, he turned toward the tree. Shadowy shapes moved under its limbs. He kept up his pace but kept quiet, too. He couldn't help Angel if the mob turned on him. They weren't right fond of him just then either.

He saw her. He'd been sickened earlier that day, but this went beyond anything he could have imagined. A burly brute held her upright by a thick braid, the hemp rope around her neck.

She was innocent, yet they wanted her to pay for another's crime.

It wouldn't be the first time in history it happened, but it was the first time Jeremy saw it up close. It shouldn't happen, couldn't happen. Wouldn't happen.

He wouldn't let it.

He'd trade places with her—if they'd let him. He'd do anything to keep Angel from suffering any more.

Jeremy's heart pounded. He knew how scared Angel had to be, and that hurt. He walked on, no longer worried whether her executioners heard him or not.

Pringle and the others had called her selfish. They'd lost plenty on account of the drought, but not on account of her.

He'd been the selfish one. He'd wanted his dream ranch, dream life. But it had been just a dream, and he'd gone after it half blind. He'd seen only what he'd wanted to see.

He'd needed water, so he'd decided to buy Angel's, never reckoning on her love for the land her father had left her. When she'd refused to sell, he'd turned his eyes to Dahlia.

He shuddered but didn't slow his steps.

How could he have thought, even for a minute, to hitch himself up to that rude, spoiled child?

Thank you, Father.

He hadn't deserved it, but the Lord had spared him a right miserable life. He now knew that life would be unlivable if he didn't keep those killers out there from working their worst on Angel.

He sneered at his own stupidity. He'd felt so righteous to offer her marriage—the Christian thing to do, he'd thought. Oh, he'd been dutiful, all right. But wrong and sinfully proud. He had a wagonload of sins to confess.

He'd been of two minds, even after they wed. He'd done what he knew to be the right thing, but he'd done it to ease his conscience. And then, worse yet, he'd resented the lost chance at a "good" marriage to Dahlia.

He'd even closed his heart against the feelings that sprang up between him and Angel. Even after those sweet, moving kisses, he'd told himself he was only acting as a godly man, as a good Christian, doing for another as he'd want someone to do for him.

"A man can stay blind only for so long," he muttered. And he wasn't about to any longer.

He braced his feet wide apart and crossed his arms. After a prayer for courage, even a small part of the courage Angel had, he called out. "Do any of you know how Almighty God looks on this?"

Someone yelled, "Go home, Johnstone. You can't just up and stop justice like you tried to before."

"Justice? Murder's what it looks more like."

The mob began to grumble. Out of the corner of his eye, Jeremy saw a man approach the table, his movements quiet so as not to draw attention. Had the Lord sent him help? Jeremy prayed He had.

"This ain't no murder," Pringle objected. "The jury said she oughta hang, and hang she will. We hang thieves here, you know."

"She stole nothing." A hand clasped his shoulder. Jeremy turned for a fight.

"Relax," Eric whispered. "You're not alone, and Douglas and Adrian are on their way, too."

Thank you, Father.

". . . she done stole Pringle's stock," a man said, his voice full of hate. "Then she kilt them. And when that weren't enough for her, she came back and kilt some more. She's gotta pay for that."

"I paid Pringle for his losses," Jeremy countered. "Even though Angel did none of it, nothing at all."

"She really didn't," Wynema called out.

Everyone turned toward the young photographer who, head high and leading with her chin, marched right up to the mob. A look at the tabletop made Jeremy's gut thump down to near his toes.

Angel was gone.

Had she escaped? He chose to take comfort in the empty noose, and he asked the Lord to keep her safe.

". . . I can tell you who did shoot the stock out near Angel's ranch," Wynema said.

"Now, there's another one of them unwomanly women for you," Pringle called out. "Go home, you confused critter. We know who did it." He pointed to the noose. "And it was her—"

Gasps hissed out.

"She's gone!" someone yelled.

"No, I'm not," Angel said. "I didn't hurt Mr. Pringle's stock, and I won't run away either. Someone did it, and I won't rest until that person's caught. I will prove my innocence."

Men hooted. More than one moved toward her. Jeremy ran to his wife before anyone else got close.

"Who do you think did it?" he asked Wynema, who came to Angel's other side.

"I don't think," the photographer said. She waved something pale in the moonlight. "There's only one person in these parts this can belong to, and I figure anyone here will know straight-away who that is."

She walked toward Adrian and handed him her evidence. "Who do you know who buys more mauve thread than anyone else in town?"

"Oh dear!" Phoebe, who ran the mining company's general store for her husband, covered her mouth. At her side, Letty, Randy, and Mrs. Stone all nodded.

"Well, Phoebe?" Wynema asked again. "Tell everyone who stole the stock."

The blond woman shook her head. "I can hardly believe it. That's . . . that scrap of handkerchief belongs to Dahlia Sutton. I can't keep enough of that shade of floss in the store, she goes through so much of it."

The crowd began to whisper. Questions flew. Everyone wanted to know how Wynema had found this bit of cloth, and where.

Before Jeremy could stop her, Angel darted away. He took off after her, while behind them, cries of "Catch her!" and "Don't let them get away!" followed.

Then he saw why she'd run. Ahead of them, a familiar figure sped toward town, but Angel ran faster than the man. She caught up to him as Jeremy reached her.

Sheriff Dowd, on his way out to the hanging tree, blocked the man's way.

"What is the meaning of this?" the lawman asked.

Voices chimed out excuses, explanations, stories, and tales. The only one who kept silent was the man whose mask Angel had ripped off: Marcus Sutton.

Wynema ran up. "It's not at all about the land or the water or even those poor dead animals. It's all about—"

"The train, Papa!" Steven cried from behind the sheriff. "It's all on account of the railroad coming to meet up with our line in Hartville."

"There are plans for new track in these parts?" Eric asked his son. "I haven't heard of it, and I usually hear about these things for the paper."

"I heard them," the boy said. "I did. And they said they'd make sure the line went through their land, on account of the railroad would pay for the land they crossed. They also said it'd be bad if'n you got a whiff of any of it."

Eric rubbed his forehead.

Angel released Sutton's coat sleeve.

The banker harrumphed. "You know your wife's friend has made serious accusations, don't you, Johnstone? And she doesn't know what she's saying."

Jeremy narrowed his eyes. "Same accusations as were made against my wife, I reckon. Someone's done the stealing and killing, and it sure wasn't her."

Steven pointed at the banker. "It was him. Him! Him and some other fellow, a short, stumpy cowboy I seen around town. I promise, Papa, I'm telling the truth. And that pretty Miss Sutton was with them both. I saw them, all three of them. I did. I really, really did."

The sheriff took Sutton's arm. "We'd best head down to my office to sort it all out." He turned to Eric. "Hope you don't mind, Mr. Wagner, but we're going to need your boy."

Eric looked at his wife among the clustered women, and then both he and the doctor nodded.

Jeremy took Angel's hand. "I'll never forgive myself, but I pray someday you'll find it in your heart to forgive me. I shouldn't have left you tonight."

She looked away. "It would have been no better. There were too many of them, and if you'd tried to fight, it could have been worse."

"Still and all, I haven't been much of a husband, even if we only wed less than a day ago."

"I don't reckon we're married at all."

That didn't sit well with him. He ticked off fingers as he spoke. "There was a priest—a man of God. I said I'd honor you, and then you said I do. More than one town's worth of folks witnessed it all. So, by my counting, those four things call it a wedding."

"It's not a wedding when a man weds a woman who's nearly hanging from a tree, especially not on account of a crook telling him to do so."

She finally looked at him, and what her eyes said convicted him more than anything else could have. He had to set things straight—at least, he had to try.

"I didn't marry you on account of Sutton's business dealings."

"Did he tell you to marry me so you could get my land?"

"That's not why I wed you, and you know it."

"Did Mr. Sutton tell you to marry me?"

"That's not how it happened."

"Did he tell you?"

He had to speak the truth. "Yes."

She took her hand away. "Then there's no marriage at all."

"Yes, there is, Angel Rogers—Angel *Johnstone*. And I'll prove it to you one way or the other. Make you believe it, too."

"I'm not for sale, Jeremy Johnstone. Never was, never will be. I'm not some poor soiled dove back on Hartville's East Crawford Street for filthy men to buy for a couple of bucks. And even they, like me, are children of the King of Kings."

He waved in exasperation. "I know that, you stubborn woman. I would love you either way."

"What?" she asked, her cheeks pale against the fresh bruises. "What did you say?"

His cheeks flushed. "I do—love you, that is. Don't rightly know how it happened, but there you have it. You're my wife, and with God's great mercy, I reckon we can make something out of a life together."

She glared. "I pegged you for a fool when you said I ought to sell my ranch because you wanted it and I'm a woman. Now I *know* you're mad. A man wants me hung—a whole mob of them do. There's another one who might be guilty of what folks say I did. On top of that, you went and cooked up a marriage to get hold of my ranch or because you felt you had to save me or for some other such reason. And you still think we can make a life together?"

Jeremy went to speak, but her glare made him stop.

"Don't say a word, Jeremy Johnstone. I don't know how I'll fix this mess you've made of my life, but one way or another, and with God's help and blessing, I reckon I will. I'm no one's bought flesh."

19

Angel dragged herself to Sheriff Dowd's office, her exhaustion almost as powerful as her determination. If she could just withstand a little longer, she would see the ugly matter to its bitter end.

Bodies packed into the plain room, and she had to fight her way inside. But since she was the accused—or had been until Wynema's latest discoveries—she did find her way to where Sutton and the sheriff stood.

Eric asked Steven to tell everything he'd seen and heard. The boy had nothing new to say, but he spoke with clear conviction. No one could doubt his word despite his youth.

Except the banker.

"I deny every one of that upstart's words," Sutton said with disdain. "You can't listen to an urchin who up until a short while ago caused more trouble than he's worth."

Rage burned in Eric's brown eyes.

Sheriff Dowd held up a hand. "Now, Mr. Sutton, it would seem to me that the boy has nothing to gain by lying, while you, sir, have everything to lose if he's not."

The banker's features hardened. "I have nothing further to say. I'll need my attorney, if you please."

Angel heard a disturbance at the door, and she looked. Robert

Andrews led Dahlia through the onlookers, his expression mild and bland—perhaps a mite too much. The foolish girl at his side simpered and preened, unaware of what awaited her.

"How very kind of you, sugar," she said with a pat to his jacketed arm, "to bring me here. I've never in my born days been to this kind of place, and I've been called so's I might clear up this teeny tiny misunderstanding for my dear papa straightaway."

His lack of response led her to bat her long, black lashes. She added, "Now, don't you go running off without me when it's all over, you hear?"

With a flounce of lavender dress, the banker's daughter turned to Sheriff Dowd. "Dear me! What have you done to my poor, poor father?"

The lawman tightened his jaw. "It seems to me, Miss Sutton, that we need to know what your father has done. He stands accused of stealing and killing Mr. Pringle's stock—"

She smiled. "Why, that was Miss Rogers who did that, sugar."

"Her guilt is now in question," Sheriff Dowd said. "New evidence was found that points to Sutton involvement."

The banker's daughter grew petulant. It didn't look good on her. "What new evidence?"

Sheriff Dowd beckoned Wynema. "Show Miss Sutton what you found, if you please."

The photographer thrust the torn handkerchief at Dahlia. The brunette paled. "I don't understand—"

"I think you do," the lawman cut in. "There's a number of good witnesses who can identify this as your handkerchief. Care to know where Miss Howard found it?"

Dahlia began to shiver. Her eyes filled with tears.

Wynema didn't wait for an answer. "It caught on a scrub brush right where Mr. Pringle's cattle were killed on the border of Angel's ranch. No one would ever think Angel owned this stupid handkerchief, especially seeing as you make such a stink about having Phoebe order this color floss for you."

The pampered young woman's lower lip trembled. "I . . . Papa—"

"Don't say a word, you fool!" her father ordered.

His insult cut deep. Dahlia squared her shoulders, and in a stronger voice than Angel had heard her use, she said, "Miss Howard's right. Papa had a man kill Mr. Pringle's stock."

In the uproar that followed, Dahlia spared a look at Angel. "And that's who . . . who stabbed Miss Rogers, too."

Angel gasped. She looked at the banker, who retained his unrepentant front. She shook her head. "Why? What did I do to them?"

Dahlia lowered her head. "Nothing. It was the money they wanted to make from the sale of your ranch to the railroad. And then Papa also said water rights bring in a pretty penny."

"Stop this ludicrous mockery!" Pastor Bloom demanded from the crowded doorway. "And let me in."

A narrow path opened, and he followed it to the front. "This is utterly ridiculous," the reverend said. "I'll have you all know that Marcus Sutton is a solid citizen of Hartville, a pillar of our community, and these scurrilous accusations must be dropped."

The sheriff turned to the newcomer. "Do you have evidence to counter what Sutton's daughter has just said?"

"I don't know what Miss Dahlia said," Pastor Bloom replied. "But I can tell you this: Marcus Sutton and I have established a friendship as well as a business partnership—"

Murmurs rippled around the room.

The reverend raked everyone with a contemptuous look. "Mr. Sutton can't be guilty of anything but the utmost integrity. Besides, I can show you the guilty one." He pointed at Angel. "Just look at her! That poor excuse of a woman's the one. Done up like a man, she's nothing if not a sinful, wrongheaded crook."

Jeremy stepped up, the muscles in his cheek tight against his tanned skin. "I reckon you need to defend Sutton here if you've been making pacts with the sorry devil."

Gasps burst in the air.

Jeremy didn't seem to hear.

He went on. "And I'd urge you to mind what all you say about my wife. There's few here who don't know she didn't do a single thing wrong. She's no crook, but if you're looking for one, well, then I reckon you can just look over there. Marcus Sutton's your man."

The pastor's mouth opened and closed. "B-but . . ."

Eric scribbled in his black notebook. "Do you have a statement for the paper, Reverend? Anything I can include in my article?"

The sheriff waved his deputy toward Pastor Bloom. "You'd better keep him for questioning. I don't know if he can tell us much more than the pack of lies Sutton might have sold him, but it's worth our while to find out."

Pastor Bloom argued and waved the deputy away, to no avail. He was led past many of his congregants, and never once did he stop his defense of Marcus Sutton.

"Miss Dahlia," Robert Andrews said, "you've yet to say who your father hired to carry out his crimes. I'm sure he didn't get his hands dirty, did he? It might go easier on you if you told."

Dahlia's black eyes flashed. "I can do that. I'm tired of the lies and the secrets and all the rest. I'll take you to where you'll find him. After all, I led him to Rogers Ranch, paid him, did all Papa's bidding. And for what?"

"In that case," Sheriff Dowd said, "I figure Miss Rogers—"

"Mrs. Johnstone," Jeremy said, his blue eyes on Angel. "She's my wife, remember?"

The sheriff nodded. "Mrs. Johnstone, then. You're free to go, ma'am. And I'm sorry for all you've gone through. Please forgive us, if you can."

Angel's heart beat hard. "I can," she whispered, and her knees gave way.

Angel's trip home was a blur of faces, places, and talk that only left her more tired than she'd been since her attack. She remembered going to Letty's clinic, but then she'd closed her eyes and given in to sleep.

For the second time, Angel awoke in the clinic. This time, however, Jeremy sat with her on the bed instead of in the armchair in the corner. He had a firm grip on her hand.

"I'm sorry," he said.

She shrugged.

"I've made a right ugly mess of things, and I have no right to ask your forgiveness, but I will—again."

She looked away.

"You don't have to look at me, but there's plenty I have to confess. Just listen to me."

Angel waited for his confession.

"I did come to you at first for all the wrong reasons, you know that. And it took me a while to get things straight in my thick head. Yes, I wanted to care for my stock, but I also wanted more."

She peeked at him, and his obvious remorse did something to her anger and hurt.

He ran his fingers through his hair. "I let my greed take over my common sense. Your ranch is a fine piece of land, and you know it, but I had no right to demand that you sell."

When she didn't respond, he tightened his lips, thought for a moment, and then continued. "That's not even the worst thing I did. When you turned down my offer, I let my fool pride get the better of me. Miss Dahlia looked right fine, with her fancy clothes and daddy's dollars, so I went a-courting."

"It would serve you right if she'd married you."

He winced. "Maybe it would've, but I'm glad she didn't. I reckon the Lord knew what He was doing when He made it clear I had to marry you instead."

"How so?"

Jeremy stood and started to pace. "The Father's taught me a lesson on prayer these past few months. It doesn't make a bit of difference how hard or how much you pray if you don't pray the Father's will."

Angel waited, uncertain.

"I spent more time than I should've begging for what I wanted the Lord to do for me. I never once thought to learn if what all I asked for was in His will." He gave her a crooked grin. "It's no wonder He didn't answer a single one of those fool prayers of mine. A fella's gotta remember what Jesus prayed."

"Which time?" Angel asked.

"Oh, when He said He'd rather not be crucified, but that He'd rather the Father's will be done than His."

Angel nodded. Hope bubbled up in her heart, but she didn't dare speak. She didn't know if Jeremy had said all he needed to.

He came back to her, regret on his handsome face. "I'm sorry, Angel. Real sorry. I reckon I hurt you pretty bad, even though I told myself over and over again that I only wanted to look out for you." He shook his head. "I've never been a fancy man or thought much about things and stuff, so I don't know how I let myself go so far from all's I've always known."

The bed dipped as he sat beside her once again. A gentle finger, rough from ranch work, touched the freckles on her cheek. "These are real," he said. "A lot prettier than Dahlia's curls and lace and painted face. Now that I'm seeing clear again, why, I reckon I've ruined my chances with you. I know we had us a strange wedding there, but we can always do that over—if you'd want to try."

The knot in Angel's throat didn't let her speak, and the tears in her eyes made it hard to see, but she could still hear, and she listened to Jeremy's every word.

He scoffed. "I knew how stupid I was when the sheriff came up to arrest you. I couldn't let them hurt you any more than you'd already been hurt. I told myself it was all on account of my guilt. I didn't do a thing when Eric, Douglas, Adrian, and Pastor Stone said I should."

He wrapped a long strand of copper-colored hair around his palm. "It's as soft and warm as the color, you know."

"It's red, Jeremy. I know that."

He blushed. "I tried to tell myself you were a stubborn redhead with no common sense. It only worked for a short while."

"I am a redhead, and I'm as stubborn as a mule, my mama always said."

"I reckon you wouldn't be you if you weren't stubborn—or redheaded, too."

His warm blue eyes made hope spring to life in her heart.

"I told the truth when I said I love you," he said. "It's right strange how it came about, but I do. And I'm not likely to stop pestering you until you agree to be my real wife."

He cupped her cheek in his warm hand. "Do you think you might someday get by the hate and see me like the man who'll love you for the rest of his sorry life?"

"I don't hate you, Jeremy. I never have." She reached up and covered his hand with hers. "You're a frustrating man once you make up your mind, but that's no cause for hate."

He waited. "So . . . ?"

"What?"

"So, do you reckon you might someday find some love in your heart for me?"

"I think some's already there."

Joy sparked in his eyes.

She hurried to add, "But I think we need time to see this through, to get it right this time."

"I'm not a patient man, and you know that right well, but I reckon you have a good point there." He outlined her brows, her nose, her lips with the tip of his finger. "There is one thing a fella has a right to know though."

"What's that?"

"Will you do me the honor and marry me twice?"

Angel laughed and cried as emotion burst fresh and free from that spring of love she'd held so tight and so long in her heart. Tears of relief, of joy, of wonder and love bathed her face until Jeremy's lips dried every one.

"Does that mean yes?" he asked after a particularly tender kiss.

Angel did something she'd itched to do since the very first time she clapped eyes on this crazy maybe-husband of hers. She ran her fingers through his blond hair and found it softer than she'd expected. This could become a hard habit to break.

"Ask me again," she said. "Give me some time."

He grabbed her wrists, turned her hands, and then planted kisses on her palms. "I'll give you time, but it won't be much. I'm wanting that answer an awful lot."

"In God's time, Jeremy. In His perfect and wise time."

Three weeks before Christmas, Angel pushed the last pin into the crown of copper braid atop her head.

"How does it look from behind?" she asked.

Phoebe smiled into the looking glass. "Lovely, and Jeremy's going to know he's wedding a real angel when he sees you walk up the aisle."

The bride blushed. "I reckon he doesn't know which one of me he'll see when I do. Do you think he's worried I might wear trousers to our wedding?"

Wynema tapped the toe of her shoe against the floor. "I still say you should. That's what you intend to wear on the ranch, isn't it?"

"Yes, but—"

"But nothing," the photographer argued. "It's plumb madness what you're about to do. How many times did you say you weren't the wedding sort?" She didn't wait for Angel's answer. "That cowboy said and did a passel of stupid things, and now you want to reward him and marry him."

"I love him, Wynema. He loves me. He asked forgiveness, and I obeyed the Lord."

"More like he wheedled and pestered and flattered you until you caved in."

"It wasn't like that one bit," Angel protested.

"It was too like that." Wynema planted her fists on her hips. "And that's why I've decided to take the opportunity *New West* magazine offered me. I'm making a life for myself, and I don't want or need some man to come to my rescue or any such thing."

Angel studied her friend over the froth of veil in her hands. "You never said a thing about a magazine offer."

"I wanted to wait until I knew for sure what they'd need, and now I know. They've retained me for a pictorial essay about Indians who live on reservations. It seems folks back east have begun to collect the Indians' artifacts, and they're interested in pictures and stories about them."

"What about your house?" asked Phoebe, who looked about ready to pop with the child she carried. "Have you decided to sell it?"

"No," Wynema replied. "I figure it's best to rent it out. That way, if this job isn't right, I can always return to Hartville—but don't expect me to stay. I'll only last as long as it takes me to land the next project. I'm sick of the gossips and hypocrites in this town."

Letty walked in. "Don't expect to find any fewer wherever you go. People are the same everywhere. That's what salvation's all about, dear. Without Christ's sacrifice, we're all lost in that sin and evil we carry in our souls."

The photographer shook her head. "Hartville must be the worst place for all that, and I'm stuffed right up to my eyeballs with it all. I'm ready for something new, an adventure and different folks to meet."

Angel gave her friend a hug. "I wish you well, all the best in your new work. I only ask that you remember to write. I'll miss you more than you'll ever know."

"I'll miss you, too." Wynema looked away. "You've been a dear, dear friend." Her voice grew thick with emotion. "You're all splendid, strong women, and I don't want to leave you behind. It's those who've hurt you that I can stomach no more."

"I understand," Angel said, "and I hope you understand my choice as well. Jeremy is a good man, and we've agreed to build a life based on our love. It did spring up out of trouble and grief, but the Lord can redeem even that."

"I still think you should come with me." Wynema's expression turned beseeching. "Oh, do! Leave that cowboy to his cows. Come with me. I've yet to meet the man who can rival the promise of an adventure out in the world."

Letty chuckled. "Just you wait, Wynema Howard, just you wait. I'm sure the Lord has just that man waiting for you just around the corner. I only regret that I might not be around you when it happens."

"Don't waste a thought on that notion, Doc. I'm not the wedding sort."

"But I am now," Angel said, her pulse fast. She was about to finally become the real Mrs. Jeremy Johnstone. "I don't want to make my groom wait, and seeing as we're ready, I reckon we'd better head to the front of the church."

The four friends joined hands and prayed and then left the pastor's office for the upcoming event.

Angel couldn't wait for the Lord to bless her marriage.

❦

Mrs. Stone's nimble fingers coaxed a hymn from the church organ, and Angel's eyes brimmed with happy tears. She stood at the end of the aisle, poised to start the walk that would make her Jeremy's wife once and for all.

He waited for her at the altar, his blond hair like shiny gold, his dark suit pressed and well fitted. The Lord would soon make them one.

It had become Angel's dearest dream.

At the end of the hymn, a young man crossed the front of the church and took his place at the pulpit. Angel didn't know the new minister well, but any nephew of her much-loved Pastor Stone would do her just fine.

The Blooms had left shortly after the reverend was cleared of wrongdoing. His defense of the crooked banker hadn't endeared him to anyone, and no tears fell upon his departure. Angel figured they'd reached Boston, where they belonged, by now.

Thaddeus Stone nodded to his aunt, who then turned and winked at Angel. The processional's notes rose in the church; it cued Angel to begin her walk.

At the foot of the altar, she paused, tears of joy on her cheeks. With a smile for Jeremy, she took note of his damp eyes. She took his extended hand, looked at their entwined fingers, and understood what it meant for two to become one. They'd still be themselves, as their fingers stayed separate, but together they'd gain the strength neither had alone.

"Who gives this woman in marriage?" the new Pastor Stone asked.

"The Lord does," Angel answered.

The simple ceremony moved her, and her tears persisted to the end. When the reverend invited Jeremy to kiss her, she met her husband halfway.

This was good, it was right, and she would treasure for the rest of her life the bonds she and Jeremy had just begun to form.

"I love you," he whispered.

"I love you, too."

"If you'll indulge me a moment," Mrs. Stone said as she rose from the organ's stool, "I've a prayer request."

The curious congregation leaned forward.

"Dreadful behavior has plagued our town in the recent past, actions the Lord condemns in His Word. I'd like to call on you to pray one for the other so that godly values might prevail."

Some wriggled in their seats. Others blushed.

Mrs. Stone continued. "My dear husband often reminded us that we've many members in the one body of the church. Much of what happened came about because some failed to accept others' eccentricities and peculiarities."

Angel heard Wynema's amen.

"We can confess, start over fresh," Mrs. Stone said. "This time with soft and tender hearts. No body or land or heart or mind can stand divided."

The silent congregation followed her dignified return to the organ, her husband's memory warm in many of their thoughts.

Pastor Thad, as he'd asked to be called, cleared his throat. "I can only echo what my dear aunt has said and urge you, brothers and sisters in Christ, to remember the words of the prophet Isaiah."

He paged through the large Bible before him and read in a calm, steady voice. "The LORD shall guide thee continually, and satisfy thy soul in drought, and make fat thy bones: and thou shalt be like a watered garden, and like a spring of water, whose waters fail not."

Prayer, heartfelt and sincere, brought the service to a close. No one moved, their attention on the couple who still stood at the altar, hands clasped between them, eyes only for each other.

"The Lord's the spring that feeds my love," the groom whispered. "It took me a right long while to recognize that, and only after I did could I love you like I do now."

Everyone heard and took the words to heart.

The groom kissed his bride once again.

"Oh!" The shocked cry came from the center of the choir. "I've . . . my . . . it's happened," Phoebe cried. "Oh dear. My water broke. Our baby's on its way."

Instead of repairing to the fellowship hall, where a splendid spread awaited the wedding guests, everyone followed the soon-to-be mother and her petite physician, who, also expecting a blessed arrival, waddled at her side.

The bride and groom were among the first to reach the clinic, ready to share their joy with that of their friends.

Faith, hope, and love shone like silver in Hartville on that magnificent, miraculous day.

Ginny Aiken, a former newspaper reporter, lives in Pennsylvania with her engineer husband and their four sons. Born in Havana, Cuba, and raised in Valencia and Caracas, Venezuela, she discovered books at an early age. She wrote her first novel at age fifteen while she trained with the Ballets de Caracas, later to be known as the Venezuelan National Ballet. An eclectic blend of jobs, including stints as paralegal, choreographer, language teacher, retail salesperson, wife, mother of four boys, and herder of their numerous and assorted friends, brought her back to books in search of sanity. She is now the author of nineteen published works.

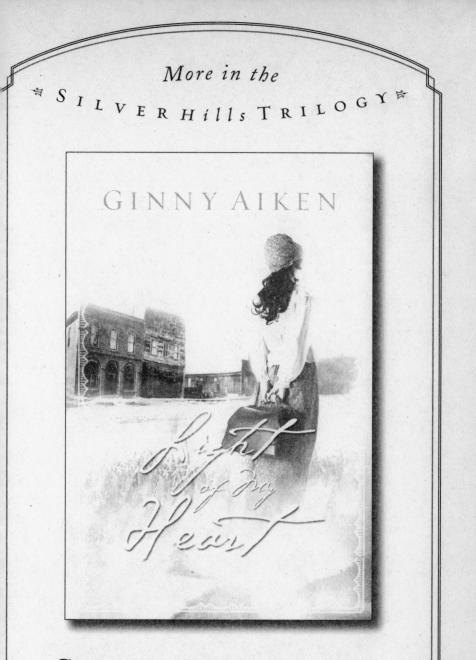

GINNY AIKEN

S he wanted to change the course of her life, but this lady
doctor didn't know what she was up against. Dr. Letitia
Morgan had a God-given calling to heal. But when she moved
to Hartville, Colorado, in 1893, she unexpectedly encountered
controversy—and a surprise romance.

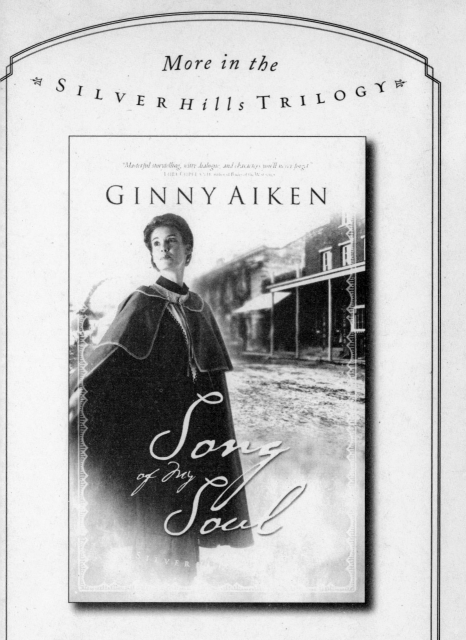

"*Masterful storytelling, witty dialogue, and characters you'll never forget.*"

GINNY AIKEN

Song of my Soul

When you're running from your past, it always catches up to you. Adrian Gamble just wanted to disappear. But while trying to make a new start in Hartville, Colorado, he realized he must confront his past in order to face his future.